More Praise fo[r]

Life After Kafka

"*Life After Kafka* is not just a fictional quest to find out who Kafka's fiancée, Felice Bauer, was and what kind of life she led after their five-year correspondence ended. In it, 'life after Kafka' is the existential situation into which a community of Prague-based, Jewish intellectuals were thrown . . . capturing the living conditions and possibilities of the refugees after the loss of their homes and relationships, after the shattering of the world whose ruins each of them took with them in a few suitcases." —**Magnesia Litera jury citation**

"In *Life After Kafka,* Platzová movingly portrays Felice Bauer's valiant efforts to forge a new life for herself and her family in the wake of historical catastrophe, even as she grapples with whether to reveal an intimate and painful chapter of her past in service to Kafka's literary legacy. This meticulously researched and vividly imagined tale peels back the layers of cultural myth, offering a testament to a different kind of heroism."
—**Ross Benjamin**, translator of *The Diaries of Franz Kafka*

"Franz Kafka is a universe that resists any attempt at interpretation. Platzová's novel offers a new key to Kafka's world: we look at it through the tender and sorrowful gaze of the people whose fate had been marked by him personally. An utterly touching book!"
—**Agnieszka Holland**, award-winning filmmaker and president of the European Film Academy

"*Life After Kafka* is a thrilling detective story about one of literature's most celebrated names, a haunting family saga about preserving our legacy during the darkest turns of history, and a thought-provoking exploration of the rippling impact of famous artists on the people in their lives. Platzová's masterful merging of fact and fiction, in Alex Zucker's artful and inspired translation, carries us across decades and continents to prove that our connections can be abandoned and yet unbroken, and that even the briefest encounters—in love and in art—can shape us forever." —**Jaroslav Kalfař**, author of *Spaceman of Bohemia* and *A Brief History of Living Forever*

Life After Kafka

Also by
Magdaléna Platzová

The Attempt

Aaron's Leap

Life After Kafka

Magdaléna Platzová

Translated from the Czech by
Alex Zucker

Bellevue Literary Press
New York

First published in the United States in 2024
by Bellevue Literary Press, New York
For information, contact:
Bellevue Literary Press
90 Broad Street
Suite 2100
New York, NY 10004
www.blpress.org

Originally published by Argo in Czech as *Život po Kafkovi*

This is a work of fiction. Characters, organizations, events, and places (even those that are actual) are either products of the author's imagination or are used fictitiously.

Library of Congress Cataloging-in-Publication Data
Names: Platzová, Magdaléna, author. | Zucker, Alex, translator.
Title: Life after Kafka / Magdaléna Platzová ; translated from the Czech by Alex Zucker.
Other titles: Život po Kafkovi. English
Description: First edition. | New York : Bellevue Literary Press, 2024.
Identifiers: LCCN 2023043655 | ISBN 9781954276291 (paperback ; acid-free paper) | ISBN 9781954276307 (ebook)
Subjects: LCSH: Bauer, Felice, 1887-1960--Fiction. | Germans--United States--Fiction. | Women immigrants--United States--Fiction. | Kafka, Franz, 1883-1924--Relations with women--Fiction. | LCGFT: Biographical fiction. | Novels.
Classification: LCC PG5040.26.L38 Z3613 2024 | DDC 891.8/636--dc23/eng/20240327
LC record available at https://lccn.loc.gov/2023043655

Bellevue Literary Press would like to thank all its generous donors—individuals and foundations—for their support.

The publication of this book is made possible by the support of Jan & Marica Vilcek.

This project is supported in part by an award from the National Endowment for the Arts.

This publication is made possible by the New York State Council on the Arts with the support of the Office of the Governor and the New York State Legislature.

Book design and composition by Mulberry Tree Press, Inc.

Bellevue Literary Press is committed to ecological stewardship in our book production practices, working to reduce our impact on the natural environment.

♾ This book is printed on acid-free paper.

Manufactured in the United States of America.

First Edition

10 9 8 7 6 5 4 3 2 1

paperback ISBN: 978-1-954276-29-1
ebook ISBN: 978-1-954276-30-7

Dedicated to the descendants of
Felice Marasse, née Bauer,
without whose helpfulness and trust
this book could not have been written.

Contents

Life After Kafka

New York
October 15, 1975

Dear Mr. Canetti,

I read your book about Franz Kafka and my mother, Felice, née Bauer. I wish I had never gotten hold of it. Unfortunately, there is always some "friend" who comes along and hastens to inform me of the latest achievements in Kafkology (or is it Kafkography?), which evidently—to judge from the number of titles at least—is a highly profitable business.

I will not dwell here on the personality of Franz Kafka. I have nothing more to add beyond what you yourself quite accurately described in your book. Whether he was a great writer, I honestly cannot judge. What I know beyond a doubt is that he was a neurotic, a masochist, and, in regard to his relationships with women, a sadist as well.

Every one of the letters that you quote from so extensively would, in my opinion, be worthy of psychiatric evaluation, and any one of them would have been reason enough for my mother to break up with him as quickly as possible.

Why she did not, I truly have no idea. I have not yet had an opportunity to explore this aspect of my mother's personality. I expect the fashion of the times may have played a role, an echo of fin de siècle decadence. My mother adored Strindberg, who, as you will admit, is also quite morbid in some respects. But even I only found out about this "love" of hers from Kafka's letters, when I read them—along with everyone else—after my mother's death. My parents were from the old school and maintained a certain distance from me and my sister. We knew very little about their inner lives. But enough that I feel it necessary to object in the strongest possible terms to the way you dealt with my mother in your rash and sensationalistic book.

Already the false, pseudoscandalous revelation on the opening page betrays the superficiality of your approach: So, at long last, we know the name of the woman who until now has been hidden behind the initial F.!

Dear sir, if you had actually cared to find out, you could have known my mother's full name years ago, even without the use of any detective methods. You had only to read the readily available biography of Kafka written by Max Brod, of whom I also have no great opinion, but at least one cannot deny his goodwill and—at least as it relates to my mother—a certain sensitivity.

My mother was a woman of many talents. She leaned more toward a practical orientation. A no-nonsense person, as they say in this country. Yet she was always deeply influenced by art. Literature, theater, and music as well. My father, a banker by profession, was an excellent pianist, and had circumstances in his youth permitted, he would have devoted himself to music.

Art was one of the "charms" with which Kafka impressed my mother. He was, after all, a published author, as people say nowadays. That certainly played its part.

My mother did not receive a formal education. At the age of fifteen, she had to leave school and take on employment, by her own efforts working her way from the lowly position of typist all the way up to head of sales. But she always took great pleasure in reading and enjoyed being enlightened. When we fled in the thirties, first from Berlin to Geneva and then to America, instead of valuables, she took books with her. She had a special collection of volumes dedicated to her by Kafka, which she kept grouped together, some sixty titles in all. There was even a copy of the Bible among them. After her death, I sold them to the Fischer publishing house in Germany. It was the only money I made on Kafka at a time when every Tom, Dick, and Harry was making a killing on him.

My mother was very emotional, a warm and generous woman. When she was still single, she cared for war orphans at the Jewish Home in Berlin, and even after she was married and had a family, she maintained close relationships with them. Her "girls" would come to visit, and she helped them in all sorts of ways.

She was enterprising, resourceful, optimistic, and cheerful. She refused to let anything break her. Anyone who knew her couldn't help but love her. She had a talent for organization and business. In the end, it was she who supported the family after our immigration to America. Especially the last twelve years, after my father suffered a heart attack and could no longer work. I, too, did my best to help, of course, to whatever extent I was able, tutoring other students, getting scholarships, and so on.

My mother took courses in massage and hairdressing and opened her own beauty salon. She also baked and sold cookies with her sister, eventually expanding the range of products they offered. Then she opened a yarn store, selling knitting supplies and notions. But it never, I repeat *never*, would have crossed my mother's mind to try to make money from Franz Kafka's letters, which she kept hidden away in secret for forty years.

I myself only came to know of their existence from a relative, when I was eighteen. Before then, I had no idea that my mother had had a relationship with anyone named Kafka. I only knew his name from the spines on the books we had at home, which I had given a cursory glance, but they had never captured my interest. Brod's biography of Kafka, published in Prague before the war, didn't find its way into my hands until the fifties, when it was reissued in expanded form in Germany. Like everything else that had to do with Kafka, I didn't discuss it with my mother. But I do know for certain that she read Brod's biography, as well as Kafka's diaries and *Letters to Milena*. What she thought of them, I have no idea. I can only guess.

You, sir, wrote that my mother "had the heart to sell the letters." In this way, you indirectly accuse her of being insensitive and self-serving, even mocking her. How heroic! Taking swipes from a safe distance at a woman about whom you know not one whit and who cannot defend herself.

How could anyone know anything about my mother when the recipient of her letters so carefully destroyed them, whereas she preserved every postcard, every telegram, even letters that didn't belong directly to her and weren't written by Kafka but touched on their relationship in some way. Like the letters Kafka's mother, Julie, wrote to my grandmother Anna. I've often wondered why she saved everything so meticulously.

It's true, my mother was very fastidious. Every scrap and sheet of paper had its place with her, carefully labeled and classified. It was a habit, a passion of sorts, probably one that she took home with her from the office. Reading Kafka's books, it even occurred to me that this fascination, one might call it, with modern bureaucracy was something the two of them had in common. Yet each approached it from a totally different perspective: my mother from the standpoint of efficiency and reason (though every passion also exposes the irrationality within itself) and Kafka from the standpoint of madness. Which did nothing to change the fact that he was a very capable clerk, as all of his contemporaries attested to. But I don't mean to dabble in your profession. You are the one who's here to interpret Kafka! I'll stick to my mother.

It also occurred to me that maybe for her that bundle of letters was sort of a legal document. Whether a defense or an indictment, who knows? Probably both. But either way, it had to be complete.

As I already said, she never spoke to me about Kafka and their relationship, even when I was an adult. But from the way she clung to the letters, it was obvious it wasn't a dead issue for her—that unhappy five-year period shaped the rest of her life in a fundamental way.

For most of her life, my mother enjoyed complete anonymity. Nobody took any interest in her; nobody knew who she was. It wasn't until a few years after the war, when Kafka began to get famous and a mad dash was unleashed for every word he ever wrote, that she began to worry, and rightfully so, that some information she regarded as intimate might be made public. She had made up her mind to destroy the letters before she died, and she truly wanted to go through with it. But she couldn't work up the courage, so she kept putting it off.

In the end, she did dispose of some of them, which I know not from my mother (who at the time suspected me of conspiring with Schocken), but from her best friend.

She clung to Kafka's letters with an incredible stubbornness, and it wasn't easy getting her to sell them. Mr. Schocken and Max Brod spent years trying to persuade her. Ultimately, she gave in. Not for the money, although she was sick and in need of funds, but at a certain point she realized that she wouldn't be able to destroy the letters as she had planned and, if she died, she would lose control over them.

I explicitly threatened to sell her letters once she passed away. And the truth of the matter is, I coerced her into selling them.

Her pangs of conscience at betraying Kafka (no one could ever convince her that it wasn't a betrayal) were presumably mitigated by Schocken's promise that he would donate the letters to the National Library in Jerusalem after they were published.

Alas, Mr. Schocken passed away in 1959, a year before my mother, so he was unable to honor his promise. Whether or not his heirs kept his commitment, I have no idea. I would have hoped they would have let us know.

I am not happy to return to all this and would just as soon have forgotten it. But I must stand up for my mother. If not in front of your readers, then at least in front of you.

No, my mother did not, as you wrote, have the heart to sell Kafka's letters. Not only that, and I say this only to you, with shame and great pain, but I believe the loss of those keepsakes killed her prematurely.

My mother had actually been dying since 1955. She suffered her first stroke, with only minor consequences, in 1953. In 1956, she had another stroke, but even after that, she still had a partial recovery and came home from the hospital. My mother had a very hardy constitution. But she was no longer able to live on her own, so I convinced her to leave L.A. and move in with us, in New York. She had been with us several months when she suffered the third, fatal blow, from which she never recovered. She was hospitalized in Rye for a year and a half. We couldn't keep her at home, since she needed constant care.

In those final months, she was unable to speak or move, though she was lucid and understood everything. She was literally a prisoner in her own body. What must have been going through her mind?

That, to be frank, is the hell I inhabit on nights I cannot sleep.

An efficient businesswoman, eh? A woman without a heart.

In Max Brod's melodramatic book about Kafka, I learned that Kafka, too, was unable to speak at the end of his life, due to tuberculosis in his throat. Unlike my mother, however, at least he was able to write, as long as he could still hold a pen.

So you see, there is some hint of symmetry; I wouldn't call it justice. The meaning of which escapes us, of course.

I end with the wish that the facts I have shared with you here will burden your conscience enough to ensure that you will be more cautious in your fabrications next time.

I cannot write either "Respectfully" or "Cordially," let alone "Yours," so you will have to make do with my signature.

Joachim M.

New York
May 18, 1987

Dear Mr. Canetti,

Consider this note of mine an addendum to the letter I wrote you twelve years ago, to which I never received a reply. As you may recall, I wrote you about the promise Salman Schocken made to my mother, which was what finally convinced her to entrust her letters to him. Namely, that he would donate the manuscripts of Kafka's letters to the National Library in Jerusalem.

I have just learned from an article in the paper that my mother's letters were auctioned off at Sotheby's in New York for $605,000. Reportedly a record-breaking sum, at least so far as manuscripts go.

Over a half million, sir. And they gave my mother eight thousand! The deal of the century, don't you think?

The buyer was neither a library nor an archive. Where would a place like that come up with that kind of money? It was a private party, whose identity was not revealed. The letters have vanished into a private safe, maybe forever. So that's the end of the matter. They cheated my mother even in death. What a disgrace. She was absolutely right to want to destroy Kafka's letters. Pity she didn't succeed.

Regards,
Joachim M.

1935

Geneva

THE THIN MASTS OF SAILBOATS bristle at the end of the street. As the wind blows from the northeast, strong and steady, every line in the anchorage whistles at a different pitch. The boy stops and listens. Sharp white-crested ripples play across the lake, the sky pale, clear, cool.

For four years he has been walking home from school the same way, twice a day. In the other direction, he usually runs. He knows the lake in every weather and time of year, at twilight, in the dark. Darkness falls early in winter. The scraping of wood. The hollow lapping of water against the boats' flanks.

His mother and aunt have already begun to sort and give away the things they won't be taking with them. The only thing going in the suitcases is clothing; books, porcelain, paintings, silver, rugs, and furniture will make the trip later, once they have settled in. Moving from Berlin had been worse; even his mother had cried then. But his father had insisted, and now he was dragging them away yet again. Away from Europe, where the ground was disappearing underneath the Jews' feet.

The street leads along the park, the surface of the water hidden behind the trees. He turns the last corner. Their apartment building has the air of a seaside hotel, with its long, decorative balconies, colorful shutters, and niches galore. They have already moved three times since leaving Berlin. When they first came to Geneva, his father rented a villa. Then his mother was badly missing Berlin, so they returned there for a while. That turned out to be a mistake. The second time they fled, they lost a lot of money, having to pay a special tax to be let out. Next they rented a smaller apartment in the center, and it was only when his grandmother came to stay with them that his father found the place on rue de Montchoisy, by the park near the lake. The rooms weren't large, but at least they offered some privacy. And now, since his grandmother had passed away, there were seven of them at home: Father, Mother, Joachim and Lily, Aunt Else, cousin Hana, and Berthe, the maid. They didn't have a governess or a cook anymore.

On the third floor, outside the door to their apartment, Joachim catches the aroma of roasted meat. All of a sudden he realizes how hungry he is. He presses the doorbell button. There are voices from inside, but no one comes to open the door. After the second ring, he hears the sound of sharp footsteps, followed by silence. The door slowly opens.

"Oh, come on!" he says, throwing himself on his sister.

"Stop that. And don't shout. Mom has company from Berlin."

"Who?"

"Some lady named Margarete. We're supposed to call her 'Aunt,' but I don't remember meeting her. She won't stop talking. They shut themselves in there."

Sunlight streams through the glass panes of the drawing room door, casting dapples of blue, red, and green on the white wall. The parquet floor creaks, the colors dancing before his eyes.

"Home already?"

His mother has on a dark blue dress with a low-waist pleated skirt and a string of red coral beads wrapped twice around her neck. Her dark blond hair, graying at the temples, cropped just below the ear, blazes ginger red in the sun.

A petite brunette woman in a light-colored dress rises

from the sofa behind her, outstretched hand holding a lighted cigarette.

"Why, you must be Joachim!"

He has to walk over and say hello. The top of the woman's head barely reaches his chin, but she tugs him down toward her and plants a kiss on both his cheeks, leaving behind a trace of red lipstick.

"You're all grown-up! Do you still remember me?"

She ruffles his hair with her hand.

"We used to be practically neighbors. I lived on Sedanstrasse, a little way down from Hilda Hildebrand, the famous actress. Professor Einstein lived near me, too. He's in America now. Everyone is running away. Maybe you'll be a Hollywood actor. Such a handsome boy! He takes after Ferri."

The visitor gives a loud laugh, takes a drag on her cigarette, exhales a cloud of smoke. She smells of sweet perfume and the herbal liqueur his mother likes to offer guests before lunch. Two cut-glass tumblers containing the remains of an electric green liquid stand next to the ashtray on the table, one on either side, like an honor guard.

"I'll go see what's happening with lunch," his mother says. "The children have to get back to school. As long as you aren't too hungry, we'll wait for Robert to eat. I'll have the table set in the dining room."

"Oh, I'm never hungry. Look at me. I couldn't gain weight if I tried."

How could he not remember her. She always talked too loudly and had never missed a party that his mother threw in Berlin. That nervous, high-pitched laugh of hers reminded him of honking horns. He was shy around her and didn't like her. Especially the way she embarrassed his mother in front of other people. Apparently, his mother didn't mind, though, since she kept inviting her over. No dinner party on Viktoria-Luise-Platz was complete without her presence. The red beads were also a gift from her.

"Excuse me for a moment," his mother says. "Play something on the piano. Or have a look at the latest fashions, I have a whole stack of magazines there."

"Don't you worry about me. I won't be bored. I'm too busy counting my losses." Again that obnoxious laugh. Grete takes a drag of her cigarette and walks to the window. "Pity you don't have a view of the lake."

The only person home when Joachim and Lily return from school that afternoon is Berthe, the gloomy-faced servant girl. She warms up some milk for the children and puts a plate of buttered bread out on the table, then rushes straight back to the stove.

Usually no one cooks in the afternoons at their place. Lunch is the main meal, and for supper they make do with a piece of bread with lard or a bowl of soup from lunch. But today, apparently, there is a feast being prepared. They can smell their aunt's pulled strudel from the oven, and Berthe is angrily banging pots around.

"What am I supposed to do when they leave me all alone like this?" she grumbles. "I'm not some fancy chef from Berlin."

"You're doing just fine," says Lily, trying to calm her down. "Do you know where my mom is?"

"The ladies went for a walk in the park," Berthe hoots. "In this wind! And you, young master, had better be careful, too. Your cheeks are blooming red. This springtime sun is fierce."

"Did they tell you how long that lady was staying?" Lily asks.

"They just told me to make up a bed in your grandmama's old room. I haven't got round to it yet, seeing as I've been shut up in the kitchen all day. But those are some right big bags she's got. Looks to be she's moving!"

"I hope not in with us," Joachim blurts.

A door slams and the sound of voices carries from the hallway.

"They're back." Berthe breathes a sigh of relief. "Now maybe the madam will help me out with supper."

The boy quickly finishes his milk and carries his empty plate, along with the mug, to the sink.

As he walks out the front door, he almost collides with his mother.

"Where do you think you're going?'

"Can I go out for a while?"

"Don't you have homework?"

"It isn't due until Monday."

Tobacco smoke wafts from the half-open door to the drawing room. With the sun shining from the west now, the colorful panes of glass have dimmed.

"Supper is at seven."

"Can I eat at the Weinbergers'?"

"No."

"Please, Mom? They invited me."

"No, we have guests."

"All right, Mom."

He slips past her and hurries out the door. It's five o'clock; he can still catch the evening service at the synagogue.

The only part of Shabbat that Joachim's family still keeps is lighting the candles, which his mother does before supper. Apart from that, Friday evenings in their home are the same as any other.

But at his best friend Leo Weinberger's, the family has a silver cup, over which his father, wearing a yarmulke, recites *"Baruch ata Adonai, eloheinu melech ha'olam, boreh pri ha'gafen"* before passing it around. Then he says the blessing of the hand washing and the sweet challah bread, and only after that do the Weinbergers tuck into their meal. And how cheerfully they eat, even though they really have no reason to be happy.

Mr. Weinberger had told Joachim the story of how they

escaped the first time, during the war, fleeing the eastern front and the pogroms, to Berlin. Mrs. Weinberger was pregnant with Leo at the time. There they survived both the postwar flu epidemic and the inflation crisis, but no sooner had Mr. Weinberger, a teacher by profession, found a better job and begun to bring home some money than Hitler came to power. They didn't want to give up everything all over again, so they missed the right moment and got to Switzerland just as the laws against refugees, whose numbers were constantly growing, began to appear. Among other things, they weren't allowed to work. Mr. Weinberger taught Hebrew clandestinely, his pupils paying him in cash, one class at a time, and Leo's mom worked as a cleaning lady. Leo shared a room with his two younger sisters in the small dark apartment, near the synagogue, where the five of them lived.

Yet the mood there on Friday nights was always more joyful than it was in Joachim's household. The only time it was cheerful in the splendidly furnished dining room on rue de Mo tchoisy was when their father wasn't home.

On those rare occasions when their father was away on a trip or eating dinner out, their mother and Aunt Else spoke at a higher volume, reminiscing about their childhood in the town of Neustadt in Oberschlesien and moving to Berlin. They told stories about their crazy uncles and aunts—there were plenty of them in the family—and going out to dance in Berlin, all the different dresses they had and the suitors who tried to woo them. They would laugh, though it wasn't clear what about, and after dinner they would play games: hide-and-seek; duck, duck, goose; red light, green light. Or Aunt Else would sit down at the piano, which she didn't dare do in front of their father, and play Viennese waltzes and old Jewish songs and also a few Hungarian tunes, which she'd learned when she was still living with her husband in Budapest. They rolled back the rug and their mother taught Lily and Hana to dance. They tried to convince

Joachim, too, but he refused. He didn't have to skip around like a madman to feel happy.

Grete isn't the only company they have today. Seated at the table is another old friend from Berlin, Herman Eisner. Even the children are allowed to call him by his first name, as "Uncle Eisner" hardly seems appropriate in his case.

Herman is a psychiatrist, originally from Prague. It was he who scoffed the most on September 15, 1930, when their father announced to the guests one night, during a dinner party on Viktoria-Luise-Platz, that the next day he and Felice and the children were leaving for Switzerland.

"Forget Switzerland, Robert. Just come stay with me in Grünewald. It's much closer." The room exploded with laughter. Grünewald was where Herman had his private sanatorium for the mentally ill.

They dined on stuffed quail and drank champagne for their farewell supper that evening.

Herman Eisner believed in German humanism and democracy, and was convinced that Hitler and his gang of convicted criminals, as he referred to them, were not to be taken seriously. No one could force dictatorship on the nation that had given birth to Goethe and Heine. And if anyone wanted to try, they would have to be of higher caliber than an uneducated psychopath with an inferiority complex.

Having deftly assembled a diagnosis of the Führer, Herman predicted that soon he, too, would end up in Grünewald. They all laughed over their quail.

As late as January 1933, Herman wrote an essay for a newspaper in Berlin about the invincibility of German democracy. Less than two months later, on March 6, just before midnight, he was pounding on their door in Geneva. He had come to apologize.

This evening they dine on chicken soup with dumplings, then stuffed veal, with a light Burgundy to accompany it. They are celebrating the arrival of Grete, who just the day before (was that even possible?) had still been in Berlin. They reminisce about their favorite cafés, bakers, and tailors, milliners, pastry chefs, waiters, even benches in the park. The city's fabric of faces and places, creating a feeling of safety and home.

Much of it even Joachim remembers. For example, the zoo, where he used to go with his nanny. And the aquarium, where he'd stood gaping at the colorful fish darting to and fro, and the delicate sea horses with their elongated noses and curlicue tails, fluttering up and down in the glass tanks like miniature fairy-tale dragons.

Grete says there are some parts of town they would hardly recognize now. New buildings have sprung up all over Berlin, and what with the preparations for the Olympics, the city has turned into one big construction site. Hitler is determined to dazzle the world.

The two women had changed outfits for supper. Grete now has a lacy shawl thrown over her shoulders.

To her right sits Joachim; to her left, Robert, with Herman seated in between Lily and Felice.

"How long will you be in Geneva?" Herman asks.

Good question. Joachim gives Lily a kick in the shin under the table. Now, at last, they'll find out.

"A couple of weeks. I need to enjoy some time with Felice before she vanishes over the ocean. Who knows when I'll see her again."

"And after that?"

"I have a brother in Palestine."

"In Jerusalem?"

"No, Tel Aviv. You might have heard of him. Hans Bloch. He's a doctor. We're very proud of him."

"When did he leave?"

"Two years ago. But he wanted to leave much sooner. Hans is an ardent Zionist."

"Do you intend to stay there permanently?"

"Please, what is permanent nowadays?"

Grete takes a sip of wine and languidly lights a cigarette. The serving of veal on her plate is untouched.

"Of course, silly question," says Herman, turning red. "I ask mainly for my own sake, since I myself don't know where to go next. I can't stay in Switzerland. I haven't got enough money and I need to work, which I'm not allowed to do here. The problem is, language is key in my line of work. I don't know Hebrew, and while there may be plenty of people in Palestine who speak German, I'm not so sure they would want me. Does Palestine need psychiatrists? Or just bricklayers, peasants, and soldiers? What do you all think?"

"You don't know Hebrew yet, Herman. Not yet."

"For once, Robert, you're an optimist, but in this case I'm afraid your optimism is misplaced. Maybe you can learn English still, but Hebrew? Me? Hardly. I've never had a head for languages, and Hebrew's just too different. Reading and writing from right to left?"

"I speak English," says Grete. "I led the foreign sales division at Adrema. You may have heard of them."

"Typewriters."

"That's right. I was with them nineteen years. That's a long time. Not having a job feels like not having hands to me. Like the death of someone close. Or a divorce."

"What are you going to do in Palestine?"

"Does Palestine need typewriters? Or just shovels, hoes, and rifles? What do you all think? Typewriters are all I know. I can support myself as a typist. If nothing else, it will be warm there. We were frozen solid today by the lake."

Shivering, she pulls her shawl tighter around her shoulders.

"You were the one who insisted on going for a walk, Grete."

"Yes, Felice, and it was gorgeous. The snowy mountains in the distance, the blossoming trees, the ripples racing over the surface . . ."

"I'm considering Italy," says Herman. "Everyone is fleeing to France, but I've heard Mussolini is treating the Jews decently."

Grete exhales a puff of smoke. "Good idea, Herman. I have an invitation to Florence. A former colleague of mine married an Italian, a lawyer. They own a banking house. She has a gorgeous villa overlooking the city. We could go there together and pretend to be engaged."

"You aren't afraid of Mussolini?"

"Oh, Bob!"

The boy's ears turn red. He can't believe that lady is calling his father "Bob."

"Mussolini isn't Hitler. And after all, there are Jewish fascists, too. The Italians don't much go for all that Nordic race talk, you know." She arches her back like a cat. "I simply adore Florence. I went there on vacation right after the war, couldn't wait. Everyone warned me how much they hate Germans, but they were utterly sweet to me. I don't think the Italians even really know how to hate, not like the Germans. That former colleague of mine had Mussolini and his mistress over to her villa. And his mistress, who was a journalist, was actually a Jew."

Else's strudel appears on the table. The warm sour-sweet taste of apples, walnuts, raisins, and cinnamon, enfolded in a delicate doughy crust, baked to a golden brown, yet white and soft at the center.

After dessert they pass into the salon, planting themselves on the sofa and armchairs around the low-set table. Berthe offers coffee and tea; Robert, cognac. Grete makes a request for Robert to play Beethoven.

"For old times' sake."

He takes a while to be convinced but then sits down to the piano and raises the lid.

The opening strokes of the *Pathétique.* Joachim studies his father's face. When they lived on Viktoria-Luise-Platz, he used to play every evening after supper. But here in Geneva, he rarely sits down at the keyboard, almost as if he is avoiding it. Maybe he doesn't like the pianino as much as the grand piano they left behind in Berlin.

The boy reflects on how little he knows the man at the piano. How different he is from his father, demanding, strict, and, more often than not, morose. For the first time in ages, at supper tonight, he had laughed the way he used to, his laughter rumbling pleasantly through his square-shouldered body.

Now he sits playing, eyes closed, with an almost imperceptible smile, fingers moving rapidly up and down the keys.

The boy remembers how last year at the synagogue his father beamed with pride when he, Joachim, read his Torah section without stumbling once.

Yet the boy had had to beg for a bar mitzvah. At first, his father didn't want to hear of it. It was only after several long discussions with his mother, who laid it out in practical terms, that his father finally gave in, even paying Mr. Weinberger to teach Joachim Hebrew.

He justified it to himself as a farsighted investment in his son's future rather than a concession to obscurantism on his part.

Palestine wasn't for him and Felice; he was clear on that. That would have been like jumping out of a frying pan into a boiling pot. But who knew where his children might end up? And if his son had a desire to study, it was important to support him in that, whatever subject it was. But he drew the line at buying him pants for the ceremony. On that he would not budge. He didn't care if Joachim could get married at thirteen under Jewish law. Under the rules of civilized Berlin society, of which he considered himself to be a part, you didn't buy a boy his first pair of pants until his fourteenth birthday. And so, on that famed Saturday when Joachim was to become an adult, he walked into temple in wool shorts and knee-high socks. Luckily no one made fun of him. He recited his text flawlessly, and after the ceremony he could see with his own eyes how moved his father was. He didn't give Joachim a hug, since Robert never hugged his children, but he patted him appreciatively on the shoulder and smiled the whole way home.

His mother, Aunt Else, cousin Hana, and Lily had the table set and waiting when they got home. Lunch was a feast, and his aunt had baked his favorite walnut cake, with soft chocolate frosting and currant preserves. From his father he got a watch as a bar mitzvah gift.

Second movement, Adagio cantabile.

This must be good-bye, thinks the boy, looking around the room.

Aunt Else sits on the sofa, and sensing his gaze, she turns her eyes to him and smiles. She and his mom look alike, but his aunt Else is older, her hair already completely gray. Joachim has always been fond of her. His beautiful cousin Hana leans her head on her mother's shoulder. She isn't going with them to America, instead staying in Switzerland to finish medical school, which she just began a year ago. Grete sits reclining in one of the armchairs, head resting on the seat back, eyes closed. With the bluish shadows around her eyes, she looks like a cadaver. She has even forgotten to smoke for once, her motionless fingers clutching an unlighted cigarette. Herman stands at the piano, turning the pages of the score.

In the other armchair his mother sits, Lily at her feet. Lily's head, with its two thick, dark braids, rests against her mother's knees, her mother's warm palm caressing her forehead.

In two months, Father and I will be setting out on our journey, the boy thinks. His stomach tightens in excitement, the way it does every time the thought crosses his mind.

They will embark in Genoa. Spend a week aboard the ship, then another week in New York, where his father is hoping to contact some old friends. Then they will travel by train to Chicago, where his mother's younger brother, Ferri, lives. From Chicago, they will head to the West Coast, then down, via San Francisco, to Los Angeles, their destination. He and his father will travel alone. His mother and Lily will come afterward, once they've found an apartment. The last one to make the trip will be their aunt Else, who's going to have a hard time saying good-bye to Hana.

His mother's cousin and his wife had been settled in Los Angeles for a year.

"It's a simple life," they wrote to Felice. "Beaches, palm trees, sunshine, cheap housing—you'll save a lot on heating. You pay less here for a small house with a garden than for a one-bedroom apartment in New York."

Joachim sweeps his gaze across the room again, trying to impress it all upon his memory, like the boat masts and the lake earlier today, creating a collection of impressions to take with him. He learned at least that much from leaving Berlin.

He hadn't formed any impressions then, and as a result his childhood home, apart from a few fuzzy snapshots still lodged in his mind, had fallen into oblivion.

Not until much later, once Joachim himself was married and had secrets of his own, did it dawn on him that *he* had been there with them the whole time. His mother's whispering with Grete. A word frozen on Aunt Else's lips. Books that mysteriously appeared and disappeared again before anyone had a chance to get their hands on them.

He remembers precisely the day when he first found out about him. It was in 1938, in Los Angeles.

His aunt Sophie invited him to an ice-cream parlor on Pico, and as soon as they had ordered, she pulled a book out of her handbag and laid it on the marble table between them. It was in German. The author, Aunt Sophie's brother, was someone Joachim had only heard tell of. He didn't remember the man's visits to their place on Viktoria-Luise-Platz.

"This book came out in Prague," Aunt Sophie said. "And your mom is mentioned in it."

Joachim picked up the book and leafed through it. The biography of a writer he had never read anything by.

"Franz Kafka was Max's best friend ever since they were little. He used to come over to our place practically every day. That was how he met your mom, long before you or your sister, Lily, were born. Your mother was on her way to visit your aunt Else in Budapest. Or maybe she was going to Vienna on business. I can't remember now. But either way, she was at our place for dinner, and Kafka happened to come, too—that was how they met. They began corresponding, and then they got engaged, but the war broke out and nothing came of the wedding. In the end, Franz got sick with tuberculosis and died soon after. And your mom got happily married to your father.

"Kafka was a kind man and very educated," his aunt continued. "Max always insisted that he was a genius, but that's not for me to judge. His books aren't for everyone, that I can tell you, though supposedly he's quite famous now in Germany. Mainly due to Max, who handles his estate.

"I wanted you to hear it from me, since sooner or later someone was bound to tell you about the book. I don't understand why Max felt he had to dredge up these personal matters. What is the point of dragging living people into literature?

"I'll have a talk with Lily about it, too," Aunt Sophie said. "I don't want you two to feel like your mom is keeping secrets from you. But it would be best if you didn't ask her or your father about it.

"You have no idea how brave your mother is," she went on. "All she did for her parents, and for Ferri and Erna and Else of course, how much she sacrificed. You really need to honor her for that."

It didn't surprise Joachim that before his mother got married she had had a courtship, as they used to say in those days. But he never would have taken her for the type to date a writer.

She had married at age thirty-one. A matchmaker in Berlin had helped her find a groom, and Felice was very grateful for the efforts she had made. She never forgot to send the woman a New Year's greeting card.

For Joachim and Lily, there was something fairy tale–like and mysterious about their mother's life before she was married. She had told them stories about her job at a company that manufactured office machines and how her boss had gradually promoted her from assistant typist all the way up to head of sales. How she had traveled to trade fairs and attended social occasions, more than once dancing the night away and then in the morning going straight to work in the office. How her mother, Anna, had scolded her for ruining her health, but she didn't listen. In those days she had strength for four and didn't need to sleep.

As for Brod's book, it was really none of his business.

It was the start of summer. And he was eighteen years old.

It was only after the war, when he lived in New York and all of a sudden his mother's old acquaintance was on everybody's lips, that he was forced to deal with it to some degree. On the outermost, graying edge of his memory, associated with a colorful pile of dry leaves into which he had jumped, leading his mother to chastise him (dirty pants, dusty shoes), he recalled the shadow of a tall man in a dark coat rising from a bench and doffing his hat.

A few months before his death, from fall 1923 to spring

1924, Kafka had lived in Berlin. Could she have encountered him there? Had Joachim been there when it happened?

She must have known that he had moved. Their mutual friends had his address, and presumably his telephone number as well. Surely they had told her he was struggling. The prices went up so fast that winter, it would have been laughable if people hadn't been starving to death. A piece of bread or a half liter of milk cost a thousand inflationary marks, and the pension for a retired clerk from an accident insurance company would have been barely enough to cover rent. His parents were sending him food from Prague.

Meanwhile, Felice and her family were doing better than ever before. When the German mark collapsed, it took the big banking houses down with it, and private bankers like Robert had no more competition. Thanks to personal contacts abroad, they were able to get investors for the failing German state and its industry, and they made a lot of money on it. For the first time since she was fifteen, Felice didn't have to go to work, and it shows in the photographs from that time. After the birth of her second child, Felice was full of life, her hair and complexion glowing with health. Who would have taken her for the aging, careworn, teary-eyed girl boarding the train in Prague in late 1917?

Of course she would have wanted to show up for Kafka. And probably help him, too. Compassion for her was a temptation stronger than vanity, and one she could never resist.

But there is no evidence of their meeting at that time, apart from a memory that may be just a figment of Joachim's imagination.

1938

Paris

As the Dakota detached itself from the runway with a sudden lurch, Felice barely suppressed a whoop of joy.

"Your champagne, madam. Madam?"

She accepted the glass offered her by the flight attendant and took a sip.

The captain announced their planned trajectory, including speed, altitude, and wind strength. With the sun setting directly behind them, the metal wing through the window blazed like heated copper. The hills beneath them, covered in dry grass, were pink, the sky tinted green.

She should not have been feeling happy at all. Even if it was her first time on an airplane. A woman in her situation should not have been smiling blissfully, nose glued to the window.

The ticket had cost her three hundred dollars. An enormous sum in light of the expenses now awaiting her and Robert. But by plane she could cross America in a mere sixteen hours, so tomorrow she could still catch the fast ship that sailed from New York once a week and covered the overseas journey in five days instead of seven.

By train, it would have been much cheaper, but the trip cross-continent would have taken three days, and meanwhile the ship would have sailed without her. She would have made it to Paris in two weeks at the earliest, which was far too long for someone waiting in a hospital.

They had also drunk champagne before Robert's departure.

Would she have let him go if she had suspected what danger he was in? How was she supposed to know? Robert hadn't told her a thing. Yet the whole time he had been carrying around in his pocket the vial of nitroglycerin pills that had now saved his life.

He must have known about his illness ever since Switzerland, where he underwent his last exam. It was after that appointment that he suddenly stopped smoking overnight.

When they arrived in America three years earlier, Robert was over sixty; now he was sixty-four. They were down to their last three thousand dollars of the savings they had brought with them from Europe, and that was off-limits. Felice covered their day-to-day expenses by giving massages and baking cookies, and Joachim chipped in as well, tutoring his classmates in French and German.

In late spring, Robert had been contacted by a former business associate from Berlin who fled to Paris when Hitler came to power. Several of his clients were looking for the most profitable way to invest their money in the United States, and they were offering a big commission. They were interested in the film industry in particular, but he said it could be something else, as long as it had a future.

Following Nazi Germany's annexation of Austria, there was no longer doubt in anyone's mind that war would break out in Europe. Those who were wealthy but for whatever reason were unable to make the trip themselves sought to place their savings in reliable hands overseas.

Robert predicted that it would take a while still before Hitler could sufficiently arm himself. Long enough to capitalize on the situation financially. He had managed to turn misery to their advantage once before, during the inflation of the twenties. Why shouldn't he be able to again?

"It has to work," he told Felice.

His former business partner was leaning on him as well. His clients had confidence in Robert. This kind of operation was right up his alley. They were willing to entrust him with a large sum of money in cash, provided he would come to Paris. But he needed to get there ASAP. If the Czechs' dispute with the Sudeten Germans were to escalate, there was a risk that France would declare war on Germany, significantly complicating everything.

Robert got to work. Billy Wilder, their former neighbor from Berlin, not yet famous but on his way to success, introduced him to Ernst Lubitsch, who took him around the offices of the movie studio heads and executive producers. Cash money was in demand everywhere.

In between the ashtrays and glasses of whiskey, their desks were overflowing with scripts, budgets, profit forecasts, movie star headshots. In one office Robert even shook hands with Marlene Dietrich, but he didn't let it dazzle him. His hunting instincts were on high alert. He couldn't sleep at night, with all the profitable combinations bouncing around in his head. And he still managed, the week before his departure, to have the piano tuned, which he hadn't touched since the movers unpacked it.

He didn't say a word about anything wrong with his heart.

"This trip," he told Felice, "is my last chance to get back into finance."

She wasn't worried. She baked a batch of pastries, bought a bottle of champagne, cooked a festive dinner, and, finally, drove her husband to the station, where he climbed on board a new silver pointy-nosed Pullman car headed for San Francisco.

She was a little envious that he got to ride the express.

She had been sitting at Robert's bedside since morning, and also kept him company during lunch, but then the staff sent her away.

"Why don't you go for a walk, madame?" said the attending nurse. "It's such a beautiful day. Go enjoy Paris. Don't worry, your husband won't run away. He'll be back home in a week, and then you'll have your hands full taking care of him. Do a little shopping. Let the monsieur get some rest. Even just talking tires him out. Don't move and get plenty of sleep, that's the best heart medicine there is."

Robert told her it had felt like there was a claw stuck in his chest. Unable to breathe, he had tried to sit up, grasping for the vial of nitroglycerin on the nightstand. He put a pill beneath his tongue. Five minutes. Another pill. The claw was still there. He groped for the phone. The receiver slipped out of his hand onto the bed. The night receptionist picked up . . .

"Talk about luck," said Felice. "If he had been asleep . . ."

The nurse, a pretty young blonde about half Felice's age, always stopped to talk with her when she came by. She wanted to know about Hollywood. Was it true even an ordinary girl like her could become a movie star? Had Felice met any movie stars yet?

In the pretty young nurse's imagination, Los Angeles was a place glittering with gold. It was no use telling her about neighborhoods like Boyle Heights, where you didn't see any movie stars, but every day you encountered a multitude of poor immigrants from Europe, most of them Jews. Even the main shopping street, with its one-story homes, cheap eateries, tiny stores, barbershops, and auto garages, looked more like one of Berlin's forever unfinished working-class suburbs than a city center.

It wasn't until Felice unexpectedly found herself in Paris that she realized how much she missed a real European city.

She walks out the hospital gate. To her left is the entrance to Notre-Dame Cathedral, in front of her the embankment of the Seine. It's so bright out that she has to squint even under the brim of her hat.

Felice stands on the bridge, watching the river with its colorful tour boats. Then she crosses to the other side and, feeling a sudden urge for a coffee with cream, finds a café and takes a seat at a round marble table. Directly across from her, on the other side of the street, busy with cars and trams, a stone Archangel Michael perches atop a fountain, finger pointing skyward. In his other hand he grips a sword, keeping in check the devil writhing at his feet.

It's Saturday afternoon and men stand around the fountain dressed in their holiday best, some holding flowers. The women and girls they are waiting for are almost always late. The men shake their heads, pacing impatiently back and forth, checking the time on their watches against the time on the corner clock. When their sweethearts finally arrive, they give them a kiss on the cheek or the lips and walk away, arms around each other or hand in hand. . . .

How uninhibitedly the youth of today behave, thinks Felice. Compared to how we lived. Dragging around a chaperone with us everywhere we went, and then when we did find ourselves alone, we were too nervous to talk. The war certainly put an end to that. With all the killing going on, who cared who was married or not? When we took rooms next to each other in Marienbad, no one asked us a thing.

She hadn't gone on dates with Robert, either, or left him waiting with a bouquet in his hands. The reason for their marriage had been clear from the start. To start a family, not to wander around holding hands, staring up at the clouds.

Felice finishes her coffee, leaves the change on the table, and sets off uphill, along the boulevard Saint-Michel.

The hotel where she is staying, by the Luxembourg Gardens, isn't too expensive, and is quiet, considering how centrally it's located. Her third-floor room is spacious and looks out into the treetops. Robert will be able to recover well there, and as soon as the doctor allows him to get out of bed, they can go for walks in the park. She paid for the room through the end of

October, though it's clear now they won't be leaving any sooner than mid-November.

She saunters along the sidewalk lined with restaurants and shops, observing the Parisian women. Their skirts are longer than last year's, and their hats are bigger, too, with a broader brim than Felice's fall bonnet, which she bought in Geneva before they left for the United States. Straw hats and berets are also back in fashion, in every color imaginable, with decorations that strike Felice as eccentric. She prefers a short feather or simple ribbon. Then again, some of the chapeaus passing by are entirely bare, with no decorations at all, like a men's hat. On this warm day, there are even women going hatless. Strolling along with uncovered heads, a coat draped over their arms, even those clearly not students, laundrywomen, or maids.

The café terraces are filled with merry, noisy people, and they are right to be that way. You can't stop living just because Hitler is on a rampage in Germany and Europe is on the verge of war.

Felice decides to stop in at the Galeries Lafayette before Robert is released from the hospital and buy herself a new hat and maybe a light autumn coat. She normally never buys clothes off the rack—in Berlin she'd had them sewn, and in Geneva and Los Angeles she had simply refashioned them—but why not pick up something nice as long as she is in Paris?

She stops in front of a display window. Looking at herself reflected in the shiny glass, her graying hairs and wrinkles are not actually obvious, and as she stands there, handbag pressed to her hip, she is quite content with what she sees.

Suddenly she snaps to attention. Is that just a trick of light? Or is there someone on the roof of the building across the street?

She turns around and squints her eyes, sharpening her focus.

A man stands in front of a garret window, balancing on the steeply sloping tiled roof. He is naked, with a bare head and a black patch of hair around his genitals. Pale skin shining white in the afternoon sun. He grips the window frame with both hands, shouting something, but his cries are drowned in the racket from the cars and trams below. Felice sees his mouth open and close, the muscles on his neck tensing; then either his foot slips or he jumps. A white flash, the impact of body on pavement.

She wants to run to his aid, but the road is too busy to cross. People gather around him on the other side of the street.

"The Austrian Jews got here in the spring, and soon the Czechs will be here, too. It isn't just Paris, the whole country is bursting at the seams. You can't imagine the situation."

She is sitting in a restaurant with Robert's business partner from Berlin. Given that it was he who lured Robert to Paris, he feels somewhat responsible for the unfortunate situation that Robert now finds himself in. Although it wasn't as if it had been deliberate on his part, he reasons with himself.

Nevertheless he still feels guilty, even after paying Robert's hotel bill, packing his things with his own hands, taking them back to his place, and telegraphing Felice to come. Now on top of everything else, he is treating her to dinner, again another expense.

Yet he had incurred losses, too. Due to Robert's sick heart, he had missed out on an advantageous deal. All that had been left to do was sign the contracts and scoop up the money.

The negotiations with the clients were going swimmingly. He had wanted to celebrate—prematurely, he could see now—by inviting Robert to the Café de La Rotonde, in Montparnasse. They ordered an aperitif, a bottle of wine to go with the food, and champagne at the cabaret to top the evening off. But they hadn't gone overboard with their carousing; by eleven thirty Robert was home. That is, in his chilly hotel room on avenue des Gobelins, where the bathroom stank of sewage and the curtains of stale tobacco smoke.

"It's a farshtinkener pit!" he told Felice after she arrived. "And the money it costs!"

In any case, his heart attack had probably not been caused by either the heavy food or the alcohol he drank, but by Robert's habit of reading the newspaper before bed. Already during dinner he had gotten upset over Hitler's brash ultimatum and Chamberlain's willingness to negotiate on the Sudetens.

As if it weren't obvious to everyone that there would be a war—it was what Hitler had wanted all along. What was there to negotiate? Phooey! There was no negotiating with a dreykop like that.

"You've got to hand it to him," Robert's associate tells Felice, "your husband was prescient in a way. Everything he predicted has come to pass. He got you out of Germany in time, while it was still relatively easy. I used to see him as a pessimist, but clearly his pessimism has paid off. The optimists, who are fleeing now, are having a much harder time of it. In France there are some departments that aren't taking Jews anymore. England doesn't want them, either, and America has cut back on its quotas. Nobody wants us, my dear, and that conference in Évian that got so much press is a total bluff. It's just for show, so the world can't say they don't give a damn. Hundreds of thousands of people, Felice, surviving from day to day here in Paris only thanks to charities. Even famous people, successful people, you wouldn't believe it. Do you remember Dr. Weiss?"

"Is he in Paris?"

"Oh, yes. Physician, successful writer. Now, of course, he doesn't exist in Germany. His books have disappeared from shops. They aren't allowed to be published or sold. Every so often he writes something for the exile newspapers, but from what I've heard, the pay is hardly worth mentioning. I always enjoyed reading his work. I liked the way he complicated things. You know, I ran into him just a few weeks ago, on the street, right here, by chance. I invited him to lunch. He didn't let it show, but it was obvious he hadn't had a proper meal in a long time."

"Do you know where he's staying?"

"The last time we spoke, he had a room in a hotel not far from yours. He lives modestly, but even so, he sometimes has to stay with friends, to economize. Do you know him personally?"

"A bit."

"I'll write down the name of his hotel for you, but I can't guarantee he's still there. It's been three weeks or so since the last time we met."

He writes a name down on a napkin and slides it to Felice.

So Dr. Weiss is also in Paris, waiting for a miracle.

Felice can pick them out now when she sees them on the street.

The quick-stepping men with the briefcases under their arms and a busy look on their faces who suddenly stop mid-stride, unsure which way to go. The painstakingly dressed and groomed women who avoid the eyes of passersby as if they are ashamed.

The man on the roof was surely one of them. Perhaps a former neighbor from Viktoria-Luise-Platz. An actor, journalist, insurance agent. Maybe she used to see him in the park. Or she bought gloves from him.

Cheap boardinghouses, attic rooms—for the poorest, alcoves and under bridges. Lines in front of charity agencies. Lines in front of public lunchrooms. Donated clothes and shoes that never quite fit.

If not for Robert, she might have fallen into that trap herself.

Up to now, her only regret had been losing her homeland. In Los Angeles, living among the other refugees, who carefully preserved their bubble of the old world, she had dreamed Hitler would fall and they would return to Germany.

Now in Paris, in October 1938, for the first time she sees her situation differently.

Her Berlin exists no more and never will again.

Here in her handbag, though, she has a round-trip ticket to America. All she has to do is walk into the shipping company office and announce her date of departure. And waiting for her at the other end of her journey, tucked in between an orange tree and a stunted palm in Boyle Heights, is her home, with Else and her children inside.

Suddenly she feels impatient. She just hopes there won't be any hitch and Robert will be back on his feet as soon as possible, so the two of them can return home.

The lobby has a certain elegance to it, and the hotel's first two floors do their best to give the impression of an establishment that provides its guests with more than the bare necessities. If the yellow carpets aren't sparkling with newness, they aren't entirely trampled bare, either. The armchairs and tables with flowers mask the stains and cigarette holes, and the curtains on the windows are trimmed with gold fringe.

On the third and fourth floors, the fringe, armchairs, and flowers are gone, while the burn holes and stains are decidedly higher in number. On the fifth floor, which is the shabbiest, the cage elevator comes to a stop. From there on, you have to walk.

The boy who rode up with her points to a door, behind which there is apparently a hidden staircase.

"Room six oh eight is up the stairs. Shall I escort you the rest of the way?"

They ascend to the attic. A narrow corridor with a row of numbered doors and a shred of gray daylight falling through a single unwashed window. From one room she hears a child crying as two grown-ups quarrel, the thin walls only slightly muffling the noise. From somewhere else the peals of a woman's high-pitched laugh.

Felice pulls out her wallet, finds a few coins, and hands them to the boy.

"Would you be so kind as to tell the gentleman I'll be waiting downstairs. Felice Bauer, from Berlin."

It hadn't occurred to her before how awkward it would be. Standing at his door, knocking, waiting for him to open.

The first time it had been him knocking on her door, in Berlin, more than twenty years ago. He had shown up at her office unannounced, as she was today, bringing an urgent message from Prague. She had seen him several more times after that. In Berlin, it was impossible to avoid running into each other. He had been living with a well-known actress at the time.

By the time Felice makes her way down the stairs to the ground floor, the boy, who rode the elevator, is already waiting, and hands her a piece of paper:

"Dear Felice, what a lovely surprise! I had no idea you were in Paris. I'll be right there. Give me a half hour or so. Wait for me by the Grand Bassin in the Luxembourg Gardens."

"The gentleman wasn't alone," says the boy with a grin, holding out his palm. She decides to pretend not to notice and exits the hotel.

She is already frozen through by the time Weiss appears, having waited over an hour.

In the meantime, she walked the loop around the pond, watching the children in their berets and fall coats, chasing one another in circles around the green metal chairs where their mothers and nannies sat. An old woman in the kind of hat still worn before the war shuffled from one seat to the next, collecting the rental fee in an old-fashioned fabric drawstring purse, the type once known as a pompadour. The change made a jingling sound as it dropped on top of the other coins.

Despite keeping an eye out, she failed to see him coming.

All of a sudden, he is standing right in front of her, smaller than she remembered, with a thin, long face, dark eyes, and a vertical wrinkle between his eyebrows.

"So, what do you say to all this, Felice?" He runs his eyes over her, from her hat down to her shoes. "You haven't changed a bit."

A compliment? From him, hardly.

"Forgive me for making you wait. The lady dawdled getting dressed."

Still one to provoke, even now. He always had taken her as the petit bourgeois type, easily disconcerted by comments about sex. But Felice doesn't fall for it. She never had. Nor does she wait for him to offer his arm, taking hold uninvited. "It's chilly. Shall we go for a walk?"

They slowly make their way in a large semicircle, climbing the white staircase, then submerging themselves in an allée of trees already turning yellow.

"If only he could see us now," says Weiss. "Two archenemies on a stroll in the Jardin du Luxembourg. While we were fighting over his soul, his body vanished into thin air."

"If I felt a need to reminisce, I wouldn't do it with you. I have no desire to speak about the past. I sought you out because I happened to be in Paris. But we live in Los Angeles now."

"Lucky you."

"Maybe we can help you get out of here. I'm not sure how, but there must be a way."

"How do you know I want to leave?"

"Everyone wants to leave."

"I'm not everyone, though of course I do, too. And I know you're in America. The gossip gets around here as reliably as in Berlin. Miss Bloch is in Italy now, for a change."

"I believe that she's in Florence. She hasn't written in ages."

"I hear she's headed to Palestine, or maybe England. But she hasn't left yet. There is a love interest involved. She's living with a musician, much younger than she is. You see, I know everything. Though I haven't a clue what you're doing in Paris when everyone else is fleeing in the opposite direction."

"My husband is in the hospital here. He traveled here on business and had a heart attack. That's why I came."

"I don't know your husband, but he has my sympathy. It is actually a miracle that we haven't all died of a broken heart."

As he leads her down the long allée, the darkness thickens, the light from the electric lamps shiny on the damp yellow leaves. It rained a bit that afternoon and the air smells of decay.

"I am honestly glad you sought me out, Felice. A messenger from that old, happy world, which seemed so unbearably unhappy to us at the time. Little did we know what lay in store. I often wonder what he would say to all this. Though I'm sure it wouldn't surprise him. He suffered no illusions when it came to the human race. I sometimes argue with him in my mind. But everything he faulted me for, I fault myself for now. 'The measured leaps of a grasshopper,' he said about my writing. Writing is increasingly difficult, but the most difficult thing of all for me is getting up in the morning and keeping my wits together. Though apparently I do possess a certain tenacity—I wouldn't call it courage—that won't allow me to give up completely. Do you remember Hanni?"

"The last I heard of her, she got married. It was in the papers."

"The wedding changed nothing between us. Her husband knew about me. He didn't much understand Hanni, but he appreciated that she was an exceptional woman, an artist, with particular needs. As long as he wanted her, he had to accept my existence. He works in finance, like your husband. The two of us are friends now. We've even seen each other here in Paris a few times."

"They're here?"

"He is. Hanni died. I was with her. Just me, by myself. I returned to Berlin on a Czech passport. Then I buried her. That was two years ago."

"I'm so sorry."

"Of course. I also felt sorry for you at one point. Though it might not have seemed that way to you. So, how are you doing? Over there in America?"

She tells him, truthfully, how she took the massage and cosmetic courses, how she's been learning English, how she and Else bake custom cakes and cookies, and that as soon as she saves up enough, she wants to open a shop selling notions and knitting supplies. Both of her children are fine and in school. But Robert hasn't caught on there yet. His trip here to Paris was sort of a test run.

"Else is your sister from Budapest?"

"She lived with her husband in Budapest, but it's been years now since she divorced him. Then she lived with us in Berlin and Geneva. She and Hana, her daughter."

They walk slowly out of the park and come to a stop at the wrought-iron gate on boulevard Saint-Michel.

"I remember he was very fond of one of your sisters."

"Erna. She got married and stayed in Berlin. He was fond of Toni, too, but she died."

"Did you know he's been translated into French? Schocken published his collected works. You probably know about that. It appears he's going to be as famous as Brod predicted. You know what Klaus Mann wrote about his books? He said they were the most noble and significant publications to appear in Germany recently, a spiritual event spawned from the splendid isolation of the ghetto. He meant well by it, Klaus Mann. He was doing his best to help. He's been helping all of us, actually. But in this case, all it accomplished was to draw the censors' attention. They probably wouldn't even have noticed his books otherwise—they were below their resolution threshold. But an intellectual event from the ghetto? *That* they had to prohibit and burn immediately. On the other hand, it was great publicity for him abroad."

"I don't dwell much on the past," says Felice. "I don't have time. I don't read much, either."

"I would love to take you out for dinner, but honestly, I can't afford it. Maybe next time. I just finished a novel and entered it in an international contest. If I win, I'll get a visa to America and my troubles will be over."

"I'll keep my fingers crossed."

"Of course, why not? There's a young lady here as well—married. The woes of love. I never have known how to be alone."

Felice opens her handbag and takes out an envelope.

"I hope you won't be offended, Doctor. It isn't much."

The vertical wrinkle between his eyebrows deepens. It looks like it was cut with a knife.

"I'm not offended at all, Felice. Why should I be? I thank you with all my heart. I used to tolerate hunger fairly well, but now I've developed a stomach ulcer, and it hurts if I don't give it something to eat. It doesn't like everything, either. It's a picky ulcer."

"I used to get stomach cramps when I worked in the office. I don't know if it was an ulcer, but it hurt an awful lot."

Weiss pauses, turning the envelope in his fingers. "I'm sure you think I hated you. But that isn't true."

"You needn't explain a thing to me!"

"On the contrary, I quite liked you. You weren't my type, but I understood what he saw in you, what he admired in you."

"Really? Then why did you meddle in our affairs? Why did you talk him out of the wedding?"

"I was frightened of you."

"Frightened?"

"He never should have stayed at that dreadful insurance company. It was killing him. And you acted like you didn't see it. He never should have stayed in Prague. And you, you wanted to move in there with him. How could she be so bright and yet so deaf and blind? I thought. Why does she insist on having her way?

"I was so angry at you for being so obtuse.

"He was begging, Felice. He knew his life was at stake. He wanted nothing but to leave his job at the office and write, but he couldn't. No, not as long as he was strong and healthy, not until he was dying. But you, you could have helped him. He wasn't wrong about that. If only you had wanted to. You were solid as a rock. You helped everyone else. Why not him?

"I did hold that against you. And I confess, I was delighted when the two of you broke up. If the war hadn't broken out, it might all have turned out differently. He already had his letter of resignation written. I helped him with it myself. He was determined to leave the company and settle down in Berlin. He was still healthy and I could have helped him. Lots of other people, too. He had plenty of literary friends who believed in him. And at that very moment they closed the borders. That's what I call 'bad luck.'

"But don't just stand there. Defend yourself."

Felice has her head bowed, hat shading her face. The man grasps her by the elbow.

"Go ahead and tell me how awful I am. You've been kind. You sought me out. No one forced you to do that. You gave me money. And here I am, causing you pain. What kind of man does that? A beggar, and an ungrateful one at that. I've gotten used to begging, though. It doesn't bother me anymore. I have an ulcer and my books don't sell and I can't open a practice—where would the French end up if every Jew here opened a doctor's office? But the worst part about it is, I can't write. That novel I told you about fell apart, just like everything else in my life is falling apart now. Maybe the jurors won't notice, but what does it matter?

"Why am I even alive, Felice? Love since Hanni's death isn't love anymore. It's just fear and arousing the senses. My mother passed away. No, there's nothing now for me but to write, no matter if it's good or bad.

"The truth is, I've forgotten what it was like to be someone—doctor, writer, lover, son. I only know it was nice. I live because I'm afraid to die, Felice. That's it. And the main sign of life is pain—here." He hits himself in the stomach with his fist.

Felice raises her head. Through a veil of tears she sees a man falling—Dr. Weiss hurtling down into the darkness—and she has no way to help.

She reaches out and touches his sleeve, then turns and slowly walks away, leaving him standing there with the blue envelope in his hands, next to the cart of the roasted chestnut seller.

Over the course of the fall, she spotted Dr. Weiss once more, but only from a distance, in the park. He was strolling with a woman. It was late October, when she and Robert began going on walks, as the doctor had prescribed. But since Robert didn't know Weiss personally, she decided to pretend not to see him.

The Czechoslovak crisis, as the newspapers referred to it, had by then been resolved. The French and the English settled for the illusion that Hitler got what he wanted, moving him off the front pages into the foreign section, where they hoped he would remain.

Still, Felice was careful to keep the papers lying around the tables in the hotel lobby out of Robert's sight. His heart required absolute calm. Time measured only in meals, medicines, regular exercise, and sleep.

Robert knew his life was at stake and didn't ask any questions.

Afternoons, while he rested in bed, Felice read out loud to him from *Sentimental Education*, by Flaubert, then followed it with Stendhal's *The Charterhouse of Parma.* She purchased them in German translation from the bouquinistes on the embankment.

They both were familiar with the books from their youth, and it was interesting and refreshing to read them again, together, in this strange situation in which they found themselves. Instead of Hitler, Germany, the fates of relatives and friends, instead of Robert's illness and their own uncertain future in America, they discussed the love interests of Frédéric Moreau and Fabrizio del Dongo.

On November 2, after consulting with the physician, Felice went to the office of the shipping company and booked two passages on a ship to New York.

On November 7, a seventeen-year-old German Jew with Polish roots, Herschel Grynszpan, shot five bullets into the abdomen of Ernst vom Rath, a German Foreign Office diplomat in Paris. On November 9, at 5:30 P.M., vom Rath died of his wounds, and a few hours later a coordinated pogrom was launched throughout Germany and Austria. Thousands of Jews robbed, injured, and killed, synagogues burned, shops ransacked. Felice succeeded in keeping even that hidden from Robert.

Hitler returned from the newspapers' foreign section to the front pages, apparently now for good.

On the morning of November 14, they boarded a train at Saint-Lazare station, and that same evening their ship set sail from the port at Le Havre.

They are traveling first-class, even though they can't afford it. Robert needs quiet and comfort.

Felice helps her husband change into his pajamas and puts him to bed. She unpacks and arranges everything they are going to need in the cabin over the course of their voyage. Then she puts on her coat, ties a scarf on her head, and goes out to the afterdeck.

The pilot boat has just turned around and is heading back to port, where she can still make out the windows of homes and the lanterns atop the ships' masts.

A cluster of people stands at the railing. No one says a thing, the only sound the splashing of waves and the howling of the wind.

The coast recedes into the distance. The individual lights blur, merging into a soft glow that gradually, little by little, disappears.

1944

San Donato Val di Comino

Tree, trees. Trees. Roots. She loves the trees. She can feel their strength. She is depleted.

Longing, longing, longing, longing, longing. And exhaustion.

She is going mad in an inconspicuous, invisible, pain-free way. It feels like nothing around her has anything to do with her. She has to keep convincing herself that it does. Even the desire, the burning, no longer touches her at her core. It isn't a blazing at her core, but ashes. It is ashes; everything is falling apart. Fear. Depression. Love a tree. Love a mountain.

Never again is she going to love. Never again will she find her way.

Her hip and wrist are in pain.

Everything has already been, everything has already happened, and yet at the same time it's as though none of it happened at all. That's the worst part about it. Her life has been erased. When she looks in the mirror while brushing her hair, it's there, a wide gray lock of hair, falling down the left side of her face, and then countless threads of silver mixed in among the black.

Fifty-one years old. Today, March 21, 1944. The fortune-teller in Florence told her that people born at the vernal equinox tended to be exceptional. There was nothing left but a small stack of letters and photographs, which she dragged around from place to place. Too little even for an ordinary life, let alone an exceptional one.

Parents dead. Brother in Tel Aviv. When she announced to him, at the end of summer in 1935, that she was returning to Europe after spending two months in Palestine, he begged her not to go, screaming and yelling that it made no sense to leave now, when everyone else was trying to get *into* Palestine. She should be thankful she was safe, he said. Why did she always have to have a mind of her own?

She didn't have a mind of her own; she wanted Ernst, who was waiting for her in Italy.

Just when she was feeling so old and humiliated and alone, right before her departure for Tel Aviv, the heavens had put in her path a young, talented man who was completely lost and needed her, loved her.

Who would seek to separate love from need at this point? There is no such thing as free love; anyone can tell you that. Tenderness is inseparable from necessity, whether what we need is a firm embrace, food, or reassurance that there's a point in getting out of bed in the morning, even if only for that ray of sunshine streaming through the curtains. If only for that other someone making coffee in the kitchen.

Thanks to Ernst, Grete became herself again; it didn't take very much. She was so hungry. Just a faint fragrance of love, of life, and she fluffed up her feathers. The banners were raised and the troops launched into battle, vigor renewed.

She had to be strong, for him. Five years, day after day, she wrestled with his anxieties. The situation, even in Italy, was getting worse for Jews. All sorts of measures were being introduced. The authorities had begun throwing them out of the country.

With every new order issued, Ernst suffered a breakdown.

He didn't set foot outside the building, lying in their room and smoking with the curtains drawn. Grete made sure they had food, along with everything else. Finally his relatives arranged a visa to Chile for him and sent him funds for the trip. A huge victory. There weren't many people who could legally leave the country. But Ernst was paralyzed with fear. He couldn't leave without Grete.

She was strong.

Not once did she think of herself.

Or maybe just the tiniest bit.

You see, she had no idea how long she could keep convincing her lover that the suicide of a German Jew in Italy wasn't the best solution to a problem that no one, not even Grete, had any clue how to deal with.

Her strength was slowly diminishing, too.

In the end, she packed his bags for him. She spoke to him like a child at the dentist, holding his hand on the train to Genoa. She took him all the way to the ship. She even made sure he got on board and was with people he could trust. And then . . . *Ernst ging nach Chile.*

Alone on the train back to Florence. Outside the windows, a landscape with touches of spring, despite its being only February.

Alone in the rented room she had shared with Ernst, in one of the Renaissance buildings on the Piazza Santa Croce. She was expecting loneliness, but also relief. Yet what came was not relief. Her life was over.

Four years ago, in the room with a window on the Piazza Santa Croce, she had ceased forever to be the funny, quick-witted woman that she once was, the woman who worked as head of the trade division at Adrema. And like flames creeping along the edges of a sheet of paper before they swallowed it up for good, madness was creeping along the edges of her soul, while at the core it was barren and empty. The pain . . .

Never again is she going to love. Never again will she find her way.

She hardly left the building. She lay on Ernst's bed, either smoking or writing letters. Letters and official requests. She wrote by hand. Even the typewriter that had supported her and Ernst for so long had been confiscated.

I, the undersigned, Margarete Bloch, daughter of the late Luigi Bloch and Jenny Meyerowitz, born in Berlin, March 21, 1893, residing in Florence, Piazza Santa Croce, Fl. 12, hereby state that my passport (no. 573/124/132), issued 5/9/32 by the Berlin Police Prefecture, expired as of 5/9/37. Being that I am of Jewish origin, I am not able to obtain a new travel document from the German authorities, and it is therefore impossible for me to leave Italy. To this end, I most respectfully request that I be issued a new identity card by the relevant authorities. . . .

Dear sir, would it be within your power to intercede with Mr. XY, who—insofar as I know—possesses certain contacts, so that he might intercede with YZ? So that he might help? I am sorry to insist like this, but my situation is beginning to be untenable. I did not receive any reply to my last letter. Respectfully . . .

Dear Wolf, do you remember the last time we met in Prague? It seems so long ago. Our walks through that magical city, when you played the piano for me in that messy room? Florence weighs on me, body and soul.

The flames of madness. The crumbs of life she shapes into the form of a woman. She still wants to live. She clings to life like a weed dug up, over and over again, from a crack in the pavement.

The springtime sun in Italy is soft as velvet, not cruel like in Berlin. The fragrance of orange trees wafts down from the gardens above the city. But the velvetiness is torture for her, the beauty, yes, she would have felt better being in some dump, in some ruins, than in Florence, in that perfectly proportioned tomb, an oasis of ideal beauty, which at any moment, as she had witnessed, could turn into absolute ugliness and evil.

She heard from Ernst. The ship had reached its destination, and he was going to try to procure a visa for her as well. Not expecting him to succeed, she busied herself with looking into other escape routes, systematically, as she had learned to do in the office.

She compiled an inventory of anyone who might be able to help: friends, friends of friends, important people. Only one of the people on her list was famous, and he was long dead. Felice's fiancé, a writer and doctor of law from Prague. He had courted Grete's favor, too, once upon a time, but she refused him. Or did he refuse her? It no longer mattered. She had his letters, at least some of them. Some she cut to pieces, at one point, because of Felice. How young and silly they both had been.

She never would have believed that he, of all people, would become famous.

To survive meant to set oneself apart from the nameless masses. The American newspapers wrote articles about famous Jews; international rescue committees came to their assistance.

She had taken the rare letters to a law office and had them locked up in a safe. They were too valuable to lose. The only famous man she had known in her life.

In May, she received an ultimatum from the authorities. She had two months to leave Italy. Then three weeks. Finally they arrested her and brought her here with the others.

She combs her hair into a bun. She has a streak of gray running down the right. Big black eyes. She tries her best not to show her slightly crooked teeth, holding her tiny figure erect, handbag over her arm.

She refuses to give up; she has no intention of doing so.

She didn't see the request with her own eyes, but she can imagine it, typos and all.

> Addressee: Ministry of the Interior. General Directorate of Public Affairs, Department of Security. Re: Bloch Margarete, born in Berlin 3/21/1893. Transfer proposal.
>
> Jewess Bloch, Margaret, interned in San Donato 7/20/40, is causing a public disturbance through her behavior, in that she maintains an intimate relationship with one Cendrone Nazzarene, born in San Donato 12/14/08, a barber of dubious faith. Despite that Cedrone was recently called up to service, Bloch persists in maintaining written contact with him. I propose that she be relocated from San Donato, where her presence is undesirable, thereby severing any contact with the above-named individual. Proposed relocation site: women's internment camp of Pollenza.

It was pointless trying to figure out which of Nazzarene's mistresses had turned him in.

"I'm not going anywhere," she told them when they came for her from the prefecture with the official order for relocation. "I would rather hang myself on that walnut tree in the garden."

The moment they left, she dashed off to see the doctor. Dear old Dr. Massa. He gave it some thought, then pecked out a report on his typewriter: "Ovarian cancer, neural instability, risk of collapse . . . Conclusion: In view of the patient's state of health, her transfer from San Donato is emphatically recommended against."

She was permitted to stay. She just had to move out of the little room over Nazzarene's barbershop to an apartment a few streets away, where an elderly clockmaker lived with his two adult, unmarried daughters. The local authorities apparently believed that the fifty-year-old widower would be able to cope with Grete's pernicious Jewish charm. . . .

The flowers, the Church of the Virgin Mary perfumed with incense, the pipe organ and the cool water running down her forehead.

Her baptism had been proposed by by Di Bona, the parish priest himself, who was secretly aiding, who was secretly aiding the partisans. On his last trip to Rome, he had learned that the Vatican had at its disposal a certain number of Brazilian visas but would grant them only to Jews who had been baptized.

It was worth a try, he said. But it had to be for real, not just for show.

He limited his teaching of the catechism to the bare essentials: name the twelve apostles, recite the Credo and the Our Father.

Dr. Massa and his wife acted as her godparents.

There were others besides her: Gabriela, from Bratislava; Edita, from Vienna; Grete's best friend, Rosa Myler; Gabriela's two children. All of them, in the hope of escape, dressed in their Sunday best or whatever they had left of it, got on their knees, and recited in hushed tones:

I believe in one God,
the Father Almighty,
maker of heaven and earth,
of all things visible and invisible.
I believe in one Lord Jesus Christ,
the Only Begotten Son of God,
born of the Father before all ages.
God from God, Light from Light,
true God from true God,
begotten, not made, consubstantial with the Father;
through him all things were made.

By way of prayer, Father Di Bona told them, we can summon faith. Of course how that faith then operates in people is a mystery.

What she most appreciated about the old doctor and his wife was that they didn't ask her any questions. Neither before the ceremony nor afterward as she sat with them at home around the festively set table, drinking glass after glass of wine and trying not to think about her dead parents and her brother in Tel Aviv.

After lunch she played Beethoven for them on the doctor's pianino, the only one in the village.

They didn't get the visas to Brazil anyway. Cardinal Luigi Maglione in the Vatican would recognize only Jewish baptisms prior to 1935.

Still, *confino libero* is better than an internment camp. She just has to report to the police on a regular basis, not leave home after dark, not work for pay, and not consort with the local population. Which is impossible. How can she not consort with the people who are feeding her out of their own pockets, since otherwise she would starve to death?

Love can no longer be separated from cigarettes, soup, bread, and a little bit of wine. She has always known how to take care of herself, and that's what she does now; she has no intention of giving up. She may feel exhausted, but it's only mimicry, the protective coloration of a lizard scanning for weak spots and figuring out how to exploit them from its hiding place under the rocks. The danger can never be overestimated. Regulations, laws, and amendments come charging at her like a wild elephant. She ducks and dodges, never asking why. There is no answer. There is no time.

Or she could hide out in the mountains, like the Tenenbaums.

When Italy signed a truce with the Allies last September and the first Germans appeared in the valley, Mordko Tenenbaum and his wife packed up and left.

"The end of the war is in sight," he said. "I'm not about to get killed now. I'm going up into the mountains, and I recommend that everyone do the same."

Of the twenty-eight interned Jews, twelve of them took his advice. Sixteen remained in the village.

Even if her hip hadn't hurt as badly as it did, she wouldn't have gone with them.

They weren't about to drag her out of here. The Germans were losing on every front. In January, the Allies had landed at Anzio. It would be only a matter of days or weeks before they broke through the defensive line and occupied Rome. German lives were at stake; they were hardly concerned about capturing the few remaining Jews.

Refugees came pouring in from the battlefield around Monte Cassino. Women, children, sheep, hens. Every house, every cottage and courtyard was bursting at the seams. And smoke and the sound of gunfire from over the ridge. Villages in flames. The monastery bombed to rubble. Who would bother wasting time with Jews now?

Ulla Tenenbaum returns to the village in secret, sneaking in after dark, to hold her child in her arms. Katja will be two come summer, and has just begun to walk. She toddles up and down the stone steps along with the other children of San Donato, and when the inspector comes around, Catherina, a woman from the village, passes off the little girl as her own. Mordko Tenenbaum treats her for free, as he does so many other people in the valley. They are grateful to him, and everyone is fond of Ulla, too. She's a midwife, and there is always a need for them, the same as there is for doctors.

Given all the official correspondence they are handling now,

Grete is certain they could use a typist, too. If only her beautiful typewriter hadn't been left behind in Florence.

She stands on the highest spot in the village, by a stone tower dating back to the Middle Ages that looks like it sprouted out of a huge lichen-covered boulder. It stands in a clearing, now in spring still green and damp with rain, in summer seared brown by the sun. A forest climbs the mountain slopes. Oak trees, hornbeams, elms, and, still higher, pines. And beyond the bare, rocky peaks, in one of the mountain passes said to be impossible to traverse even in summer, so steep and jagged are they, the Tenenbaums and the others who took to the mountains with them have been hiding out since autumn. She has heard there are English soldiers and Italian deserters from the front there with them, too, and even a stray group of Yugoslavian women.

Only women and children remained in the village, all of them stateless Jews. Poles, Czechoslovaks, Germans, Austrians. *Ebrei stranieri.* Trapped at the end of the valley, with no way out. In a charming, quaint little town that in peacetime would have been a lovely place to go on vacation. Feasting your eyes, as she is now, on the view of the wide valley with its colorful mosaic of little fields and olive groves, the dark fingers of the cypresses and tops of the cedars serving as a benevolent hand shielding against the sun. The hills with their gray-and-white bald patches of limestone, for centuries carved by the local masons into balustrades, porticos, spouts, and fountains. The oleanders and bougainvillea and orange trees, just now starting to bloom, with a fragrance like sweet girlish dreams.

Yet to be trapped here in this little town, against one's will and destitute, is absurd.

At the rear of the German line, which, a few kilometers to the south, separates the occupied part of Italy from the free, dividing life from death.

The soil is cool and muddy, damp on the soles of her feet.

Bending down and running a finger over the tip of her shoe, she feels a hole. Might that still be repaired?

Her shoes are falling apart, like everything else. She has already sold or given away her better items of clothing, except for her coat and her one best dress, now mended at the neck as well. Lace, jewelry, velvet jackets, silk blouses, fashionable trousers, all gone. Exchanged for money or food. At this point she has nothing left for anyone to take. She is teaching English to Arturo's two daughters. In exchange, they share their soup, bread, and sheep's cheese with her. Arturo has bottles of wine and olive oil buried in his barn, and sometimes traps a bird or wild rabbit in a wire noose that he sets in the hills. He was forced to surrender his rifle ages ago.

He jokes that Grete eats like a bird. Living off of smoke. He scrounges cigarettes in the village for her.

He treats her with the respect of someone who has never set foot outside the valley and barely learned to read and write. But his fingers are delicate, and he knows all there is to know about clocks, including the church clock, which he repairs. He learned the trade from his father, who, in turn, learned it from his. Besides that, he has an olive grove and a flock of sheep as well, and knows all about the life cycles of birds, bugs, and herbs. On the other hand, he hasn't the slightest idea who Beethoven was.

One winter's day, he was already dressed and on his way out when Grete, standing by the door, suddenly pulled him close, and, clasping his left arm in both her hands, pressed against it with her chest and face and lips. He was wearing a sheepskin coat, and in that one arm he had strength enough to keep her from the abyss.

He continues to use the formal *you* with her even after they become lovers.

Her body, arching underneath his, still fills him with astonishment. So white and fragile—he has never seen anything like it. Even the little ladies from Rome who came for the summer before the war were not as white as she is.

She is a strange one, perhaps even a bit mad.

Before coming, she shouts German words, and once satisfied, she bursts into tears.

"Sono infelice," she whispers in his ear.

"Va bene. Va tutto bene."

2019

Lyon

Finally I sit down to write again. The children's vacation, trips, visits. And there she is, waiting, on the hill in San Donato, where I left off last time. Waiting insistently. It is her story, after all.

Grete Bloch.

Old Dr. Massa called her "La Blok." To her last lover, she was "La Passioncella."

How important are names?

Why in one book was I able to rename Emma Goldman "Louise G." and Alexander Berkman "Andrei B.," while Felice remains "Felice" and Grete "Grete"?

Also Felice's son, Henry, let me change his name to Joachim, and his wife, Annette, willingly appears under the name Nina Perel. Moritz Marasse, Felice's husband, hides behind the character of Robert. But Felice and Grete refuse.

It may be because Kafka introduced them to literature long before I did, via his letters. Felice and Grete have become literary characters, and characters can't be renamed; their names are what define them. Hamlet may appear in plays other than the one that Shakespeare wrote about him, but he still has to be called Hamlet. Which doesn't mean that there isn't a different, living human face hiding behind his name in every play.

Felice's family, or at least a part of it, consented to my writing about Felice. I hope their consent applies to her name as well.

Why write about Felice anyway? Who cares about a woman like Felice?

I find no great story here, just an everyday courageousness that manifests itself mainly in perseverance. Withdrawn, hard-working, unliterary. This is how I imagine her. A woman with the ability to organize and straighten out the world around her, care for it.

She reminds me of the women in Sarajevo who once so fascinated me.

At the time, my first husband and I were moving from one city to another, all over the former Yugoslavia. He was a film editor, and whenever he had a job somewhere, we would go with him: me, our son, who was still too young to go to school, and our dog.

We arrived in Sarajevo in October and left after Christmas. This was ten years after the end of the war there, and there were still land mines in the mountains above the city. It was forbidden to stray from the designated trails.

The producer found us a place in an old apartment building with its plaster pocked by gunfire, near a city park that used to be a cemetery. What looked like milestones from a distance were actually the gray stelae of Muslim graves. When it snowed at the end of November, it made fluffy little caps on the stone turbans, which my son and I knocked off with our hands.

The apartment was on the fifth floor, with no elevator, so I had to lug the shopping and the stroller up the stairs, and sometimes our son, too, when he didn't want to walk. I remember the nameplate on the door of the apartment one floor below us said Gavrankapetanović, and the windows on the landings wouldn't close all the way, so when winter came, the snow gusted onto the staircase. The apartment looked out on a busy street on one side, and on the other it gave onto the courtyard, where a family of cats lived in a collapsed shed. People threw their leftovers down to them from the windows.

In Sarajevo, people do most of their shopping at the marketplace, just as they do in Belgrade, Zagreb, and Ljubljana. I went there every day. Some days went better than others. I got cheated often. Not badly. Pieces of rotten fruit mixed in with the good ones, things like that. I think they did it mainly for educational reasons. Because if you're going to shop at the market in a city like Sarajevo, you have to know the rules. You need to know when to haggle and when not to, and that undervaluing quality goods and overpaying for junk amount to the same thing from a moral point of view.

The local women, whom I admired from a distance but tried in vain to emulate, never got cheated. None of the vendors would even dare. Women here learned to shop from their mothers, who had learned it from theirs before them, and you could tell. It isn't the kind of thing you can learn from a book. You have to feel a tomato, a head of cabbage, a chunk of meat, weigh it in your hand.

Every day, after coming home from the market and an early lunch, I would put my son to sleep, so I had at least a while to write. By that point he was two and it wasn't as easy as when he was a baby. I practically had to force him into the stroller; then I would cover him up, put a cap on his head, and open the bedroom window wide to let in a stream of icy air. That usually did the trick. Then I would roll him back and forth, between the door and the bed, until he was overcome by sleep.

There was a homemaker who lived across the courtyard from us. She had a glassed-in balcony that she used as a pantry during the colder months. There were braids of garlic and onion hanging from poles, shelves of canning jars, stores of potatoes and vegetables. She would often appear on the balcony while I was putting my son to sleep, and stride assuredly back and forth through her kingdom. Pick something here, rearrange something there, cut off a stalk or sweep the floor. Slide open the glass panel and hang the laundry on the line running off the balcony.

I followed her movements with envy. How completely everything obeyed her.

Whereas my own material life, as Marguerite Duras called it in one of her books, was a half-tamed beast, which only occasionally feigned obedience.

It wasn't a question of my knowing how to cook or do laundry. Things didn't beam as I approached them. Entrust themselves to my protection. Breathe a sigh of relief when I was near, feeling that they were in good hands.

And they were right not to trust me. I didn't trust them, either.

That was what hit home for me in Sarajevo.

Three years later, I moved to New York, along with my son, to be with my new love.

I had been teaching a course on Franz Kafka at an American university in Prague before I left, and in New York I got an offer to continue teaching.

Leaving aside the difficulties that Kafka's writing presents, no matter what context you study him in, I have to say that teaching young Americans in Prague was easy. With a mere four months for their European adventure, their main priority was to have a good time. Staggering from one hangover to the next, they were always grateful when I took them for a walk.

In New York, touring sites connected with Kafka was no longer an option, and the students who showed up for my course, titled "Kafka and His Context," were likely to be readers of Deleuze and Guattari, for the most part not hungover. I had to keep up with them, and ideally stay a step ahead. It was October 2010, our second fall in the States. My son had just turned six and my first daughter was soon to be born. The semester started in January.

I was reading Kafka, and about Kafka, while attempting to make headway on a novel of my own about anarchists, which was fighting back against me. I was having a hard time entering into the text, finding the right pitch. It was like I had lost my tongue. Not Czech, the language I speak, but a language of my own.

Clearly it was a result of the previous two years I had spent working for a magazine in Prague, writing articles of my own every week, and editing other people's, with no time left for anything else. My tongue had become an effective, reliable tool, nothing more, serving a purpose that didn't extend beyond the next deadline. Returning to free writing was much harder than I had imagined.

There were good days, when I bobbed along the streets of Manhattan like a gull on the waves, grateful for all the diversity and the love that had brought me here. And then there were bad days. Instead of me, a ghost of myself walked my son to school, did the shopping and went to the playground, studied Kafka and attempted to write, but none of it had the right weight or fit the way I wanted it to, and what weighed least of all was my dislocated, transplanted self, which hurt so much, even in spite of its obvious insignificance.

And it was then, in fall of 2010, that a question surfaced in my mind: Who really was Felice Bauer? Who was the woman a generation of Kafka fans knew only as a lover of meaty dishes, heavy furniture, and precisely set watches? Who was hiding behind the poised exterior and hearty laughter to which many had testified?

The Kafka scholars have never deemed her worthy of study in her own right. Little is known of her life after Kafka. She got married, had two children, immigrated to America. Did she leave any traces behind?

Felice Bauer and Franz Kafka.

On the one hand, certainty; on the other, a permanent and potentially destructive uncertainty, which—for the sake of his writing—must and should be preserved.

She sorts, decides, plans. For him everything, from the smallest details of daily life to the loftiest symbols, has the same intense, unsettled quality. It is all part of a single organic, shifting whole, from which perhaps something may be created, but not according to a predetermined plan.

She brushes her teeth, rinses out the sink, and puts the toothpaste and toothbrush back in their place. He, on the other hand, is constantly at risk of having the tube of toothpaste suddenly leap into his face and reveal one of the secrets of the universe.

Could the two of them ever live together?

I picture myself at my desk, a small Ikea dining table, in the living room of our third-floor apartment on Eighty-sixth Street. Outside the window, the branches sway on the trees, which have grown markedly in the three years that we've been living here. The room—spacious, not too bright, in part thanks to the trees—serves as bedroom, library, dining room, and two studies all at once. The other room is for the children.

My internet search turns up contacts for two of Felice Bauer's great-grandsons. One a musician, the other an astrophysicist at the University of Texas. The second one replies to my letter. He says he is currently in Austin, doing his Ph.D., but his parents live in New York, and his grandfather Henry, Felice Bauer's son, is staying, along with his wife, in an assisted living facility on the Hudson.

His name is Joel and he was my link to the family of Felice Bauer. Apart from his career in astrophysics, he plays oboe, clarinet, and alto sax. He has long since completed his Ph.D. and gotten married. The last time I wrote, he was working on a project with a space telescope.

I don't know what I did to earn his trust, but after we had exchanged several letters, he called his grandfather up from Texas and talked him into letting me visit. Maybe he hoped I'd be able to wheedle some information out of him. Because though he had taught Joel stamp collecting and taken him on walks as a boy, he had never talked to him about his past life. Joel lamented to me, first in his letters, then eventually in person, that he actually knew very little about the most interesting part of his family.

During one of his visits to his parents in New York, Joel introduced me to his mother, Henry's daughter. Her name was Leah and she was a child psychiatrist, having inherited the calling from her father.

Leah still had memories of her grandmother Felice, and I turned to her with questions when I first began to write this book. By that point, we—my husband and I and our three children—had left New York and were living in Lyon, France.

I can never be grateful enough to Leah that she didn't tell me to go to hell, as I deserved—as anyone would who contacts you out of the blue, prying into your private life and memories. She did her best to answer every one of my questions, and then, one day, she invited me to her home, on the nineteenth floor of a high-rise in midtown Manhattan.

It was July 2018. Horse-drawn carriages weaved their way through the honking taxis and screaming, sweaty tourists at the building's base, but up above, in her apartment, it was quiet and cool. The treetops of Central Park rippled beneath her windows, a layer of green in every shade spreading into the distance. The room was dominated by a life-size standing Buddha statue and, on the wall, an Oriental rug that she said Henry had brought back from one of his trips.

"My father collected rugs. He traveled a lot, all over Asia and Europe, and he took my brother and me with him. The only place we never went was Germany—he wouldn't take us there."

In the entryway of Leah's apartment, right next to the door, hung a portrait of her grandmother Felice in a blue dress, with a string of red beads around her neck. I had seen that one before.

Leah was a petite, good-looking woman with long gray hair. She had reserved precisely one hour of her time for me, just like her father years before. On the living room table, a stack of mementos sat laid out and waiting: a photograph of Felice and her husband in Los Angeles from 1937, an old Hanukkah menorah, a small album containing blackened photographs of relatives from Germany whose names were now forgotten, and the envelope from a letter handwritten by Franz Kafka.

I had brought her a box of fine chocolates from France. She was extremely accommodating. Though she admitted she didn't know much about her father, or Felice. She had been much closer with her grandmother on her mother's side.

"My grandmother on my mother's side," Leah told me, "came to America at age seventeen. Didn't know how to read or write. She fled to escape the pogroms, but the interesting thing is, all she remembered was the nice things from Russia. Even when she spoke about the pogroms, she wasn't bitter. She had the instinct of someone who'd been through a lot, and didn't let things get to her. People who've been through a lot re-create their past, leaving out the things in their story that are painful. If they didn't, the past would kill them.

"As for my grandmother Felice, her most striking quality was probably the way she reassured and encouraged everyone. 'It'll be fine, don't worry,' she would always say."

Leah added that she imagined Felice's letters to Kafka—which, unlike his, had not been preserved—as being in the same spirit.

"I'm sure she was reassuring and supportive of him," Leah said. "My grandmother Felice never spoke about unpleasant or difficult things. She didn't feel it was proper. If she couldn't say something positive, she preferred not to talk at all. But she was great fun to be with. She loved to laugh and think up games. She adored parties and celebrations. We were staying with her for my birthday once, and she baked cookies and served them to me on a silver tray. They were these crunchy butter cookies with almonds, melted right on your tongue.

"My father always said he had a rich childhood.

"My father had a sister, Aunt Ursula. She married badly, it was an unhappy marriage. She died of breast cancer relatively young. She and my grandma Felice never got along too well. My aunt used to tell us about how she went to my grandmother's store to show her her new daughter, Susan, when she was born, and Felice threw her out. Supposedly, she said she was too busy working and didn't have time for children.

"Of course I have no idea what actually happened," Leah said, "but that was how our aunt told it, and she never did forgive her. My grandmother had a better relationship with my father. Whenever he went to visit, she would ply him with home-cooked food. Meatballs in caper cream sauce, that was his favorite dish. Or breaded cauliflower. She would send us homemade jams, too, and at Christmas and on birthdays we would get packages of cookies and marzipan.

"None of us knew about Kafka's letters. Not even Grandpa Moritz."

Joel and Leah. It was generous of them to allow me to write about their family. I hope they realize there is a lot I can only guess at, and I'll be touching on their lives, too.

And meanwhile, Grete is still waiting.

1944

San Donato Val di Comino

THE GRASS, REFRESHED BY SPRING RAIN, moist underfoot. When do the violets bloom in San Donato? Maybe she could pick a few; it's her birthday today.

There they are, right by the wall. She plucks one and smells it.

Fifty-one years old.

Despite having less than a month left to live, she firmly believes that she will survive the war. The Americans are just over the hill; the Germans are on their last legs. Who would want to transport a sick, aging woman halfway across Europe only in order to kill her? It didn't make any sense. Whom could she matter so much to, and why?

She heads back downhill, the soles of her shoes slipping and sliding. In her hand she clutches a bouquet of violets. On her way home, she stops in at Dr. Massa's place. She gives the violets to his wife, drinks some tea, and runs into her friend Rosa Myler from Vienna. Rosa has a gift for her, a lace collar. And Dr. Massa's wife has baked a pie. It is her birthday, after all.

That evening Arturo will dig up a bottle of wine and roast a bird he caught in the hills. La Passioncella will get drunk and reminisce, taking out one of the books written in German that she brought in her suitcase, and reading from it to Arturo.

"You see, this famous writer loved me, too. I was his wife."

The photographs that he has seen several times before make their way from the leather bag onto the table: young Grete with a child in her arms and a boy with his head bandaged on a hospital bed.

"That's him," she says. "My son. He died in Munich, poor thing, far away from me. No one ever knew about him."

She sobs.

This woman is crazy, Arturo thinks.

"What was his name?"

"Who?"

"Your son."

"Casimiro." She prattles on about Vienna and Berlin. Balls, dresses, lovers, trips she took, representing a firm called Adrema as her boss's right-hand woman. "He alone," says Grete, "knew everything about me. Him I could trust. He was so kind, so discreet. It was a disaster for me when he died. Ach, hold me close."

He strokes her hair and back, feeling her sharp, tiny bones under the tips of his fingers.

1944

Los Angeles

Felice takes a left at the house, then another left, and a few blocks later she is on West Pico. There she has a choice. Either turn the steering wheel to the right and head west, along the line of slender palms to Santa Monica, toward the ocean, or go left. Then, after a few miles, that will connect her to Venice Boulevard, which runs right past Rosedale Cemetery, loops around downtown Los Angeles, and veers north near Boyle Heights.

She opts for the latter.

Past the new General Hospital, which towers over the low-standing buildings around it like the Great Pyramid, all the way to Raymond Hill, where she can get on the new freeway and streak along the blacktop, as fast as her Ford will carry her, into the mountains.

So Dr. Weiss had slit his wrists. He got out of Paris the only way left to him, four years ago now. The news had been late in reaching L.A.

This section of road, wide and smooth, hugging the riverbed of the Arroyo Seco and connecting East Los Angeles with the town of Pasadena, had been opened by City Hall only recently. It led through dry grass and bush–covered hills up into the bluish mountains. The drive took only twenty minutes, but it was intoxicating. The freeway ended in Pasadena, and connected up to the highway that stretched across the United States, linking the West Coast to the East.

Felice toys with the idea that this time, instead of slowing down and turning the car around, she'll just keep on driving, continuing on to cities with fairy-tale names like Flagstaff, Santa Fe, Tulsa, Phoenix, Oklahoma City. She could drive for days and nights on end across this vast and endless land, under skies as insatiable as her longing for the open road. Leave it all far behind, with nothing left but speed and space made up mostly of sky.

1944

Long Island

LISETTE HADN'T WANTED TO MARRY. But he insisted, so finally she gave in.

Lisette.

Joachim had only to whisper her name, and she was lying before him, fixing him with her warm brown eyes. Whenever they made love, afterward her cheeks glowed red and her forehead glistened with sweat. Lisette held nothing back and was not shy or embarrassed. Lying there, body relaxed and satisfied, eyes open wide, reaching out her hands to him.

The freshly mown grass on the baseball field where Joachim lay stretched out was drying in the June sunshine, giving off a delicious scent. And what was that other smell he detected? A sweet, familiar fragrance. He didn't know much about flowers. In Europe he had summered with his parents by the seaside, and winters they had spent in the mountains. He had traveled to Paris, Florence, Venice, but only seldom had he visited a forest or a meadow.

He remembered his cousin Hana dragging him along with her once on a trip with her friends to the mountains. "All this beauty right in front of your nose and you just sit at home," she'd said.

They took the train to a village high up in the mountains, and then spent half the day trudging uphill. He could still recall the feeling of lightness and radiance, the meadows dotted with pink, yellow, white, and blue flowers that he had never seen before, the tinkling of cowbells down in the valley.

What was that fragrant smell?

As a child, he had loved the month of June. He didn't remember it much in Berlin, but June in Geneva, yes. He had always looked forward to the end of the school year, going to swim in the lake, eating strawberries, then cherries and apricots and peaches, which his mother brought home from the market and held to her nose, sniffing with pleasure. When they moved, she complained that the strawberries and peaches in America didn't smell strongly enough. Contained in that scent was all the splendor of the start of summer, the joy of having made it through the winter and a sickly spring, the relief of the first truly warm days and light evenings.

He sat up and looked around. On the left side of the baseball field, a few linden trees were in bloom. They must have just blossomed that morning, since he definitely hadn't noticed their fragrance yesterday evening when he went for a walk after work. In Geneva they had had linden trees on the street where they lived. The staircase in their building, even their apartment itself, had been filled with their scent.

His white hospital coat was making him hot.

He had just dashed out after lunch to clear his head for a while, but he wished he didn't have to go back to work at all. It may not have been as hot as Los Angeles, but it was definitely hot enough to swim.

He closed his eyes and, half asleep, again pictured the naked Lisette. A painful pressure below his navel. Like he was caught on a hook and being dragged.

He would rather remember his mother.

One time, early in the morning, he saw her walking around the garden with a hose, spraying the grass and trees; then suddenly, like it was the most natural thing in the world, she pointed the hose in the air and, standing there under the glistening stream, let the flow cascade over her head.

Afterward, when she called him in to breakfast, having changed her clothes and dried her hair, he didn't let on what he had seen. Spraying yourself with the hose was exactly the kind of thing that she had forbidden him and Lily to do when they were children.

But better to leave memories behind and get back to the hospital. There were patients waiting for him.

His patients cried all night long, smoking and wandering the corridors. Some of them couldn't stand up straight; others twitched their heads or stuttered or had lost their memory—and almost all of them felt guilty and afraid. Not of death—for them, that was attractive. What they were afraid of was shapeless, hanging in the air. A catastrophe from which there was no escape.

They were young men and boys, soldiers. But they were unable to return to the battlefield, so here they were, in a military hospital on Long Island. The field doctors had sent them home, not knowing what to do with them. Amytal Sodium, sleeping pills, rest, even a hearty diet, none of it worked for these patients.

The first and hardest task was getting them to speak. They were incapable of talking about themselves or their problems. These men were so ashamed, it hurt. That's how they were raised. Stop complaining. Be a man. Don't be a bother. Their whole childhood they had lived in fear that their parents would find out what was going on inside them, and their parents, for their part, hid both from them and from each other.

Every family was similar in that respect, reflected Joachim. When the men in brown shirts had paraded past their building in Berlin, his father had simply remarked that they were madmen and chased Joachim and his sister away from the window. When they heard gunfire in the city and asked what it was, he told them they were busybodies and said they would find out when they were old enough. Their father's illness was also taboo. His mother's life before she was married. The problems with their relatives. Their Aunt Else's divorce. Aunt Erna's illegitimate child, whom Joachim only knew about from vague allusions.

Yet their mother was neither cold nor reserved, quite the opposite. Her demeanor was warm and compassionate; there was no one who wasn't fond of her. But serious and unpleasant matters weren't spoken of at home. School and classmates, yes, but even there the conversation never went too deep, for fear of what they might stumble across.

Where did this passion for hiding everything come from? Joachim wondered. Was it fear of emotions? Or a defensive strategy?

Stick to the surface and keep quiet, even if everything is collapsing on the inside. As long as it isn't spoken aloud, it's as if it doesn't exist. But actually, that isn't true, and these men were the best proof of that.

They were so ashamed of themselves that first they had to be drugged. Only then would they talk about the horror they had experienced, the feelings of fear, guilt, and hopelessness.

Later, once they had made some progress in their treatment and were able to open up in a group, they discovered, to their amazement, that they were not alone. The others had had similar experiences. They loosened up and began to talk about their childhoods, about parents, siblings, wives, children, lovers, and the jobs that were waiting for them. They established friendships among themselves. Even their bodies transformed.

And that was when Joachim—who, in order to make it easier for the men, had begun to call himself Joe—knew that victory had been won. It didn't work with every patient, though.

In the previous war, they had called it "shell shock." Now it was known as "battle fatigue" or "exhaustion." True, it sounded better. A person can sleep off fatigue. The word doesn't call to mind the rattle of a machine gun, the screams, and the stench of burnt flesh.

Language in general had adapted to the needs of war. The young men who were required to enlist had had it pounded into their heads by parents and teachers since childhood that killing was bad, and yet now those same people were sending them to kill, calling it their "patriotic obligation" or "noble work for their country."

Estimates were that, today, two years since the Americans had entered the war, one out of every five soldiers in the U.S. army was affected by some form of psychiatric disorder. It was an epidemic, and the battlefield doctors, most of them surgeons, hadn't the slightest idea what to do. At first they had regarded the men as malingerers and cowards, and sent them back into combat. But the commanders didn't want them, since a mentally unstable soldier is a danger to those around him. He makes mistakes. Or shoots himself and ruins the other troops' morale.

How much human material had already gone to waste in this way.

The army was unprepared. It was a full-blown crisis. The government hastily began casting about for experts who could come up with a unified strategy and train the number of doctors needed. The whole thing was carried out in a state of urgency, in fact emergency, since by this point there were thousands of sobbing, shaking, raging wrecks—there was no other way to put it—who were refusing their patriotic obligation.

Joachim had studied general medicine, and underwent a crash course in psychiatry only after he enlisted in the army. It lasted twelve weeks and qualified him to examine patients on his own, though solely in an army setting. When it came to treatment, he was still required to consult with a superior.

If he wanted to continue in psychiatry after the war, he would have to complete his education and do a residency in a hospital.

He really needed to get going, though. It wasn't just patients waiting for him but also Major Bloomberg.

He leaped up, dusted off his smock, and quickly headed back to the main building.

The curtains in the examination room are drawn. Joachim stops on the threshold and blinks, waiting for his sun-dazzled eyes to adjust to the floor lamp's yellow light.

Major Bloomberg sits in a swivel chair, back to the door. All Joachim can see of him is the shiny bald spot atop his head. A patient lies on the examination table, twitching sharply every few seconds. Standing beside him is a nurse, keeping an eye out to make sure that he doesn't fall off.

"You're late, Doctor."

"I apologize."

"Let's begin. Medical history."

Joachim steps to the desk where the major is sitting and opens a folder bearing the patient's name.

"Take a look for yourself. I already read it," old Bloomberg says. He seems annoyed.

As Joachim concentrates on the details in the patient's file, he suddenly remembers. He has examined this man before. The man mumbled so badly, he was practically unintelligible, and despite being in sound physical condition, he was unable to walk. A classic case of hysterical paralysis in both his lower limbs. Not sudden onset, but delayed and gradual, after a combat mission in the Philippines.

"All yours, Doctor," the major says.

The man's name is Richard.

"Rick? My name is Joe. Dr. Joe. We met once before, remember?"

"Yes, sir."

"How are you doing?"

"Good, sir, thank you."

"I see you're talking better now. How about sleep? Are you able to sleep at night?"

"If I take my medicine, yes, sir. Otherwise, I can't get to sleep."

"And how are your legs doing?"

"I still can't walk, sir."

"Do you want to?"

"Of course, sir. Who wouldn't want to walk?"

"Well then, let's have a look."

He wishes he could imitate the fatherly tone that Major Bloomberg uses with the soldiers. But the major is over fifty, whereas Joachim is probably younger even than Rick here, and has hardly been through anything in life compared to him.

"So you can't walk. And you can't sleep at night. Just lie down for me a moment, and don't move."

Rick twitches even lying down. Giving him an injection isn't going to be easy.

"Could you be still a minute?"

"I can't, sir, I'm sorry. Believe me, it's not on purpose."

"I believe you. I'm going to give you a little injection now, just some medicine. It's going to make you feel good. You might even feel a bit tipsy. Have you ever been really drunk?"

The nurse hands Joachim a tourniquet and a full syringe.

Major Bloomberg doesn't say a word. Apparently, he has decided to leave Joachim on his own.

The Amytal Sodium takes effect immediately. The patient relaxes, his panic-stricken grimace slackening.

"How do you feel?"

"Like I'm floating on air."

"Could you count down from a hundred for me, Rick? Nice and slow."

"One hundred, ninety-nine, ninety-eight . . ." His voice drops off.

"Can you hear me?"

"Yes, sir."

"You can't walk. Why can't you walk, Rick?"

"I don't know."

"What comes to mind when I say the word *legs*?"

"Scared. I can't move my legs. I'm scared."

"When did you start being scared, Rick? When did you first feel that way?"

The experiences the soldiers relate under the influence of the drug are similar to one another. They all include gunfire or exploding grenades and mines, and dead buddies. Some also involve planes being shot down or burning jungles. Rick and his buddy were on lookout when they got jumped by a unit of Japanese troops. His buddy got killed by a hand grenade, but Rick survived. His squad came back for him after they withdrew from the attack, but it took a long time and Rick spent all day lying in a trench, wounded and covered in mud.

"Where you are now, Rick?"

"I'm in the woods."

"What are you doing?"

"Sitting in a hole. Jack is here with me."

"Are you hiding?"

"I'm on watch. Those were my orders. It's awful quiet. Whenever it's quiet, that's when things happen. Jack, look out!"

"Where are you running?"

"Away."

"What happened?"

"Help! I can't move."

"Why can't you move? Are you wounded? Does it hurt?"

"Mud, I've got mud all over me. They're here."

"Who, Rick?"

"The Japs. A whole platoon. They'll kill me if they see I'm alive."

"They didn't see you?"

"No. But they might come back."

"And what about Jack?"

"What about him?"

"Jack. Can you see Jack?"

"Jesus Christ, I left him back there. His stomach."

"What's wrong with his stomach?"

"It's torn wide open. Oh my God!"

"It's okay, Rick. Go ahead and cry. Cry all you want."

Rick covers his face with his hands and sobs.

"Now come back here again, Rick. Come back. You're not in the woods anymore. You're home, Rick, home in America. You're safe. Your buddy is dead, but it isn't your fault. You're alive, and your legs are healthy and strong. All right, Rick, now when I tell you to, you're going to stand up and walk. Are you ready?"

"I don't know, sir."

"All right, Rick. Sit up. Now stand for me, please."

Joachim's stomach is tied in knots. What if it doesn't work? But Rick obediently gets to his feet and staggers across the exam room and back, the nurse at his side.

"There, you see? You can walk. How does it feel?"

"Excellent, sir."

"I'm sure. Now lie back down and get some sleep. We'll discuss your memories again in therapy. What you went through is normal in war. But it's gone now. It won't haunt you anymore."

Joachim strokes the man's forehead as he lies down on the table. "Just go to sleep. Relax. Nurse, can we get a blanket? Wake him up in about half an hour, okay?"

He turns to Major Bloomberg, who sits quietly at the desk, smoking a cigarette.

"Not bad. But you need to work on your self-confidence. The patients can sense your uncertainty."

Joachim walks out to the corridor, leans against the wall, and lights a cigarette.

What he did with Rick just now is called "constructively reliving the past." When Rick wakes up, they will review the whole traumatic experience together, point by point, once again. Only this time they will embed it in a story. The main character will be Richard Crow, a soldier who went overseas to fulfill his patriotic obligation. He conducted himself bravely, lost his best friend in battle, and then came home, to his family, to enjoy the peace and build a future life for himself. Included in that will be what Rick might like to achieve. Before the war, he was an auto mechanic. Maybe now he'd like to open his own garage, or a gas station, or even go to college?

Together they will construct a story, which Rick can churn over and over again in his mind until he comes to believe it. Then the memory will lose its emotional charge, and maybe Jack and his blown-open stomach will finally leave his buddy alone.

Joachim works on the sixth floor of the new army hospital, a tall redbrick complex whose towers and pointy roofs rise above the flat landscape like a modern-day ark of fools.

There are still visible signs of construction around the building, and the freshly planted saplings have not yet had a chance to grow. The grassy plane with its vast sporting grounds is yellow in spots from the drought.

It's going to be a desert by end of summer, thinks Joachim.

From the upper stories you can see the ocean.

Maybe he should get hypnotized, too, he muses. If it did the trick for dead buddies, why not for Lisette? He didn't get a moment's rest from her, either.

There is another method of course, and a much more enjoyable one. Fight fire with fire. Find another woman as quickly as possible.

What came to mind when he said the name Lisette? Fucking, kissing, loving, pain, craziness, love, betrayal. Color, always just red. Like his ears and her cheeks, the Communist banner, a heart, blood.

He met her in spring 1942, on the campus in Los Angeles.

She sat down next to him, on a bench, with a book he himself had just recently read, Freud's *Interpretation of Dreams.* She was petite but well endowed, with black curly hair and suntanned legs without stockings. Full red-painted lips and a pointy nose, her cute little fingers smudged with ink. He asked her how she liked the book. She said she was just getting into it but it was intriguing. She could see why Freud was all everyone was talking about.

He told her he was studying medicine. She was in art school. Two years older than he was, but just starting her studies. She asked him how he'd gotten so far ahead. He explained that he'd had a head start thanks to the schools in Europe.

Her name was Lise, but ever since she was little, she said, everyone had called her Lisette. Her major was painting, but she had doubts whether she was talented enough. She might end up being more interested in policy and social work.

Her parents had pushed her into painting. Mainly her mom, who was a painter herself. She was French, her father American—a writer, but not well known. He taught literature at the university. Neither one of her parents could imagine there might be anything more important than art in the world.

Such as?

Social justice.

Then he, in turn, without any obvious connection, told her about how his family had moved from Berlin to Geneva and how his classmates there had bullied him because he was Jewish and got better marks than they did. How he used to go down to the lake and cry and reminisce about Berlin. He resented his father for having taken him away from there. As if his happy childhood had been stolen from him by his father.

He said he kept asking his father, "Why does Hitler hate us so much?"

"Because we're Jews," his father had replied.

"But how can he tell? We don't even go to synagogue. I'm not even circumcised."

"Do you want to go back to the Middle Ages?"

"But how can you tell someone's Jewish?"

"You can't. That's what makes the whole thing even more absurd."

"And what if I want to be a Jew?"

"You can be a Hottentot for all I care!" his father had yelled. "Just give me a rest with the questions!"

From then on, Joachim was clear: If he'd lost his home for being a Jew, then he was going to be a Jew, a Jew with a capital *J*, in spite of his father and Hitler.

He told her about Leo Weinberger, too. How they'd promised to meet up in Palestine, and now Leo was writing and asking him when he was going to get there, but Joachim wasn't going to go.

"Why not?" she asked.

"I stopped believing in God."

The words just slipped out. He dropped the sentence in front of her without even realizing that he had had it in him, ripening on the inside, and all of sudden out it came, just plopped to the ground and lay there, this small, empty nothing, teeny-tiny yet heavier than the Moon and the Earth together.

His secret. He hadn't even acknowledged it to himself ever before, and now this girl, this total stranger with big brown eyes, whom he had just met by chance in the park, had drawn it out of him.

He was thoroughly bewildered by what had happened, but Lisette didn't notice a thing. She just calmly replied that she didn't believe in God, either—God was an instrument of power invented to control people, and believing in God was sheer nonsense.

She believed in revolution. And in a more just world.

She said she fully understood why Joachim's father rejected his Jewishness. Of course he found it repulsive, since all it had ever meant to him was humiliation and injustice. Especially since it had always been forced on him.

"Your father is a proud man."

He was intrigued that this girl with the beautiful eyes was standing up for his father, when all he ever did with him was argue. He didn't agree with his father on anything, from the actions of the Allied forces to the latest Ernst Lubitsch film.

From that first afternoon on the bench in the park, with Freud's *Interpretation of Dreams*, the two of them became inseparable. Their conversation continued on into the night. They wrote each other letters, which they would exchange with each other on their way in to class in the morning.

Joachim spent most of his afternoons in the reading room, or with the pupils he tutored, but evenings he would accompany Lisette wherever she went, including to meetings of young Communists, though he himself would wait outside. And on Sundays, provided he didn't have too much studying to do, he would take Lisette to the mountains or the ocean. They would borrow Felice's Ford and take along food for the whole day.

And so the spring and summer passed.

When fall came, Joachim was drafted into the army. He hadn't received his order to report yet, but he was expecting it any day. He loved Lisette so much, wanted her so badly. Soon he would be going to war and maybe he would be killed. She had to become his wife.

But Lisette wasn't like other girls. She said formalities didn't matter, that they were already like husband and wife, and had been for a long time; they belonged to each other.

He insisted. They needed to do it for real.

Maybe he hoped that once Lisette got married, she wouldn't be so interested in politics anymore and would stop going to meetings with all those young men. That crew she ran with was constantly getting up to something. She had already been arrested once by the police, for handing out flyers on the street against the war.

He thought, he assumed, he wanted to believe that every normal woman, once she got married, turned her thoughts mainly to her husband and their children to come, and everything else faded in importance. That was what he had seen in others. Why should Lisette be any different?

He spent hours trying to convince her, emotionally blackmailing her with the war and the chance that he might die, until finally she agreed.

They were married at the town hall instead of by a rabbi. Felice and Robert didn't approve of their decision, but they came to the wedding and drank a toast of champagne with Lisette's parents and the newlyweds. Then Joachim packed up his few possessions and moved in with Lisette, in her tiny room in the city, which up until then she had shared with a girlfriend of hers.

Their honeymoon was a weekend in bed. Folds, hollows, smoothness, curves, her weight, his weight, their shared saliva, hair, fingernails, her cute little fingers. Each for the other a rich and inexhaustible landscape they had only begun to discover, and now, suddenly, they had plenty of time, without the threat of someone walking in on them. They could be an arm's length apart, fall asleep and wake up again, and the other one was still right there. A feeling of abundance. A shared comforter. And fried eggs with toast at night when they got hungry.

"My honey, my sweet . . ."

They slept and woke in sync with the tides of desire. At one point, Lisette got up, walked across the room naked, and took a box of paints and brushes from the closet.

"Come on," she said. "Let's preserve this moment for eternity."

"But I don't know how to paint."

"Sure you do. Everyone does."

They dipped the brushes into the colors and painted all over the room's white wall: multicolored butterflies and flowers and exotic birds, and a sea horse that floated up from Joachim's memory.

But then came Monday, and with it the regular meeting of the young Communists. Of course Lisette was going. Was he going to walk her there?

"Do you really think you should go?"

"What do you mean?"

"I mean now that you're married and all."

She laughed. "What's gotten into you? Wait for me after the meeting." And with that, she left.

He wasn't her first lover, either. Her first had been someone from the organization, a married man; that was why she was so well versed in making love. The two of them were still in touch. They were comrades, after all.

He waited for her in front of the building where they had met. He wasn't about to go inside.

The truth was, he was afraid. He didn't want anything to do with Communists. Not Communists, not fascists, none of them. He was grateful America had granted him citizenship. He just wanted to get his degree and do his work in peace. Wasn't that enough?

At the end of the second semester, Lisette dropped out of school. She hadn't done a single one of her assignments.

Joachim passed all his exams with honors and started his residency at the General Hospital. He bought himself a used car, so he could drive to work.

Lisette brought home stacks of political flyers and pamphlets on the world revolution, and read from them to him at night. She talked at length about poor people, her eyes swimming with compassion. Whenever Lisette spoke about the suffering of others, her big round eyes would get even bigger and her gaze would soften, turning warm and heavy. He had to hold her close and cover her with kisses.

Then she started to take an interest in psychoanalysis. She attended lectures by a European psychiatrist who had worked first with Freud and later on with Wilhelm Reich. In the fall, she applied to a full-time program in psychology.

She often turned the conversation to the sex life of adolescents, and drew bold connections among capitalism, patriarchy, sexual dysfunction, and war. Terms like *sex economy* and *the sexual revolution* began cropping up in her vocabulary. She read all of Reich's books, and longed to go to New York so she could study under him.

A child would keep her at home, Joachim thought. But Lisette didn't want children, and it even occurred to him that she might not be able to have them. They made love all the time and he wasn't always careful, so how else to explain why she hadn't gotten pregnant?

He was insanely jealous. One night, when Lisette was asleep, he found himself rummaging through her purse. It made him blush with shame, but he had to find out what and how. He didn't have time for lengthy interrogations, he was constantly at the hospital.

When his draft notice finally appeared, it came as a relief.

The army stationed him on the East Coast, in New Jersey. He was supposed to undergo a twelve-week course in psychiatry and then depart for Europe, but it never came to that. There was a greater need for doctors on the home front.

As soon as it was clear he would be staying in the United States, he urged Lisette to move out east. She was his wife. It was her duty to follow him.

She came two months later, but only for a visit.

Three days on a bus, three days with him, and another three days on the journey back to California.

"Bubele, you know I love you. I wouldn't have come all this way otherwise."

"Bubele" was what Felice would sometimes call him when she was in a joking mood. But coming out of Lisette's mouth, it somehow sounded fake. She was just trying to appease him.

"I'm sorry, but I can't leave L.A. now. I need to study."

"Since when do you care so much about school?"

"I care. You'd be surprised how busy I am."

Busy in bed with other men, he thought.

"You're my wife," he said. "I'm not going to wait. Stay here with me or it's over."

They got a long-distance divorce, by proxy. Some things are more complicated in wartime, but then again, some things are much simpler.

1946

New York

ANOTHER ONE READING KAFKA. The guy was everywhere all of a sudden.

Riding the subway, on his way in to Bellevue, the hospital where Joachim was doing his residency, he saw one sensible-looking girl after another, students at NYU or the New School, furrowing their brow over *The Trial* or *The Castle*, the latest release from Schocken flooding the U.S. market. Even the bartenders in New York were quoting Kafka. Yet in Germany, before the war, he was practically unknown. The Nazis wouldn't even have bothered to ban him if someone hadn't called him to their attention. If not for the concentration camps and the German Jews who had flooded the United States, he would probably still be unnoticed today.

The doctors at Bellevue were reading Kafka.

Kafka's books stared out at him from the nightstands of his lovers.

Even Nancy, the hale and hearty long-legged blonde from Minnesota he had invited to the party with him, felt the need to mention she had recently read Kafka.

She sat on a low velvet sofa, squeezed in between Joachim and his colleague Ralph Kubicek, who had just come back from Europe before Christmas. And who, despite being well aware that Nancy had come to the party with Joachim, had just laid his hand on her thigh. Strong and solid, unlike her literary theories.

"You know, Nancy, in Germany, girls like you offered themselves to soldiers for four cigarettes or a bar of chocolate. 'Madama Butterfly,' we called them, because they were always waiting for something. A visa or a boat ticket to come in the mail. I have one who writes to me, 'Honey, don't forget.'" Ralph burst out laughing. "Honestly, I don't know how I could! Especially the stink of those dead bodies!"

Nancy started as though she were about to make a run for it, but Ralph, by this point thoroughly drunk, grabbed her by the shoulder, pressed her against the sofa back, and kissed her on the lips so violently, she yelped in pain.

"There."

He propped himself up with both hands until he managed to stand. He had gotten a lot fatter since he'd been back. He staggered off toward the bar, lined with bottles of alcohol.

Nancy got up as well, stammered something, and disappeared. It was clear she wouldn't be back.

Joachim was left on the sofa alone.

He rested his head against the lower frame of the window that took up one of the living room walls. It was a high-ceilinged room, stretching across two floors of an old brick apartment house on the west side of Central Park. At one point it had probably been a garage or assembly shop. Along one wall ran a wooden staircase that ended in a gallery opening onto the bedrooms. On the opposite wall, ten feet above the floor, hung a large mirror. It seemed an odd place to put a mirror, so high above the guests' heads, but standing on the gallery, you could see yourself reflected in it. Below the mirror was an enormous pseudo-Gothic fireplace, with crackling logs shooting sparks. The walls were partially covered with bookcases reaching up to the ceiling. A wooden ladder was propped against one. The wallpaper was dark red, with a gold pattern, and there were paintings as well: a Pissarro, a landscape by Derain, and an enormous Balthus, purchased in Paris shortly before the war.

The wife of the doctor hosting the party came from a wealthy family. The last time Joachim had seen her, she had had dark hair, but now she was a platinum blonde à la Marlene Dietrich. From the sofa where he was sitting, he had a good view of her. As the latest Bing Crosby record played again for the umpteenth time, a few couples danced a waltz. The lady of the house, in a close-fitting, open-back white-silver gown, wrapped herself around an Italian-looking man with a Clark Gable mustache, a lit cigarette balanced between her red nail-polished fingers.

Everything here was copied from somewhere; he had seen it all before, but still he liked it. Now this was living. The slow song gave way to the upbeat "Chickery Chick."

The red wallpaper, the logs in the fireplace, the heat and the alcohol and the women's fragrant skin, the snow coming down outside, buffeting the windows in clumps. The streetlamps' yellow light. The steam rising up from the pipes in the street.

He loved New York.

Neither his divorce from Lisette nor the dreadful news from Europe could ruin the joy he felt at seeing the urban canyons of Manhattan again after six years, the peaks of the skyscrapers and the ships on the Hudson, catching the damp scent of the subway tracks underground, the smell of metal, gasoline, and smoke. Before this, he had been here only once, with his father, after a trip to the West Coast, but even back then he had already taken a liking to it, and now he knew for sure: If there was anywhere in America he could feel at home, it was New York. He wouldn't be going back west.

The host kicked them out around 3:00 A.M. In the meantime it had stopped snowing, but the street, sidewalks, and front-yard fences had vanished under the soft, deep drifts.

As soon they stepped out the front door, he and Ralph sank

into snow up to their knees. Shoes soaked, they quickly sobered up, tramping through the snowbanks to a barren stretch of Broadway, where they found a bar still open.

Inside it was jam-packed. Everyone there was dressed in their evening best, and, just like him and Ralph, they were determined to stay out until the snowplows cleared the streets and the taxis started running again.

They elbowed their way to the bar and ordered a drink.

Joachim didn't even ask a question before Ralph launched into a story. No introduction, as if he had been waiting all night just for this moment.

Her name was Helke and she was from Nuremberg, where the end of the war found Ralph. The mother of two small children, a war widow. They were good-looking children; their father had died on the eastern front.

They were starving when Ralph met them. The little girl hadn't spoken a word since the battle that turned the city into a pile of rubble in the space of five days, and she slept constantly. The little boy spent his time crawling nimbly through the ruins like a small animal, looking for a bite to eat, or playing with abandoned military equipment with his friends. Ralph had access to treats that Helke and her children hadn't seen in years: dried milk, chocolate, canned meat.

When she was together with him, in his narrow little room in a hospital occupied by the Americans, a neighbor they were living with in the basement of a bombed building watched her children for her.

From a distance there was no way to know that anyone was living there. But when Ralph walked between the buildings and saw the metal chimneys poking out of the cellar windows and the freshly washed laundry hanging on the lines, it was clear to him the German women had no intention of giving up.

It was like a dream. Attractive and healthy-looking, in gaily colored dresses, immaculate and elegant, the young German women emerged from the heaps of stone, plaster, and brick, from behind the charred remains of walls, in spring high heels, some in spring hats, climbing over the mounds of debris blocking the sidewalks and roads. Helke's smooth, soft skin was always so healthy and clean-smelling. How did she do it, living amid such filth?

He loved to drink in the sight of her, and Helke was glad to oblige. In the beginning, when he was still embarrassed about it, she even encouraged him: "Go ahead, take a look."

Closing his eyes now, he could still see the fine light hair between her legs, her pale, slightly bulging belly, rosy-nippled ample breasts spilling to the side.

It was a warm spring, the lilacs and acacias blooming in the gardens, their fragrance in his nostrils and at the back of his throat mixing with the stench of sewage, of human feces and corpses, a smell that still haunted him to this day.

When he saw the first photos from the concentration camps, he spent all night crying.

But by morning he was back to being the stern conqueror in the metal helmet, no longer a medical doctor, but head of interrogations, spending each day at a table before an endless line of wretched German soldiers. Since he had been born in Vienna and spoke good German, it was his task to determine which of them was telling the truth and which of them was lying. To uncover the active Nazis, arrest them, and let the rest go.

Once, after making love, he told her he was a Jew.

She lay naked on his bed, staring up at the ceiling.

"You aren't circumcised."

"No, I'm not."

She turned her sandy-haired head to the wall.

He couldn't name the feeling he had. It wasn't hate. It was like two snapshots, one laid on top of the other, overlapping and yet having nothing at all in common. His escape from Europe, where he and his parents had been violently chased out of their home and the rest of his family had been murdered. And then his return in the role of conqueror, feeding two starving Aryan children and sleeping with their mother.

When Helke was nearing climax, she would ask him if he loved her. She would repeat it four times in a row if she had to, as many times as it took for him to say yes, and only then would she allow herself to give in to the wave of pleasure.

Helke slept with soldiers out of love. She was a good girl. And he wasn't lying when he told her that he loved her.

Even for a psychiatrist, there are times when it's truly hard to understand your own feelings.

Now, she has been writing that she misses him. She isn't sleeping with anyone else, and doesn't want to.

The children have been asking about him.

Her little girl is doing better.

What she doesn't write is that they're hungry, that their drinking water freezes in the bucket, that they don't have anything to heat or light their home with.

She says she longs for his kisses and the palms of his hands.

Women are strange.

"Why don't you bring them over here?" Joachim asked.

"I'd have to marry her."

"So what?"

Ralph glanced at him with a look of incomprehension, fiddling with his empty glass.

"If it doesn't work out, you can always get divorced. Meanwhile, Helke can find a job. I mean, obviously she knows how to take care of herself. The kids aren't yours, so they're not your responsibility, but if nothing else, at least you'll get them out of there."

"If only it were that simple."

"It is," said Joachim with conviction. "I got divorced myself."

"Oh yeah? And what is she doing now?"

"The last time I heard from Lisette was a year ago. She sent me two books by Dr. Reich. *Character Analysis* and *The Sexual Revolution*. She's studying with him now. She always wanted to."

"Isn't that guy Reich a crackpot?"

Joachim shrugged. "I don't know. He wasn't back when he was doing psychoanalysis. His older books are pretty interesting. I don't understand all that orgone stuff, or whatever it's called, that he's researching now. Haven't kept up."

The corner of Ralph's mouth twitched. "Your ex sounds like a riot. Good-looking girl?"

"I wouldn't have married an ugly one."

1950

New York

THE PROJECTOR WHIRRED TO LIFE, casting a rectangle of light on the wall where he had taken down the painting.

The reel in the first box was one of the old movies his mother had filmed while they were still in Switzerland. She had always liked taking photographs, and had bought herself a home movie camera the first chance she got.

On the wall, his little sister, Lily, who looks to be ten or so, starts off downhill on skis. Joachim glides into the frame right behind her and promptly falls on his butt. He gets up, dusting off the snow and waving to the camera. In the next shot, their father, a determined look on his face and a pipe in his teeth, tugs a sled at the end of a rope. Then Felice appears. In a semilong wool skirt and a thick turtleneck with a belt, she stands, also on skis, at the top of a low slope. She opens her mouth, shouts something, laughs, then pushes off downhill at a cautious lean. At the bottom, she manages to brake without falling, raising her poles triumphantly over her head. Next is a slightly shaky view of a village, a horse-drawn sleigh, and snow-covered mountain peaks, barely visible against the white plaster of the wall. Probably Mürren.

Joachim loaded a new reel onto the projector.

Now they're in the United States. His father sits on the back veranda of their home in Pico-Robertson, in the same armchair he's been sitting in every day for the past twelve years. He is wearing a suit with a vest and a tie.

"Who is that man?" Their daughter is only two, but she speaks very well. She's a clever girl.

"That's your grandpa Robert. And look, here comes Mommy. Look how pretty she is."

Nina Perel emerges from the house in a light-colored skirt suit (light blue in reality), with her hair brushed out. It was their first visit to Los Angeles together, right after their engagement in New York, which Felice and Robert had been unable to attend. Gracefully leaning over her future father-in-law, Nina Perel smooths a stray wisp of hair away from her face and waves to Felice behind the camera. Joachim appears in the frame, dressed in summer pants and a white open-neck shirt. He wraps one arm around the waist of his bride, resting his other hand on his father's shoulder. The camera pans up to the top of a tall palm; then the picture goes dark.

"Is that Glanpa Lobelt who died?"

"Yes."

What was it like for his mother and father living together those last twelve years?

When Felice brought Robert back from Paris, to the old house in Boyle Heights, Joachim still lived at home. But he mostly just spent the night there. The rest of his time he was studying in the library, tutoring other children for money, rehearsing with the school orchestra (he played clarinet), and going to the beach to play volleyball and swim.

Twelve years is a long time to spend in an armchair.

Wednesday evenings Felice gave Robert a ride to the movie house, and Sunday afternoons she took him to the café, where he would meet with friends from Germany. Those were his only amusements. That and the radio. Felice continued not to buy the newspaper for him until long after the end of the war, once all the uproar died down about the concentration camps and the trials of the Nazis. She did her best to shield him, but it was no use. His friends from the café read the papers, and besides, they still had relatives in Europe.

He was usually quite chipper when he left the house on Sundays, but he would return home gray with exhaustion and rage. He had to go lie down right away and take his pills. Then he would relax in bed without moving, and even having ingested a double dose of medicine, he still had chest pain and an irregular heartbeat. It wasn't even a beat so much as a wriggle, like a worm caught in a claw. But there was no talking him out of his café visits; he wouldn't hear of it.

Whenever Joachim did happen to be at home, his father latched on to him right away, wanting to talk. Robert didn't agree with anything, criticized everything, and was angry at everyone, except maybe Felice.

From the perspective of a chair on the back veranda, a person sees things that healthy people don't notice and, unfortunately, they don't want to hear about them, either. Even if you do all the thinking for them, the obvious truths are so uncomfortable, they prefer to bury their heads in the sand. But a person didn't have to be a fortune-teller to predict the problems young people were likely going to face. First and foremost, overpopulation. Now that people were no longer dying, thanks to antibiotics and the other achievements of modern medicine, they should stop having children, too. All that awaited them otherwise was famine, war, and dictatorship.

Felice might have been able to tolerate her husband's dark musings, but she had no time. Even before his trip to Paris, she had taken courses in massage and cosmetics and set up a home salon. Her initial customers were friends of Aunt Sophie's, German Jewish women to whom she offered her services at a favorable price, so they recommended her to their friends and her clientele expanded.

The ladies would lie on the sofa in the living room for a massage, or sit in the armchair for a facial and a manicure. The main reason they came was to get things off their chest, and they had no idea that everything they confided in Felice was also being heard by the seventeen-year-old boy on the other side of the wall.

It wasn't Joachim's intention to listen; he just had no way to plug his ears.

Apart from bad-mouthing their husbands and America, which they continued to compare with Europe, the women shared recipes and tips on makeup, hair, and clothes. But the number one subject, hands down, was aging—the natural changes it caused in skin and body shape, and what to do to stop or slow it down.

Then his mother stopped giving massages, and she and Aunt Else, who had come over from Europe and was living with them again, started baking custom cakes and cookies. One thing they couldn't complain about was a lack of customers. And as the fame of Else's pulled strudel spread throughout Hollywood, a Hungarian producer who was known to be particular about what he ate offered Else a job as cook. Right around the same time, Felice decided she had enough money saved up to open a shop of her own, as she had always dreamed of doing.

First, however, they moved again, this time to a house in West Los Angeles, just a few miles from the beach in Santa Monica. A lot of Eastern European and German Jews were settling in Pico-Robertson around that time; it was common to hear Yiddish spoken on the street. Felice's friend and business partner, Masha, lived there, too, and the two of them found a space to rent, not at all expensive, right on Pico Boulevard, in view of the stepped tower of Fox Stadium Theatre.

They divided up the roles. Masha, who could knit or crochet anything, advised customers, while Felice was in charge of finances and inventory. They carried supplies and accessories for knitting and sewing. Joachim was living on the East Coast by then, and every Christmas, or whenever one of them had a birthday, he, Nina Perel, and, later, their children would get care packages from Los Angeles containing not only cookies but hats, sweaters, and gloves as well, so they wouldn't freeze to death out there in the bleak winters of New York.

To cover the short distance between the shop and the back veranda, where Robert sat dozing away in his armchair, Felice drove a red Ford B, which she had purchased right after their arrival in Los Angeles and had taught herself to handle with inimitable bravura. She used it to go shopping, as well as chauffeuring the kids to the beach and Robert to his meetings. She didn't mind, just as long as she was sitting behind the wheel of her beloved car. Whenever she had a moment free, she would drive around just for fun, zipping down the new freeway at sixty miles an hour. A newfound desire had awakened within her: to reach those mountains in the distance. Being a little red dot on four fast-spinning wheels was the most intoxicating thing she had ever known in her life.

Lily stayed with her parents a little while longer than Joachim, but she got married before she had even finished college.

Felice, in tears, informed Joachim of Lily's decision over the phone: "That silly girl. Instead of getting her degree and making something of herself. Ruining her life like that. And the man is such a schlemiel, such chutzpah!"

He had no idea what his mother found so awful about his sister's fiancé. Whenever he asked her about it, all she said was, "Waste of words."

Joachim only saw his mother cry twice in his life. The first time when he was ten and they were leaving Berlin. Then now.

He didn't understand why it was so upsetting to her. So what if Lily didn't want to finish college? All Nina Perel had was a high school diploma, and she stayed at home with the kids; he was happy to take care of her. Working outside the home wasn't for every woman, in his opinion; some women just weren't suited for it. Plus, Lily was an adult. She could do what she wanted.

But Felice would not be convinced and refused to make peace with Lily. She even refused to hold her daughter's little girl in her arms when she came into the world, as if it were the baby's fault. It was unfair, but Felice wouldn't budge; there was nothing they could do. Poor Lily. In the end, the baby was all she had, since her husband cheated on her, and what was more, he was completely under the thumb of his mother, who stuck up for him against her daughter-in-law, even endorsing his infidelities, since in her eyes Lily wasn't good enough for her son. She was the fifth wheel in her own home.

Joachim listened patiently when his sister complained to him over the phone. He didn't know how else to help.

He himself got along with his mother fairly well. They didn't talk that much, but he could feel her love and support. On the other hand, he and his father got in a fight whenever Joachim went to visit his parents in Los Angeles. Afterward, he would regret it and promise himself that next time the two of them would sit down and talk everything through.

Now it was too late for that. He would never, ever forgive his mother for not calling him. That idiotic optimism of hers. "It'll be fine, don't worry." Had she honestly believed that his father would still pull through?

"Why bring the family all this way? Stay home. Papa will get well again. Don't waste your money. There's already been enough sacrifice."

She always said the same thing, without any indication of what had been sacrificed or who had sacrificed for whom.

"Papa and I can take care of ourselves!"

He really wanted to see his father—he suspected he was dying! But in the face of his mother's optimism, that hypocritical optimism of the East European Jews—basically, as he saw it, they were just petrified—Joachim backed down. He and Lily both had in them too much old-world respect for their parents to do otherwise.

They were allowed to use the informal *you* with them, but that was the only concession that Robert—who himself had addressed his mother using the formal *you* and kissed her hand—was willing to make. As children, Joachim and Lily had only been allowed to kiss their father on the cheek when it was his birthday or he was going away on a longer trip than usual. He never held their hands on walks, or took them in his lap, or hugged them before they went to sleep. If he was pleased with them, he would pat them on the shoulder. Felice liked to cuddle with them, but only when they were still little. She used to caress them at night before they went to sleep. Joachim still remembers the soft warmth of her palm.

The moment they started going to school, the cuddling came to a stop. Not with Lily perhaps, but certainly with Joachim. Even when he hurt himself or got sick, she wouldn't caress him. Like semolina porridge with butter and sugar, cuddling was for preschoolers. From age six on, results were what counted. Naturally, only the best. Anything else was unhealthy pampering. Frugality, renunciation, rigor, a certain amount of discomfort—these were what was needed for a child to become an adult. And the wealthier the family, the more attention had to be paid to shield the children from temptation.

Now his father had died.

And he, his son, had not been there for it.

2011

Hudson Valley

EVEN YEARS LATER, after nearly half a century, he was still angry at her. I know, because he told me so himself.

It poured that day, beginning in the morning. I took the train from the station in Harlem and couldn't even make out the hills on the other side of the river through the curtain of rain.

It was March. I remember Henry had kept postponing my visit all through the winter: until the snow thawed, until his wife recovered.

At 10:00 A.M., the train pulled into the station in the little town on the Hudson. Following the instructions that Henry had given me, I found my way to the taxi stand through the still heavy rain. There was one car sitting there. The driver hesitated at first when I told him my destination. He didn't want to drive that far for just one fare. But when nobody else got off the train, he had no choice but to take me.

We drove past the cemetery in Sleepy Hollow, climbed one of the rounded hills overlooking the river, passed the hospital, and stopped in front of an upscale-looking complex of buildings.

I paid the driver and dashed into the lobby. Soft armchairs and sofas, vases of fresh-cut flowers, the murmur of rain on the glass roof. A pretty woman at the reception picked up the phone: "Hi, Henry. Your visitor is here."

I can still see him, as if it were happening today. Henry,

alias Joachim, walking down the stairs, confident and erect. One of those unsentimental old men in gold-framed glasses who maintain a firm grip on life, right up to the end. He had just turned ninety, but I wouldn't have put him at a day over seventy. He shook my hand and led me upstairs.

The hallways of the home, for affluent older people who could no longer live without help, were decorated with watercolor views of the Hudson River and flowerpots with indoor plants. A fragile-looking elderly lady with carefully permed white hair and pearls around her neck inched along the wall, taking tiny steps.

"Hi, Henry."

He nodded hello to her, opened one of the doors on the hallway, and gestured for me to enter. Waiting in the entryway, which was cluttered with furniture, was another old lady, leaning on a walker: Annette, alias Nina Perel. I removed my muddy shoes and wet jacket, and fished a bottle of Becherovka out of my backpack. I had discovered it in a well-stocked liquor store on First Avenue. Surely they would remember Karlsbad, where the famous herb liqueur came from.

Annette said she would leave the two of us alone and went into the bedroom, closing the door behind her.

The living room was bright, with a view of the river. As the rain outside slowly eased, the dull sunshine came pouring into the valley, filling it with light.

I sat down on the couch. Henry settled into an armchair, where apparently he spent most of his time, to judge from the magazines and books spread open around it. On the wall, directly above his head, hung a life-size portrait of a woman in a dark blue dress and a red beaded necklace, her ginger blond hair wound in a bun. She looked prettier than she did in the black-and-white photographs. Clearly the colors were needed to bring out her charm.

"You look like your mother," I remarked, to fill the silence. It wasn't until I said it that I realized it was true. He had the same elongated face and strong jaw as she did, the short, prominent nose and high forehead.

He shrugged and asked why I had come to see him. Normally, no one came. The last person to visit had been a German scholar, ages ago, and all he had been interested in was Kafka.

When I called Henry up to arrange my visit, he had immediately asked, "Are you a literary scholar? Do you speak German?" Trying to catch me out.

As far as Kafka was concerned, he had announced to me in advance that he didn't have much to say, since he knew nothing about him.

"I came because I'm interested in your mother," I said. "I can't find anything out about her. It's like she stopped existing with the last letter from Kafka. What was she like as a woman? What kind of life did she lead?"

"Kafka was not normal."

I nodded. I was meeting Felice Bauer's son, so I was prepared to side with Felice.

"Henry, if you don't mind, tell me about your mother. What was she like?"

"My mother was a very warm and generous person. Social. Very . . . loving." He paused. "My mother was originally a secretary. She had a career in a company that made recording equipment. She enjoyed taking pictures and in general she liked gadgets—she even knew how to fix cars. My father didn't even know how to drive. She was very organized and very thorough. She filed everything away in her archive. Not just Kafka's letters but every scrap of paper, old ticket stubs . . ." Again he fell silent. "It's a shame he destroyed her letters. I'd have liked to know more about her."

"When, exactly, did you leave Germany?" I was taking notes. "Did you have a nice childhood?"

"I suppose." He shrugged. "We had everything the other children of our social standing had. A nanny, a cook, holidays by the sea. Later on, in Geneva, I was unhappy. I missed Berlin.

I remembered it as this lost paradise, and was mad at my parents for taking me away from there. They didn't explain it to us. People didn't talk much to their children in those days. Now, of course, those five years in Geneva strike me as a relatively blissful time. Our real exile didn't start until America."

"Why did your parents choose Los Angeles?"

"It was cheaper. Nicer climate. Also, the Friedmanns lived there—Aunt Sophie and Uncle Max."

"What was your father like?"

"He was a cheerful man, the exact opposite of Kafka. Before leaving Berlin, that is. He and my mother enjoyed company. They often had people over for dinner. My father was an excellent piano player. He was fourteen years older than my mother. By the time we left for America, he was over sixty. All he had left of his wealth, which, mind you, had not been negligible, was thirty thousand dollars, and it was gone within a year. My mother supported the household—she worked twelve hours a day. At one point, my father attempted to get back into banking. That was 1938. He went to Europe to look for investors, and in Paris he had a heart attack. He couldn't work anymore after that, just sat in the garden, eating away at himself.

"I don't actually know what their life was like in those last years. I wasn't around anymore. I left when I was nineteen to go study medicine and only came home to visit. In '44, I enlisted. My father died in 1950. I didn't get the chance to tell him goodbye. My mother didn't call."

"Felice died in L.A.?"

"No, here in New York. I brought her out. She'd had several strokes in a row, couldn't move, couldn't talk, but other than that she was healthy. She spent a year and a half lying in the hospital before she died. I would go and see her, but I couldn't take her home. There was just no way."

Henry glanced at his watch. He had promised me an hour.

"I can show you the photographs now."

He led me into his room. From the bedroom I heard the

sound of loud conversation. Annette was on the phone with someone named Ethel. Suddenly, it was clear to me: I had learned all I was going to learn about Felice's family. Henry had allotted me an hour right before lunch; that was it. He wasn't about to tell me anything he didn't want to, and I was too shy to try to drag it out of him. Still, at least I could see him, touch him. That alone was meaningful.

"Nice place you have," I said.

It honestly didn't look like an assisted living home. The only thing giving away the fact that we weren't in a luxury apartment or hotel were the ubiquitous bells to summon personnel.

"It's small," said Henry. "We had a house with a garden, big plot of land, a pool. But we couldn't keep up with the maintenance."

"Beautiful view of the river."

He shrugged impatiently. "Have a seat."

We sat down side by side on a narrow, firmly made bed with a white cover. He took out a box of photographs.

Pictures of his parents, friends, sister. Ursula, whom I've renamed Lily, outlived Felice by just five years. Unlike Henry, she didn't take after her mother. Lily was shorter, dark, curly-haired, gorgeous.

Felice's husband, Moritz, was also shorter than she was, and on the chubby side, with bushy black hair and round eyes. Felice apparently took to heart Kafka's advice that fat people are the only ones you can trust.

"Did your mother ever speak to you about her past?"

"No, never. Kafka was taboo for us. I found out about their relationship in 1938, from Aunt Sophie, Max Brod's sister. Brod was an awful person. And his novels!"

"Do you remember Grete Bloch?"

"Of course. She came to visit us in Geneva. My mother was friends with her, but personally I didn't like her. She would do anything just to get attention."

"She claimed she had children with Kafka."

"That's just what I'm talking about."

"Have you read Kafka's books?"

"They don't make sense to me. I find them depressing. He was crazy, meshuggeneh. He had a major problem with his father. I'm really just not interested."

"What did the two of them have in common?"

"My mother and Kafka, you mean? I guess she was impressed he was a writer. My mother was no intellectual, but she did like to read, and he tried to educate her, sent her books, about sixty or so, even gave her a Bible. She brought the books here with her from Berlin. I sold them when she died. At least I made some money on it."

"And Kafka's letters?"

"She wanted to destroy them," Henry said, "but I prevented her."

"If she wanted to destroy them, why not do it right away? Why take them with her to Switzerland, and then to the U.S.?"

"I have no idea. She insisted it was nobody else's business, that it was a private matter. I finally forced her to sell them. She was sick and needed every dollar. If I hadn't, she would have burned them. Schocken paid her eight thousand dollars and promised that he would donate the originals to a library in Jerusalem. But after he died, his heirs auctioned off my mother's letters at Sotheby's for over half a million dollars. My mother got eight thousand. I call that the deal of the century."

"But why did she bring the letters with her? Do you think that she still loved him?"

I guess he didn't hear me.

"To me, of course, it made no difference whether or not the letters were preserved for posterity. It was a bunch of nonsense as far as I was concerned. Any one of them would have been reason enough for my mother to break up with him, and I don't understand why she didn't. It wasn't about the letters for me, but the money. It would have been foolish not to seize the opportunity. My mother was sick, she had expenses."

He got up and opened the white door of a closet built into the wall. I saw jackets hanging on hangers, shelves of folded shirts, sweaters, and underwear, all in perfect order. Then, wedged in between the shelves and the jackets, a small bookshelf. My eyes flitted over the spines of the books. Nothing but Kafka and books about Kafka, in German as well as English.

Henry pulled out a thin volume with the title *Kafka und Prag*. "Interested?" He held it out so I could see, but didn't hand it to me. Then he slid it back in with the other books and clicked the closet door shut again. "I read them all, and you know what I have to say? It's a good thing Kafka wasn't my father!"

He's jealous! I realized. Jealous of Kafka, because Felice had a life with him whose secrets he couldn't fathom. Henry had tried to diminish Kafka with money, to turn his mother's love into a "good deal," but he didn't succeed. The shadow of the man who, once upon a time, had fought unsuccessfully for his mother, Felice, was still hanging over him, and his children and grandchildren, too. Kafka was more part of their lives than their grandfather Moritz.

He separated two photographs from the stack that lay on the bed and handed them to me. He told me they were for me to keep. It took me by surprise, since he hadn't been too friendly with me apart from that. Nor had his wife, who called out just then from behind the bedroom door: "Is she gone yet?"

Before I left, the two of us sat for a short while at the coffee table in the living room.

"Do you think she loved him?"

This time, he heard my question. "I don't know. I didn't really know her. My parents were quite secretive with me and my sister. They never talked to us about themselves. If you like, I can give you a lift to the station."

In the car, we chatted about Europe. He said he went to Italy almost every year.

"I only went back to Berlin once, in 1984. Four days."

"And how was it?"

He shrugged.

"So you got used to America?"

"Never."

The clouds lifted from the bottom of the valley and planted themselves around the hills on the other side of the river. A freighter skimmed along the surface; the colors were as crisp as the air. He shook my hand and said good-bye.

I learned of Henry's death, two years after my visit, in an email from Joel. Henry died of throat cancer. Toward the end, he couldn't speak, eat, or drink, and had to be fed artificially.

Joel also asked if by any chance I had recorded my conversation with his grandfather. He was hoping someday he might play it for his kids.

The truth is, I had wanted to, but Henry wouldn't let me. He didn't like the sound of his raspy old man's voice.

The photographs of Felice that he gave me are right here on the table.

The first one is a souvenir from a holiday on the Baltic. Doubtless one of those excruciatingly long vacations during which she didn't write Kafka, and if she did, at best a postcard scribbled in pencil. This was before the war—you can tell from the girls' wide-brim hats, the matrons' plumed headdresses, the laced bodices and long skirts reaching to the ground. Felice stands off to the edge of the group, in a dark, very elegant dress with a wide lace collar and a locket around her neck. She tilts her head back, showing her teeth in a wide smile. Her mother, Anna, stands beside her like a general, grasping her at the waist, apparently tugging her toward her. But Felice, to judge from the turn of her hip, is pulling away. The other girl might be Grete Bloch; at least it looks like her. She is wearing something white with frills and lace. It may be a blouse and skirt, or a dress. The straw hat on her head is as big as a wagon wheel. There is also a sour-faced older lady, with wrinkles around her mouth, evidently another mother, and four young gentlemen in walking suits. They all have canes and straw hats, and three of them sport mustaches. A merry bunch, at first sight. Beneath their feet a sandy beach, at right a colonnade.

The second photograph is a yellowed identity card portrait. In it, Felice wears her hair short, the way they did in the thirties, pulled back from her forehead with bobby pins. Although not smiling, she wears an affable look, her face, turned slightly to the side, framed by a high fur collar. Bright eyes, faintly sloping eyelids, low, well-groomed eyebrows, high forehead and prominent jaw, straight-lined mouth. It's a strong, good-natured face, a bit stubborn perhaps.

1953

Los Angeles

THE ONLY ONE OF HER SIBLINGS left now is Erna, who lives in the Soviet occupation zone. What is that supposed to mean? Has anything of her Berlin survived? Do they even speak German there still, or only Russian now?

The first to die was Robert. Then Ferri last year in Chicago. And after him, Else.

It wasn't until they buried her sister that she felt truly alone. They had had a good life together. And Else was the last person who still remembered everything, not counting Max and Sophie.

The last two years, Else's legs had acted up and her head would start to spin. She took Robert's place in the armchair on the veranda and stopped going to work, though she still sewed and cooked for herself, Felice, and the lodger. She could still manage that. And every Saturday, Felice drove her to the movies. The whole gang would go: Masha, Else, Felice, and Sholem.

Sholem was the youngest of them, not even sixty yet. She had a husband at home, but a crabby one, so she preferred going out with her girlfriends.

Every Saturday evening, they had their ritual. Ice cream on Pico and afterward a movie. Those were good times. Else, Felice, and Masha liked Gregory Peck the best, while Sholem preferred Humphrey Bogart. They all four adored Ava Gardner.

It was sad at home without Else. Now the only one left

was the lodger, the *borderke*, as Else used to say, whom they had taken in for room and board when Robert's room freed up. He was a nice-enough man, quiet and undemanding. But after she was left alone, taking care of the lodger and the house became too much for her. She waited until he found something else, then gave the landlord notice and moved into an apartment building. It was a small place, just a kitchen and a tiny bedroom, but it was enough.

During the day she was mostly in the shop anyway, and evenings she relaxed, sewing, cooking, and listening to the radio. Except for Saturdays, when she went to the movies with Sholem and Masha.

Joachim offered her to come and live with them. He and his family had moved to the countryside, to a village in the Hudson River Valley; they had plenty of room. He commuted to work by train. She thanked him kindly and declined. She was over sixty and wasn't about to change her habits now. Worrying herself over how Nina Perel ran the household and trying to communicate with her grandkids, who only knew English.

Lily didn't offer a thing.

For the first time in her life, Felice had no one to take care of but herself, and it wasn't so bad, except for the fact that she was sad.

Thank goodness she had Masha and Sholem. The last movie they went to see was *Gentlemen Prefer Blondes*, and they all agreed Jane Russell was far better in it than Marilyn Monroe.

"Marilyn is a grown woman, after all," said Sholem angrily. She followed women's issues and was a great admirer of Eleanor Roosevelt. "Why does she act like such a child? How is anyone supposed to take us seriously after that?"

When she was young, Sholem had wanted to go to college, but it wasn't meant to be. Her whole life was spent taking care of others: siblings, parents, husband, children. Sitting in the ice-cream parlor on Pico, she had heated discussions with Felice and Masha about how Americans were trying to drive women back into the kitchen, after they had only barely managed to escape. Women had done all kinds of jobs during the war, even the most physically demanding ones. No one had any doubt that they could be independent. But now the men were back, and they wanted to go to their jobs and make lots of kids, and kids needed a mom at home. Life was a house in the suburbs, two cars, and a sweet little wife in a striped or polka-dot apron, and in Hollywood they knew it, too, cranking out one movie after another about beauties waiting for their prince, and the moment he appeared—poof—they turned into happy homemakers. Any woman who wasn't content with that came to a bad end.

Luckily, there were other movies, too. *The Snows of Kilimanjaro* they saw twice. Also *Death of a Salesman* and *A Streetcar Named Desire* and *An American in Paris*—the last one they saw three times in a row. Gene Kelly. And Gershwin's melodies. Felice loved the cinema.

And the gilded youth cruised up and down Ocean Drive in their convertibles, and nearly every woman was blond all of a sudden, not only in Santa Monica but in Pico-Robertson, too. Wherever you went, there were cranes sticking up, because of new construction, and a radio or TV blasting, and lights glaring and cars driving and planes flying. Felice was old and this was a time to be young, but even for her it felt intoxicating. This was the world she should have been born into, not the gloomy, tuberculosis-ridden one of the fin de siècle.

How would *he* have liked it here?

There were times when she would imagine him here with her, in America. Taking him out on a drive. He had always loved fresh air and open space, water and sunshine.

Whizzing down the smooth-paved freeway in her Ford, her front-seat passenger trembling with delight.

For thirty-five years, she had hardly given him a thought. Not that she had forgotten, but she hadn't thought of him.

Until now. She even opened up one of his books and couldn't stop reading it. It was his first published book, his little book, as he had said when he proudly sent it to her in Berlin. He had hoped it would impress her, but the things Felice was interested in were entirely different. Dances. New dresses. The prospect of marriage. She read books, to be sure, but nothing like *Meditation.* She liked books with stories and characters. When he asked Felice how she liked his little book, she dodged the question, not knowing what to say to keep from hurting him.

Now perhaps she understood him more.

One day, while reading his brief little text about wanting to be an American Indian, it occurred to her how much pleasure he would have taken in the freeway to Pasadena. Savoring the drive along the dried-up riverbed, and begging her not to slow down, to go faster and keep on going, even all the way to the East Coast.

Her opening up one of his books after such a long time was related to Sophie's visit and the letter that she'd brought with her.

Sophie turned up a few weeks after Else's burial, on a Saturday afternoon. A knitting circle was holding one of its regular gatherings in Felice and Masha's shop. As she listened in on the ladies' conversation, Felice unwrapped a ball of yarn from a yellow piece of paper and put it in one of the pigeonholes, based on its color. It was soft, high-quality yarn from Scotland, pleasant to the touch.

Five permed, slightly tilted heads atop straight backs, five handbags leaned against chair legs, five pairs of crossed ankles in stockings, tucked ladylike beneath the chair. Knitting needles bobbing and clinking against each other.

"It's nothing but Communists now, at every turn. I don't know if you read the papers, but they want to destroy America, and rabble-rousers that they are, they might just pull it off! Why, Hollywood is full of them. They come dragging in from Europe and yet all they do is criticize. They want to turn

America into the Soviet Union! God forbid. We need to be vigilant, like they said on the radio. What are teachers telling our children in school? How do we know they're not brainwashing them with Red propaganda? Who's going to keep an eye on it if not us mothers? I'm telling you, ladies, I keep a close watch even on my own husband, and especially my father-in-law. Anything anti-American needs to be nipped in the bud, that's what they said on the radio. At lunch on Sunday, my father-in-law said this Communist witch hunt was going too far, it was threatening our democracy, so I said, 'Are you trying to tell me communism isn't a threat? And all those spies trying to poison us? I'll be damned if my little Paulie's getting vaccinated! And now they have an atom bomb!'"

"The bomb, now that's scary!"

"I hear they're firing people. Without any proof at all. They don't even get to defend themselves."

"It's true. My brother-in-law got sacked from the newspaper, and he wasn't even in the union. Now he can't find a new job for the life of him. Nobody wants him now that there's a stain on him. And he's got three kids."

"Masha, honey, how should I end it here?"

The bell on the door tinkled; it was Sophie.

"Hello, everyone. Hi, Felice. Hi, Masha. Max dropped me off here on his way into town."

"Hi, Sophie. I was finishing up anyway. Let me just straighten things up and then we can go."

It was an easy walk home from Pico; she was still living in the house at the time. For April it was warm. People were already swimming down at the beach.

She remembered that day she had on a dark green spring dress with tiny yellow and white polka dots. The jacarandas were in bloom. Clouds of heavy purple blossoms canopied the street, their petals falling off, sticking to sidewalks and cars. Gorgeous to look at, but talk about a mess. Felice much preferred the orange trees, with their stiff white blossoms hidden inside the shiny leaves. She had one growing in her garden.

When they got home, she seated Sophie on the veranda, then went to the kitchen and put water on for tea. She sliced some bread, cheese, and a piece of cold meat, took out some pickles she had brought from the Polish grocery store.

They drank tea, nibbling their snack and gazing out at the garden as the shadows grew longer. The clouds turned gold and pink in the sea of azure overhead.

"I have something I need to give you," said Sophie all of a sudden. "I would rather not, but my brother asked me to."

She pulled a folded sheet of paper out of her handbag and slid it across the table toward Felice.

Tel Aviv
March 25, 1952

Dear Felice,

How are you doing? I heard about the great loss you suffered. Losing your beloved brother and sister at nearly the same time must be very painful. I am thinking of you and wish you much strength in getting through this difficult time.

I am writing you today in regard to a matter that concerns you personally. However, it also concerns me, as well as the many other people around the world today who admire the work of the man whom we both loved.

As you surely know, I had prepared Franz's stories and novels for publication even before the war. I have also written a book about him. I have made it my life's mission to attend to his literary legacy (even at the expense of my own work), and—as you probably also know—Franz's fame continues to grow. His works today are published in translations around the world.

I always knew that Franz was a genius. Now my words have been confirmed, as so many times before. Not a day goes by that I do not think of him, conversing with him in my mind and imagining what he might say apropos of his tremendous success. He, who was so modest. So uncertain, though not of himself, not at all. He was well aware what talent slumbered within him, what treasures he had hidden within. His uncertainty was only and nothing but a reflection of his internal integrity and rigor. And of his timidness on glimpsing the heights of whose existence he was aware, yet whose attainment was so difficult. Franz worked on himself, growing, fully aware that he had yet to write his best work, and nothing that was not perfect was good enough for him. What heights, Felice, what dizzying spiritual and artistic pinnacles might he have reached had he lived longer.

About a year ago, I was contacted by my friend Willy Haas; perhaps you will remember him. After surviving the war, he returned to Prague, and he has approached me in regard to a certain matter. Milena Jesenská-Polak, a Czech journalist, whose name you would not know, and wife of a literary critic from Vienna, before departing for the concentration camp where she died, placed into his hands for safekeeping a number of Franz's letters. (She also had Franz's diaries, so you can see how he trusted her. Immediately after his death, however, she handed over the diaries to me.)

These letters I mention were private, Franz was in love with Milena. They grew close at a distance, during her translation of one of his short stories into Czech. Milena, who was not Jewish but Czech, was truly a remarkable woman, highly educated, the daughter of a prominent dentist. She was also a very unhappy person, especially during the period when Franz came to know her. I, too, have several letters from her. She loved Franz but could not bring herself to leave her husband. She even wrote me because she feared she was hurting Franz and did not know whom to turn to.

Well, I suppose you are not interested in so many details. What is important is that the letters made it through the war and Haas, who knew Milena well, has edited them. They will be published by Schocken in September. Naturally I assisted him with it. He conferred with me on everything, especially when it came to leaving out the parts that might affect people still alive. But all the work was worth it. *Letters to Milena* is remarkable reading. In places perhaps the most magnificent writing to have issued from Kafka's pen. It has inspired me to set about editing my own correspondence with Franz and what other letters that I have so far managed to acquire from his friends. I tell you, it is a labor of many years. But nothing, not even the smallest scrap of paper or briefest entry, is without meaning, Felice, when it comes to understanding the soul of a genius. Once you read *Letters to Milena*, you will see for yourself. They are already working on a translation into English.

And now, the reason why I am writing.

Salman Schocken approached me personally with a request that I contact you on his behalf. He would like to purchase Franz's letters from you, assuming that you still have them. It is a sensitive subject, I understand. To touch on old wounds is often painful for me, too. But we have an obligation. All of us who loved him. To Kafka and to the world. We must not keep the fruits of his inspiration for ourselves alone.

Schocken would put the letters in order and prepare them for printing, but of course, it goes without saying, he would not publish them sooner than the term on which the two of you contractually agree.

I have asked Sophie to deliver this letter to you personally. I have also asked her to confirm whether, in fact, you have the letters with you and roughly how many of them there are. If you want, just say the word and someone from Schocken will be in touch, most likely Salman himself. And I don't suppose that you know what happened to the letters that Kafka wrote to Miss Bloch? If my memory serves me correctly, there must have been a good stack of them. Her brother, with whom I have been in contact, knew nothing about them. You may have other information, but the latest news I have is, unfortunately, that Miss Bloch was killed in spring 1944 during a German raid on the village in Italy where she was interned. It was reported that they rounded up all the remaining Jews and took them to Auschwitz. But Miss Bloch was not on the transport. While they were being boarded into the truck bed, a German soldier beat her to death with the butt of his bayonet. Truly no one deserves such a dreadful end, poor Miss Bloch.

I heard from Sophie that Joachim got married and now has a little boy and little girl and a private practice in New York. I congratulate you on having such a son, Felice. Also I heard your daughter got married and has a baby daughter, so congratulations are in order for that as well.

You see, Felice, what good fortune life has given you. You even have grandchildren now. Neither I nor Franz was blessed with the good fortune of having children.

As a man grows old, he hopes to see some continuity. To hand over to someone his pilgrim's staff and bag, but without children, Felice, it is all nothing but a substitute. A man would like to give away, but no one wants anything from him. Thank you, they say, we will get by just fine on our own. We know what we are doing.

No one here cares too much for my books; I am not even invited to speak at the university. To be frank, I am disappointed. In the days when we were longing for Eretz Yisrael and working so hard for our cause, I never imagined how little understanding I would find here. Yes, I suppose I really did hope to find a home here in the spiritual sense of the word. A home both for myself and my work.

But home, that was Prague, Felice, that mystical city which I am sure that you remember well and which exists no more. Home today is but a memory or a dream.

I live a makeshift life here, Felice, and that is unlikely to change. Makeshift and on the margins of public interest. Materially, I lack nothing, I have found loyal friends here, that is true, and not only in the Habima Theatre. Yet, were it not for Kafka, who is my great mission, I do not know what would keep me at a safe distance from despair.

Let me know soon what you have decided.

Cordially,
Max Brod

Dusk fell over the garden and the temperature cooled. They could hear the sound of the automobiles on Pico Boulevard, the honking horns. Masha must have closed the shop by now. She would be sitting eating ice cream with Sholem, and soon they would go to the movies.

"Max will be here for me any minute," said Sophie.

"Does he know about the letter?"

"Why shouldn't I tell him, Fae? Maybe not if Robert were alive, but as it is? You still have the letters, don't you? Or did you destroy them?"

"Not yet."

"You mustn't even think of it."

"Why not, Sophie? They're private letters, after all. I would never let them out of my hands. My mother is the only one who's ever seen them, when she went poking around in them behind my back. If only for his sake I can't. It's exactly the opposite of what Brod says. Franz wrote me things that he would never have wanted made public. He never would have agreed to that."

"Think about it, Felice. You don't have to sell all of them. No one but you knows how many of them there actually are. It would be a pity not to take advantage of the offer. Think of your children."

"I am. They would want the very ground to swallow them up for shame."

"I doubt that they would mind. Where are the letters, anyway?"

"Here. Just as I brought them from Berlin."

"I'm sorry to interfere like this, but I have your best interests at heart, to hell with the letters. I'm going to be honest, Fae, as your friend and your relative. You've always been much more important to me than Kafka, and I couldn't care less what my brother thinks. Haven't you suffered enough for his sake? Five years is no small thing! I remember it well. You endured things that no woman should have to endure, and then he ditched you in the end besides. It was sheer chutzpah on his part. Even my brother thought so at the time, no matter what he says today. And you want to be respectful of him? Was he respectful of you? Everybody nowadays is going mad over Kafka. Kafka here, Kafka there. Did you know they published his diaries last year in Germany? I have the book. I was going to keep it secret from you, but now that it's out, what's the point? You'll be surprised what you find out about yourself when you read it. It's all in there! What he thought the first time he saw you, and your walk in the zoo, and your stay in Marienbad, and some 'tribunal' in that dreadful hotel in Berlin. And how you went to visit him, poor thing, in Zürau. He didn't leave out a thing. Grete's in there, too. You're already mixed up in it anyway. You're stuck with it no matter what you do, so why not take advantage? He was hugely indebted to you, Fae, and now is your chance to get some of it back. You don't think this is providence? You don't think this is justice? That chunk of money would come in handy, especially since you aren't going to have any pension."

"What does your husband say?"

"He says sell, and fast, while there's still demand."

That evening she didn't go to the movies.

Once she was alone, before anything else, she tidied up and washed the dishes from supper. Then she walked into the bedroom, turned on the light, and opened the bottom drawer, the heaviest one, on the dresser that had traveled over with them from Berlin. If she remembered correctly, that was where she had stored the box after the last time they moved. She had covered it with a layer of carefully ironed cloth napkins, embroidered with a decorative letter *F.*

Robert had had no reason to open the dresser, and he'd had no idea what was in it. The same for Joachim. Lily had sometimes helped her change the sheets or make the bed, but she was unlikely to have looked under the napkins, part of a set that they hadn't used in ages.

It was a brown cardboard box with the name Bata on it, wrapped around with string. She set it down on Robert's half of the bed, which she left made up, went to get a pair of scissors, and cut the string. She lifted the lid.

A cloying smell of old paper. The letters were in envelopes, carefully arranged by date of receipt and bound together with green ribbon. The first one lay on top. She had still been living in Immanuelkirchstrasse at the time. The house number was wrong; it had been crossed out and corrected in hand by the mailman. Everything might have been different if that first letter had gotten lost. But even with the wrong address, it had found its way to her.

She carefully untied the bow, picked up the cleanly sliced-open envelope, and removed the sheet of paper.

Prague
September 20, 1912

My dear Miss Bauer,

In the likelihood that you no longer have even the remotest recollection of me, I am introducing myself once more: my name is Franz Kafka, and I am the person who greeted you for the first time that evening at Director Brod's in Prague, the one who subsequently handed you across the table, one by one, photographs of a Thalia trip, and who finally, with the very hand now striking the keys, held your hand, the one which confirmed a promise to accompany him next year to Palestine.

He wrote the first letter on a typewriter, still feeling shy. The second one he wrote by hand.

It was Felice's first look at the writing in a long time. She knew it well. She felt drawn to and repulsed by it at the same time. Like someone you loved who betrayed you.

The bold strokes of the capital *A*, impatiently crossed at waist level. The little tail flapping from the edge of the capital *W*. The capital *L* in the words *Liebe* and *Leben*, bent forward like a falling man, head bowed to his chest.

The paper's surface was a tad rough to the touch, and in the spots where the pen had pressed down hard, she could feel the ink.

The poison of those letters.

What had she imagined, what had she been thinking when she brought them with her? She must have known there would come a moment when she would have to take them out and look them in the face again. Was that what she wanted to do? Was there really a need for that?

She had known all along that one day she was going to have to destroy them. She should have done it right away. Burned them all the moment the two of them broke up. That was what people did in those days, and rightly so. The longer she held on to them, the harder it was to get rid of them. They lived a life of their own, there, inside the box.

At the absolute latest, she should have burned them before the wedding, as her mother had advised her. Or at least in Geneva, before she left for America.

Why hadn't she done it?

Why had she dragged them around with her everywhere?

What if she were to die today or tomorrow?

She should take the box, right now, and throw it in the garbage.

Felice sat on Robert's bed, absolutely still and yet sinking little by little. *My dearest Felice. Dearest girl. My poor dearest. F.*

There were two of them, sitting at a table, one on either side. She could see their bulbous outlines, the tall hats on their heads. They were eating meat. Gnawing the bones and tossing them under the table. We don't do that in America, she wanted to shout, but all that came out of her mouth was a faint wheek.

Something pure, something so pure, she heard one of them mutter, while the other one dug with his fingernail at a piece of meat stuck in his teeth. It was a long nail on the little finger of his right hand, clearly grown intentionally to use instead of a toothpick.

But in Marienbad there was trumpeting, was there not, Miss? the cleanly man suddenly roared. And how did you actually imagine this Parlograph looking? And why on earth didn't you want to leave Prague?

Such a zaddik, the other man cried, peering closely at his fingernail. Miss, take this down! Why aren't you taking this down? Is it true I'm too thin to marry?

He grabbed the two sides of his coat and spread them like a beetle's wing cases. There was nothing underneath but a terrifying emptiness.

His heart melted, the cleanly man said. From smoking.

And now, Miss, it is time for us to sentence you.

The town square or open space where she sat appeared often in her dreams. A sun-beaten, dusty patch of ground. The train looked familiar, too. No seats, bars on the windows, a train for the condemned. Robert was here as well. What had he done? she wondered. And Grete. So she hadn't been stabbed by a bayonet? Glancing around the unfamiliar faces, she also spotted Else with her mother and her sister Toni. Meanwhile, Franz lay next to her on the ground, pressing against her, naked and cold. Had he been dragged from the grave? What if her mother noticed them? Felice held his hand in her lap, with its long fingers and round-trimmed nails.

A single word and we will be saved.

The train suddenly came to a stop. The freight car door gaped wide open, beneath them an abyss.

The word!

His raw white naked body against the graying sky.

Such a zaddik, see how he flies!

Why it is but a piece of paper, madam, only paper.

1954

Los Angeles

Sleep comes to an end around 4:00 a.m. Alertness slips into her mind like a wedge, prying open the leaves of the gate, till it flings wide open and the procession of memories sets off on its way.

She keeps seeing Grete in Geneva, pulling her lace shawl more tightly around her shoulders while she looks around the table as though she has no idea where she is.

Or the table on the balcony at the Schloß Balmoral und Osborne hotel as Franz reaches across it to take her by the hand.

Their bodies had found their way to each other with almost surprising ease. It had been cautious and a bit awkward, but immensely liberating, a relief—it had to be, it was supposed to be, she had always known it would be. It was good to be finally clear about that.

Running her fingers through the thick hair at his temples.

Where had she found the courage to go see him in Marienbad?

She had said the words to him then: exactly six of them. They had come to her simply, on their own, and he had received them with the same straightforwardness.

Everything between them was suddenly easy and clear, and it remained that way for a while, even after she left. Despite the reality in Berlin, despite her mother, despite everyone who insisted that married life in their social class looked different from the life that she and Franz had planned for themselves.

"And what about children?" her mother had said. "Where do you plan to put them in a two-room flat in the suburbs? How are they going to fit? And who is going to take care of them when you go to work—not him, I presume? What is he going to do all day long? If he quits his job with the insurance company, he'll lose his pension. Can he make a living writing? And what about the asbestos factory? Is he getting out of that, too? And what about children?"

"My children, Mother, are going to be the orphans at the Jewish Home in Berlin, whom my dear fiancé proposed I help. Children from the shtetls in the east, which have been overrun by war and pogroms, orphans at whom you turn up your nose because they don't speak German, who, as you say, don't even know how to wipe their noses, whom you dismiss with a wave of the hand, like everything that you don't want and don't intend to deal with.

"Whatever you don't want to deal with, you simply swat away like a fly, out of fear or laziness. You certainly are not about to lose sleep over it. Because you, unlike me and my lover, have an army of mothers, fathers, uncles, and aunts behind you, apartments with sturdy furniture, banks, shops, and factories. Truth and justice are on your side and Kafka is a fool. As you have insisted ever since you secretly read his letters. And yet you don't advise that I leave him. In fact, just the opposite. I can still hear you, as if it were today: 'You might yet be able to make something of him, just wait until you have children, but for now hold on to him and squeeze what you can out of him. You'll figure it out, my girl. You can't be too choosy at your age. You aren't exactly a beauty, Erna is much prettier. You can cook, though, I'll give you that, and you know how to dress—you got that from me.'

"You forgot to mention the disgrace, Mother. It's no secret in Berlin, though perhaps it is in Prague. Our disgrace, which

Father and Erna and your precious Ferri brought on us. Franz thought I was being greedy. What did I need so much money for? Why did I work as a private stenographer after my job at the firm every day? What was I supposed to tell him, Mother? That I needed to earn more than my salary because my father ran off with his mistress, my sister had an illegitimate child, and my brother embezzled a heap of money from his boss? Outstanding bunch, those Bauers! But then again, you didn't like Robert, either, though he didn't write crazy letters and had gobs of money. Your objection to him was that he was too old and disrespectful to you, and you weren't embarrassed to say it out loud, even though it was only thanks to him that you didn't have to sell your wedding ring to buy bread like so many friends of yours in Berlin."

Sophie did her best to dissuade her, but Felice read Franz's diaries, which were published in Germany. She also read his letters to that other woman, too, Milena Jesenská, who wasn't a Jew but died in a concentration camp all the same.

Then, finally, one by one, she closely reread all the letters he had written to her over those five years. As well as the excerpts of his letters to Grete, brought to her by her friend as the corpus delicti, after she had painstakingly separated out the parts that she said only had to do with her.

It wasn't exactly a nice feeling seeing the letters again. But it wasn't about feeling good, or nostalgia. She was on a mission. Provided she read carefully enough and left nothing out, she might be able to solve the biggest puzzle of her life: Why had Kafka, a writer admired around the world, yet a man she still didn't rightly understand to this day, chosen her? And given that he did choose her, why hadn't he married her? Had it been her fault?

Also, she needed to assess whether the letters were truly intended for her and her alone. In other words, whether she did or did not have the right to comply with Brod's request.

Using a pencil, she underlined the parts of the letters that seemed to her in some way relevant to her "case"—as she had begun to refer to her relationship with Kafka in her mind.

> *Dearest one! Can I really be sure of you now? The Sie glides as though on skates, it may have disappeared in the crack between two letters, one has to chase after it with letters and thoughts morning, noon, and night; but the Du stands firm; it stays here like your letter that doesn't move when I kiss it over and over again. But what a word that is! Nothing unites two people so completely, especially if, like you and me, all they have is words.*
>
> *First of all, I am delighted that you are a vegetarian at heart. I don't like strict vegetarians all that much, because I too am almost a vegetarian, and see nothing particularly likable about it, just something natural, and those who are good vegetarians in their hearts, but, for reasons of health, from indifference, or simply because they underrate food as such, eat meat or whatever happens to be on the table, casually, with their left hand, so to speak, these are the ones I like. It's a pity that my love for you advanced so fast, that there is no room left to love you more for what you eat. And you share my craze for sleeping with the window open? Open the whole year around? Even in winter? Wide open? That would be going one better than me, for in the winter I open it only a little, one tiny crack.*
>
> *Now, before I go to sleep (it is actually 3 A.M., usually I only work till 1; you must have misunderstood one of my last letters, I meant 3 in the afternoon; I stayed on in the office and wrote from there), because it is your wish and because it is so simple, I will whisper in your ear how much I love you. I love you so much, Felice,*

that if I can keep you I should want to live forever, but only, it must be remembered, as a healthy person and your equal. Well, that's how it is, and you should know it, and indeed it is almost beyond kissing, the awareness of which leaves me with almost nothing to do but stroke your hand.

How devout are you? You go to the synagogue; but I dare say you have not been recently. And what is it that sustains you, the idea of Judaism or of God? Are you aware, and this is the most important thing, of a continuous relationship between yourself and a reassuringly distant, if possibly infinite height or depth? He who feels this continuously has no need to roam about like a lost dog, mutely gazing around with imploring eyes; he never need yearn to slip into a grave as if it were a warm sleeping bag and life a cold winter night; and when climbing the stairs to his office he never need imagine that he is careering down the well of the staircase, flickering in the uncertain light, twisting from the speed of his fall, shaking his head with impatience.

Imagine, I even ate the chocolate, slowly of course, hesitatingly, anxiously; but the temptation to participate as much as possible in your life and pleasures was too great. It didn't do me any harm either, for everything that comes from you (in this you are unlike me) is lovely and good and harmless.

You have had to put up with a great deal recently, dearest, and you put up with it in a way that is incomprehensible to me on the one hand, and that I unhesitatingly expect of you on the other. Whether you complain, are weary, or even cry in your letters, I can see you behind them, so vigorous and lively that shame about myself and sadness over the contrast—I here, you there—make me want to creep into a corner. The trouble is, I am not at peace with myself; I am not always "something," and if for once I am "something," I pay for it by "being nothing" for months on end. And of course if I don't collect myself in time, my judgment of people and of the world in general suffers from it, too; my view of the hopelessness of the world is due largely to this distorted judgment which could no doubt be straightened out automatically by reflecting, but only for a single useless moment.

Of my complaints you say, "I don't believe them, and you don't believe them, either." The misfortune lies in this very notion, and I myself am not free of blame. I cannot deny that I have acquired great experience in complaining (alas, with perfect justification), so that the plaintive note is, as to the beggars in the streets, constantly at my command, even when I don't feel quite like it at heart. But I recognize the duty to convince you, which hangs over me every moment of the day, and for this reason complain automatically, without thinking, and needless to say thereby achieve the opposite. "You don't believe them," and then you transfer your disbelief to the genuine complaints as well.

My one fear—surely nothing worse can either be said or listened to—is that I shall never be able to possess you. At best I would be confined, like an unthinkingly faithful dog, to kissing your casually proffered hand, which would not be a sign of love, but of the despair of the animal condemned to silence and eternal separation. I would sit beside you and, as has happened, feel the breath and life of your body at my side, yet in reality be further from you than now, here in my room. I would never be able to attract your attention, and it would be lost to me altogether when you look out of the window, or lay your head in your hands. You and I would ride past the entire world, hand in hand, seemingly united, and none of it would be true. In short, though you might lean toward me far enough for you to be in danger, I would be excluded from you forever.

No, Felice, we cannot go on living in this way.

I love you, Felice, with everything that is good in me as a human being, with everything in me that makes me deserving of being astir among the living. If it isn't much, then I am not much. I love you just as you are, the parts of you I approve of, as well as those I do not approve of, everything, everything. You don't feel this way, even if everything else were all right. You are not satisfied with me, you object to various things about me, want me to be other than I am. I should "live more in the real world," should "take things as I find them," etc. Don't you realize that if in fact it is an inner necessity for you to want this, then you no longer want me, but are trying to get past me. Why try to change people, Felice? It is not right. One has either to take people as they are, or leave them as they are. One cannot change them, one can merely disturb their balance. A human being, after all, is not made up of single pieces, from which a single piece can be taken out and replaced by something else. Rather he is a whole, and if you pull one end, the other, whether you like it or not, begins to twitch.

Don't tell me I am being too severe with you; all the love I am capable of serves only you. But look, for more than 18 months we have been running to meet each other, yet seemed, before the first month was up, already to be almost breast to breast. But now, after all this time, after so much running, we are still so very far apart. It is your absolute duty, F., to try to know yourself to the best of your ability. For surely, when finally we are together, we mustn't batter each other to pieces; after all, we are too good for that.

For ages you were mistaken in referring so often to what had been left unsaid. What was lacking was not discussion, but belief. Because you were unable to believe the things you heard and saw, you thought there were things that had been left unsaid. You were unable to appreciate the immense power my work has over me; you did appreciate it, but by no means fully. As a result you were bound to misinterpret everything that my worries over my work, and only my worries over my work, produced in me in the way of peculiarities which disconcerted you. Moreover, these peculiarities (odious peculiarities, I admit, odious above all to myself) manifested themselves more with you than with anyone else. That was inevitable, and had nothing to do with spite. You see, you were not only the greatest friend, but at the same time the greatest enemy, of my work, at least from the point of view of my work. Thus, though fundamentally it loved you beyond measure, equally it had to resist you with all its might for the sake of self-preservation. It had to do so in every single detail. I thought of it, for instance, when having a meal one evening with your sister consisting almost exclusively of meat. Had you been there, I would probably have ordered almonds.

Felice, don't think that the impeding considerations and anxieties are not an almost unbearable and detestable burden to me, that I wouldn't prefer to shed everything, that I wouldn't prefer a straightforward approach, and

> *that I wouldn't rather be happy now and at once in a small intimate circle, and above all give happiness. But this isn't possible, it is a burden I am forced to bear, I shiver with discontent, and even if my failures stared me in the face, and not only my failures but also the loss of all hope and the steady approach of all guilt—I really couldn't behave otherwise.*
>
> *So to your main question: Certainly, I shall want to reorganize myself after the war. I want to move to Berlin, despite the official's notorious fear for his future, for here I cannot carry on. By then, though, what sort of man will be undertaking that move? To judge by my present condition, he will be a man who at best will be able to work for one week before finally reaching the end of his strength. What a night this has been! What a day! I should have left in 1912.*

And Grete! The day she came to her with his letters, so upset she was trembling.

"Felice, I have something awful to tell you. You're going to hate me for it, but I can't keep it to myself. He doesn't want to marry you! How could he write this to me if he did?"

The poison of the letters.

What was she actually trying to do? What was he trying to do? What were the two of them up to, writing each other behind her back? Franz was presumably trying to get up the courage to marry her, but Grete? Did she mean to steal Franz for herself? But she already had a lover. Felice had a hunch he was married, though Grete kept the details from her. Surely Franz knew more.

Grete was the secretive type; it had come up between them many times. She never told the whole truth, even when it came to small things. She always kept a little bit to herself.

Are not my letters more terrible than my silence? And my life even worse than that? And on the whole not unlike the tortures I inflict? But within my power and with your help I can see no remedy other than to wait, even if one is ground to dust in the process. I know of no other. What is silence compared to this kind of writing? Isn't the former more desirable?

For I am desperate, like a caged rat, insomnia and headaches tearing at me; how I get through the days is quite beyond description. To be free from the office is my only possible salvation, my primary desire.

If you, Felice, are in any way to blame for our common misfortune (omitting for the moment my own share, which is monumental), it is for your insistence on keeping me in Prague, although you ought to have realized that it was precisely the office and Prague that would lead to my—thus our—eventual ruin. I don't say you wanted to keep me here deliberately, this is not what I think; your ideas about possible ways of life are more courageous and more flexible than mine (I am up to the waist in Austrian officialdom, and over and above that in my own personal inhibitions), so you did not have any compelling urge to consider the future carefully. All the same you ought to have been able to assess or at least to sense this in me, even against myself, even contrary to my own words. In that case I would not have been against you for a moment. What happened instead? Instead we went to buy furniture in Berlin for an official in Prague. Heavy furniture which looked as if, once in position, it could never be removed. Its very solidity is what you appreciated most. The sideboard in particular—a perfect tombstone, or a memorial to the life of a Prague official—oppressed me profoundly. If during our visit to the furniture store a funeral bell had begun tolling in the distance, it wouldn't have been inappropriate. I wanted to be with you, Felice, of course with you, but free to express my powers which you, in my opinion at least, cannot really have respected if you could consider stifling them with all that furniture.

Part of the reason she didn't take him too seriously as a writer was that she didn't understand him, but it went deeper than that. To be honest, she had to confess that she hated his writing.

It was this confession that he was trying to coax out of her, that was what he wanted from her. But she refused. She couldn't be that brutally honest even with herself.

Of course she was flattered to have a writer wooing her. At the time, he wasn't yet famous, but there were people she respected, including Max Brod, who held him in high regard.

She detested his writing, though. It stood between them. He himself kept putting it there. Yet she had never been interested in his writing; that wasn't what she wanted. It was him she liked. She was attracted to him. He was a good-looking person with a gentle and kind way of speaking, which made an impression on her. Not a hint of the coarseness or boisterousness with which she had grown up. She was loud and animated, too, but that seemed to be the very thing about her he loved most.

He had forced his writing on her! With the exception of those few days in Marienbad, when he had been there for her and with her in the way she had always wanted.

No, she was judging him unfairly. After all, he had loved her and had been ready to sacrifice for her. They might still have been able to live together, if not for the war. And if not for her mother. In the summer of 1916, when they had been in Marienbad, he wasn't yet sick—or was he?

Dearest—am I overdoing the writing again, as in former days? In justification: I am sitting on your balcony, on your side of the table, it's as though the 2 sides of the table were the 2 sides of a pair of scales; as though the balance

> *established on our good evenings had been upset; and I, alone on one side of the scales, were going down. Going down, because you are far away. That's why I am writing.*

And yet he . . . who was "he," really? He went on patiently holding her hand in his, there, on the balcony of the spa hotel Schloß Balmoral und Osborne.

Sitting twisted in his seat, torso and face turned to her, it couldn't have been comfortable.

From the tips of her toes to the roots of her hair, she was in bliss.

She had traveled a long, long way from where she started out. While he had stood fast, she had struck out into uncharted territory, steering by nothing but his instructions, fumbling her way toward him.

Before they could live together, he wanted her to discover and secure for herself a world of her own making, which she would find fulfilling. To trade in her dreams of a nicely furnished home and a little family happiness in the service of a higher purpose. And he presented her with examples. The wife of his friend Feigl the painter, for one. Felice should be like her. The artist's devoted partner, supporting him with blind trust while laying no claim to his work, which might or might not come. And for the sake of his work, she should also give up on the idea of having children, which Felice wanted, physically needed, yearned for with all her heart.

The child question, as he called it, was insoluble, given that he didn't want them.

The reason he had to be selfish was not for himself, but for his writing. It was for his writing that he wanted her to sacrifice. And she was to do so voluntarily and in full awareness, together with him bearing the guilt under which he was collapsing even before he had begun, knowing that he was rebelling against the laws of nature and man alike. She was to aid him in this rebellion, serving as his pillar and accomplice. This was the alliance that he was offering her.

She agreed while secretly trusting in nature. But ultimately the solution came from the quarter where she least expected it.

If Franz had been able to write more easily, like, say, Brod, things might have turned out differently. But his writing was capricious and fickle, like a pagan deity. He may have genuinely wanted Felice, but his writing did not. The sacrifice was not accepted; his plans and projections were all in vain. It wasn't the war, or her mother, or even the illness on which he so conveniently blamed everything. It was his writing. That was why he couldn't marry her, no use kidding herself.

Munich. The debacle in Munich. She was sitting in the audience when he read; it was bad. Brod's poems, then his short story about a killing machine, too long and full of revolting details that no one wanted to hear in the midst of a war.

The audience suffered through it and he even more so. A cool round of applause at the end.

He may even have chosen the story because of her, wanting to make an impression. His description of the torture device may well have been inspired by a prospectus she sent him at one point on the features of the new Parlograph. She had written the leaflet herself; her boss had assigned it to her. And being in love, naturally enough, she had boasted about it to Franz. He diligently read over the text and praised her writing style. It had a genuine ring to it. She neither undersold the product nor begged the way that most advertising copy did. He even compared her style to Strindberg's! That was in fall 1912. He was in love with her then.

Four years later, in Munich, he detested her. Inadvertently, she had become the witness to his failure. They had a quarrel in some ghastly pastry shop, and Felice once again reproached him for his selfishness, hearing in her own voice the echo of her mother's.

He wrote her afterward about what had been going through his mind while he was reading: Why had he not chosen a different text? Why had he accepted the invitation at all, which in any case had been Brod's doing? They hardly would have invited him on their own. Why did he, who wasn't a writer, play at being one? And how, after that debacle, which was meant to be a test run for their shared life to come in Berlin, could he pack up his suitcases and leave Prague? Rely on his writing? Impossible.

And yet he continued playing his game, even going so far as to get engaged to her a second time. In the last months they seldom wrote each other, speaking more over the phone. He lost the courage to quit the insurance company and began once more to look for an apartment for them in Prague. Except that by now it was all just a lie, and so he fell ill—from the lie, not anything else. The bleeding came as a salvation to him.

Of course, Felice could have become an artist's partner, why not? She had all the prerequisites for it; he wasn't wrong about that. She had strength, courage, and practicality enough for two, was self-reliant and yet at the same time happily swayed. She had even become, inasmuch as it was possible, a dedicated pupil of his.

The sacrifice was ready to be made, but where was the artist?

Oh, him. Left in the dust far behind, like nothing at all ever happened.

When Felice fell asleep toward morning again, she dreamed she was holding a heart in her hands. Naked, hot, and twitching at regular intervals.

2019

Lyon–Prague

THE POISON OF THE LETTERS.

It might have killed V., the poet, too, had she not been so resilient.

When asked, in 1995, by a publishing house in Prague to translate the complete set of Kafka's letters to Felice Bauer and Grete Bloch into Czech, there was no way she could have known what she was getting herself into. She was flattered. There had never been a full translation before, only excerpts.

She was sixty years old and recently had begun writing poetry again after a silence of more than thirty years. She had also just returned from exile, which had something to do with it. She lived in a prefab apartment building overlooking the Prokop Valley in Prague, and shared her one-room flat with two dogs, whose presence completely filled the tiny space. Once *he* arrived as well, there was no room left at all. V. moved from her bed to the narrow couch in the kitchen as night after night the bedroom filled with the murmur of words.

"What am I going to do with you, Franz?"

The letters' addressee was reflected in his correspondence like a mirage, shimmering in the air above the desert sand.

"What am I going to do with you?"

V. enjoyed the work at first—he could be witty. He was charming and deceitful, too; she was thoroughly captivated. How swiftly he changed course. As he headed off in one direction, she would follow along behind, eyes meekly fixed on his back; what choice did she have? Then, suddenly, without warning, he would turn on a dime and stop—how many times had she nearly crashed into him? Feeling the tingling spreading up from the tips of her toes, she would think to herself, This was how it was for Felice. This and much more besides. This was how he seduced her and this was how he escaped her; this was how he belonged and yet did not belong to her—how could the poor girl resist him?

But then came a long series of bad letters. No salutations and no love. The dogs abandoned their nests and moved into the kitchen with V. Even sleeping on bare linoleum was better than being subjected to the constant stream of griping, blackmail, and laments.

V., the poet, had no choice but to endure it. She had a signed contract with the publisher and had already spent the advance. But why did Felice Bauer put up with it? What explanation was there for a healthy, sensible girl voluntarily choosing to associate with someone like him? It didn't make any sense. No wonder the letter writer grew increasingly suspicious. He couldn't figure it out, and demanded an explanation. How was it that she still hadn't rejected him? That she hadn't fled from him like any normal woman would have by now? Was it out of compassion for him? Was she hoping to save him? Did she think she could change him? Did she see herself as a heroine in a Strindberg play? Was it possible that this efficient—as he had written so many times—this efficient, strong-minded, healthy creature in fact had a craving for a bit of mental anguish? A touch of the neurasthenia that was so in fashion before the war?

She was most likely hoping to save him, the poet V. concluded, and in doing so had also hoped that she might save herself.

That was why she was unresponsive to his pleading. He wasn't the only one who needed to run away from his family. Her family was draining her more than Kafka ever could have done. The distance of Prague from Berlin was very appealing. Whereas for him it was exactly the other way around. The fact that Miss Bauer was from Berlin was attractive to him. He wanted to be there with her.

One word and they could have been saved. Or maybe not one, but six. The whole thing would have fit into a sentence of six words. He hinted at what that sentence was but had no idea how to wring it out of her, and Felice would never have written it unprompted, of that the poet V. was sure, even if she didn't have access to Felice's letters. The repercussions of such a sentence couldn't have been contained; they would have surfaced like a tidal wave in one of Kafka's replies.

What would that sentence have sounded like?

Drop everything and come to Berlin. Come to Berlin; I will help you live.

If V. hadn't been sipping white wine while she worked, the two of them—with Grete three—would have driven her insane. She brought it home in plastic one-and-a-half-liter bottles from the taproom in her housing estate. People said their wine was good, and true, it didn't sour in the mouth as quickly as other cheap wines. But it irritated her mucous membranes just the same, and by the time she was finally done with the translation, her stomach was ruined.

Six hundred and eleven letters.

An endless procession of plastic bottles, traveling from the taproom to the poet's desk, then back again, empty, for almost five years.

But V. had outlived two husbands, and she outlived Kafka, too.

After the book's release, which was significantly delayed from the originally planned date, the poison of the letters gradually wore off. And gradually she also managed to mitigate the effects of drinking all that bad white wine.

There must be a strength in that. In sticking with something. Even when your fragility escalates to the point where there is almost nothing left to break, since everything is already cracked and compromised.

The words grow out of the diary into a novel like living tissue connecting the novel to life.

The scent of the freesias in the vase on the table where I sit remembering the now deceased poet V. is the scent of my birthday in early March. It brings back the excitement of childhood celebrations, the taste of walnut cake with whipped cream, the smell of the antique puppet theater moved up from the basement to the children's bedroom once a year in my honor. The scent of freesias fills me with expectation still to this day, though I expect nothing from my birthdays anymore. I'm not ten, twelve, or even twenty years old, after all. I'm forty-eight, the same age as Felice was when she moved to America.

And suddenly, out of context, it becomes clear to me that Kafka didn't destroy Felice's letters as her family assumed. She destroyed them herself. She requested them back from him on her last visit to Prague, in late December 1917. That was why she'd come; there was no reason otherwise. Besides her pride, there was nothing left to salvage from the ruins. After she returned home to Berlin, she burned the letters.

1954

New York

A PEACEFUL AUTUMN MORNING under cloudy skies. The wet leaves on the sidewalk had the same golden-brown color and sheen of his new desk.

The desk.

That alone had him looking forward to work. Polished walnut, with three roomy drawers on the right and a lockable cabinet on the left.

At breakfast, his daughter asked why he had come home later than usual the day before, when she was already asleep.

He missed the train, he said, because he was putting things away in his new desk.

"What kind of things?"

"Pencils, notebooks, psych histories."

"What's a psych history?"

"I can explain to you later, but for now I have to run."

He kissed the inquisitive little girl on the forehead and gave Peter, studying his plate of scrambled eggs with a furrowed brow, an affectionate pat. Nina Perel walked her husband to the door. Even if she was in a rush to get Susan to school on time, she never let him leave without a kiss. As Joachim dashed off, heading down the path to the road, Nina Perel stood in the doorway, waiting for him to turn around and wave to her one last time. She blew him a kiss with her hand and closed the door.

If they were quarreling, which also happened occasionally,

Nina Perel stayed in the kitchen and his whole day after was ruined.

He took the shortcut through the gardens and bought a *New York Times* from the newsstand at the station. Hearing the train whistle blow from the platform, he had just enough time to lift his hat to a few of the people he recognized from his daily commute to Manhattan.

It was a peaceful ride along the Hudson River.

The paper was still filled with coverage of Hurricane Hazel, which had swept up from the south over the whole East Coast the week before, even striking Canada. In North Carolina, nineteen had died and the whole coastline had been flooded by a giant wave. There had also been huge losses in Maryland, Pennsylvania, northern New York, and Ontario. The Hudson rose and the railway tracks had been submerged in places. The trains didn't run for several days and Joachim had to commute into the city by car. The situation of their village, nestled snugly in between the hills, turned out to be an advantage. Apart from heavy rain and wind, which stripped what was left of the colorful foliage and knocked over a few trees onto the power lines, nothing much had happened.

A review of the new performance of *Peter Pan* at the Winter Garden reminded him that he had promised tickets to Nina Perel and the children. He ought to buy them as soon as possible.

He got off at Grand Central, rode the subway two stops, and emerged onto the street at Lexington and Fifty-ninth. It was entirely different and much more pleasant to face the big city hustle and bustle when you came from the peace and quiet of a rural area and knew you would be going back again in the evening.

It had definitely been a smart idea to buy the house, even if it did mean going into debt. Nina Perel had been worried, but it turned out there was no need. She was afraid they would be bored in the village, and her parents had tried to talk her out of it, too. They were happy having her and the grandchildren in reach.

What was she going to do all day out there by her lonesome? Who was going to help her?

Joachim's mother-in-law resented him for dragging her daughter away from the city and saw it as selfish on his part.

"What about my mother? What do you think she would say?" he retorted. "She sees her grandchildren once a year and she never complains. We have to do what's best for the children. What would really be selfish is keeping them in the city, when what children need is fresh air and room to run around. Don't you want that for them?"

She was insulted, but what could she do but live with it? Besides, she couldn't deny that Nina Perel had blossomed since the move. Not only had she joined a women's charity club and a choir but she also helped with running the local school, tended the garden, learned to drive, ferried Susan to school, ballet, and her friends' houses, and apart from that, of course, she also took care of Peter, who was only three years old. At night she was so tired, she fell asleep practically the moment her head hit the pillow, but she had a healthy color and insisted she was happy.

Joachim greeted the doorman standing out in front of the building on Sixty-fourth Street, opening the door for tenants. He rode the elevator to the third floor and stopped at the reception desk to pick up his mail and schedule of patients for the day from the secretary he shared with his two colleagues. At nine-thirty on the dot, he stepped into his office.

There it was. Standing by the window with a view of the acacia tree, his beautiful new desk.

Joachim removed his coat and hat and hung them on the coatrack in the corner. Settling into an armchair, he took a cigarette from the pack he had left on the desk the day before. He struck a match and breathed in a deep drag of smoke. The wooden surface under his hand was pleasantly smooth to the touch.

His eyes flitted across the room. A handwoven rug from Iran, a ficus in the corner, a couch with a colorful throw. He had reproduced Freud's study based on pictures he had seen, though he used the couch much less than Freud. Different methods were called for with children and adolescents.

For his youngest patients he had a little table with crayons and paper, a dollhouse with furniture and family figures, stuffed animals and colorful pillows. He had a sandbox with actual sand in it and shelves full of cars, houses, animals, toy soldiers, and other figures, which could be played with in every possible combination. He also had an Erector Set, and cheerful pictures on the walls, to help inspire trust. Though he didn't actually see little children, only those ages seven and up. And adolescents.

Women were better therapists for little children, in his opinion, since children more naturally attach to mother figures.

Joachim's experience in the children's ward at Bellevue had been of great help in his private practice, as had his treatment of post-traumatic patients during the war. He had found that what some children experienced in their families was not so different from war, especially in the extent of its destructiveness, which affected their whole internal world. The situation of a young patient whose parents had declared war on each other was comparable to that of a soldier in the field, in a way even worse, since the child, unlike the soldier, loved both of the warring sides.

In treating those children's wounds, Joachim was also healing himself; he was quite conscious of that. Contacting his own reservoirs of pain and rage, and drawing inspiration from his own methods of survival, from that meticulously interwoven web of protective mechanisms that in childhood had enabled him—but why past tense?—still enabled him to this day to function successfully in life.

Was it not a success that at age thirty he had been accepted into the New York Psychoanalytic Society? That he had been analyzed by Kurt Eissler himself and none other than Margaret Mahler had spoken glowingly of his therapeutic results? That he had been introduced at a conference to Anna Freud?

And the house with three bedrooms. And the beautiful wife. And the two healthy children.

The flow of his reflections was interrupted by a quiet knock at the door. His secretary peeked inside.

"The lady who called yesterday is here."

So she'd actually come.

He hadn't seen Lisette since the war, since they'd split up. When she called the day before to ask if she could come, he had said yes, rescheduling little Virginia and canceling his session with Luis. He hadn't even felt that guilty about it.

Last night he had slept badly. His ex-wife found her way into his dreams, and he woke at dawn feeling physically aroused.

He stood and walked out to the waiting area to welcome Lisette.

She was wearing an elegant fur-collared coat and a fashionable gray fedora. He had never known her to be concerned with how she dressed before; clearly that had changed. Yet her eyes, staring out at him, were the same as ten years ago, not quite so bright perhaps, though he might have just been imagining it—he had been in love with her then, after all, immersing himself in the healing bath of her eyes each and every time with a feeling of renewed wonder.

Sitting in the chair next to Lisette was a man Joachim had never seen. Legs crossed, on one pointy knee—it was clear at first glance it was pointy—balancing a hat. It wasn't just his knee, though. There was something off-puttingly pointy about every aspect of the man's build as he sat there playing with his hat.

When Lisette had called him up yesterday to ask about meeting, she hadn't mentioned that she would be bringing someone.

She jumped up to give Joachim a hug. As she pressed the upper half of her body against him, he could feel her warmth even through the layers of her clothing. The soft pressure of her breasts, her lips on his cheek, the flowery fragrance from her neckline—it might even have been freesias.

The man rose from his seat as well and offered Joachim his hand.

"Appelbaum, pleased to meet you." A common Jewish name.

Joachim held open the door to his office and bade them go in. "I'll be right back," he said. "I just need a word with my secretary."

He needed a moment alone to absorb the disappointment. How could he have thought that he meant something to Lisette? She didn't give a damn about him. It was obvious she had called because she wanted something from him. After all, she often came to the city; she might have even lived here. She could have looked him up sooner if she had wanted. What a foolish, pathetic loser he was! He would never learn. She probably needed help getting out of a jam that had something to do with her political activity. The FBI was chasing Communists; he had heard they were even after Reich, and things were getting worse. He wanted nothing to do with it, though. Losing his license to practice was the last thing he needed.

After a few minutes, he stepped back into his office, having fully regained his calm.

He walked past Lisette and Appelbaum, seated in the armchairs in front of his new desk, and sat down facing them, his back to the window. The lustrous surface of walnut wood shone in between them.

Lisette ran her hand over it. "What a lovely desk."

"Thank you."

"Do you mind if I have a cigarette?" asked the man. Lisette had never smoked.

She looked around the office and nodded her head approvingly.

"Nice place you've got here. So you see children?"

"Yes."

"That must be quite satisfying. I'm still working with Dr. Reich, up in Maine, at his institute. We've done a good bit of interesting work, especially on the release of muscle tension and psychic stress—that's my specialty. I treat both adults and children. Dr. Reich's focus is on orgone research now. Cosmic energy, which he discovered—I don't know whether you've kept up with his experiments. Nothing else really interests him. It's a pity, if you ask me. It only succeeds in provoking the professional community and overshadows his substantial work in psychoanalysis."

"*Character Analysis* was an intriguing book, no denying that. Even Freud thought so."

She waved a hand dismissively. "Oh, really. Do you still have to have everything approved by Freud?"

"It's not about approval. I regard him as an authority."

"Authority! I got over that ages ago. It's still a question of how to get to the bottom of things. Dr. Reich exposes things as they are. The roots of patriarchy, oppression, capitalism, the whole system of violence that Freud and his authority, as you call it, essentially legitimized and maintained. He merely treated its symptoms."

"Let's not get into politics here. That isn't why you came, is it? Don't tell me you traveled all the way from Maine to convince me that Dr. Reich is better than Freud?"

"Do you know what's going on with Reich now? Are you following this witch hunt? His colleagues need to stand up for him!"

Joachim shrugged indifferently.

"Kurt Eissler should issue a statement about the persecution of Reich, highlighting his importance," said Lisette.

"Eissler defend Reich in public? Please. Since when has Eissler ever stood up for any renegade, as he calls them? You can't even say Reich's name in front of him."

Appelbaum took a pull on his cigarette and stared out the window behind Joachim. The introductory exchange of views between the two ex-spouses clearly left him indifferent. He had come to terms with the fact that it had to happen, and made up his mind to stay out of it.

"Why are you here, Lisette?"

She sighed. "I wanted to see you. And I wanted to introduce you to Mr. Appelbaum here, whom I met in a session with Reich and who has some information I believe you will find interesting. He was planning to look you up anyway. I just tagged along, as an excuse to pay you a visit."

Joachim studied Appelbaum more closely. He looked to be around forty, dark, grayish hair slicked to his skull. Face pinched, almost shriveled, with thin lips and strong cheekbones. The face of a maniac or a sadist. Slanted eyes, like a Tatar. A strange, piercing shade of pale gray-green.

"And what does Mr. Appelbaum here want from me?"

"Well, my name isn't actually Appelbaum," the pointy man said in German, lighting a new cigarette. "Appelbaum is the name of my adoptive family. My real name is Bloch. Casimiro Bloch. I was born in Munich in 1914. My mother was Margarete Bloch. My birth certificate says 'father unknown,' but my mother never hid the fact that she knew my father's identity."

"How about that, huh?" said Lisette, bursting with excitement. She didn't speak German, but plainly she knew exactly what Appelbaum was talking about. She leaped out of her armchair, pacing around the office. "You knew Grete Bloch well. You told me about her yourself." She suddenly stopped and stabbed a finger at Appelbaum. "You know who his father was?"

"I haven't the slightest idea. How should I know who Grete Bloch slept with six years before I was born? And why should I even care? I only knew her as a friend of my mother's. The last time I saw her was in Geneva, before we left for America. I was fourteen and had other things on my mind. I hardly even remember her."

"I have good reason to believe that my father was Franz Kafka. I have no way to prove it, unfortunately. I can't even prove that my mother was Grete Bloch. All of the documents went missing during the war. My adoptive family died in a concentration camp. How I survived is a long story. But I did, even though my own mother told everyone that I died at age seven in Munich. There is one letter of hers still intact . . . Max Brod even quotes from it."

"I read Brod's book and I know he hinted at something there to that effect, but I never believed it."

"Well, believe it or not, my mother was Grete Bloch. I even vaguely remember her visiting, until 1921, when I was adopted. From that point on, I lost all contact with the Bloch family. I only know what my adoptive parents told me. They were in touch with Grete's brother, my uncle Hans, in Tel Aviv. Till they got deported in '42. But clearly they knew nothing about Kafka being my father. That came to light only later, because of my mother's letter."

"How about that, huh?" Lisette said again, now back in her seat. "You could make a novel out of that, right? He does look an awful lot like Kafka, don't you think?"

The similarity of certain features was undeniable.

"I've tried to track down the documents my mother left behind," Bloch, aka Appelbaum, went on. "I've devoted several years to looking for them at this point. Anything that could help me to prove my true identity. I found a lawyer in Florence my mother stored some papers with, most likely her personal correspondence. But he refused to show them to me. Understandably, since I have no proof I'm her son. I even visited that Italian village in the mountains—San Donato it's called. I don't know if you know, but my mother was interned in San Donato during the last years of the war, with a group of German, Austrian, and Czechoslovak Jews. I happen to speak a little Italian, so I was able to ask around. They remember her there very well."

"My mother told me how Grete died. She was very upset about it. Max Brod wrote her the news. I can't imagine why. He could have spared her the details. I suspect it was that information that caused her to have the stroke. Fortunately, it was very minor."

"I assume this was Brod's version with the bayonet?"

"Yes."

"That's just another one of those myths that Brod is so fond of spreading whenever it comes to Kafka and anything related to him. My mother wasn't stabbed to death with a German soldier's bayonet, or beaten to death with the butt of his rifle, either, dramatic as it may sound. On April 6, 1944, she and fifteen other Jews from San Donato were tricked out of hiding, loaded on a truck, driven first to Rome, then to a transit camp in Fossoli, and from there transported by train to Auschwitz. My mother went straight to the gas. Out of sixteen people deported, only three survived. Forgive me for constantly citing numbers, but I'm fascinated by them. Numbers, for me, are a way I can make things tangible. Numbers and names. For instance, Naomi Levy, a little girl, not even two years old. She was born at the internment camp in San Donato and was also among the murdered."

Bloch, aka Appelbaum, paused for a moment.

"How were you able to get such detailed information?" asked Joachim

"I did some digging. You would have, too, if it had been your mother. I managed to find one of the three survivors, a woman named Rosa Myler. She was my mother's best friend in San Donato, though she was quite a bit younger. She said she and my mother rode the whole way to Auschwitz together, and were still holding hands on the ramp. Then for one of them they pointed left and for the other they pointed right. May I ask you a question?"

"Go ahead."

"Does it make any sense to you that the Germans, who fought to the last man, despite being outnumbered by the Americans, and defended several hopeless positions, tooth and nail, that those same Germans would round up sixteen starving Jews, mostly women and children, and transport them halfway across Europe, just to murder them in Poland? Can you comprehend that? What did they get out of it? Why not just leave them be?"

"From a human point of view, it's truly difficult to grasp," said Joachim. "But from a bureaucratic standpoint, apparently it was an item that had to be crossed off the list and reported to the higher-ups."

"I guess you're right, but still it boggles my mind," said his guest, shaking his head. "It would have taken so little for my mother to survive. I'm sorry, whenever I talk about this, I always get upset."

He took out a handkerchief and blew his nose.

"Did you find what you were looking for in San Donato?"

He nodded. "It didn't do me any good. I knew her luggage had been left behind in the village, a bag or a suitcase with her ID and photographs. My birth certificate, or some other kind of proof, had to be in there as well. I was told that after my mother's sudden deportation, this bag—which I picture as red, though it was probably black or brown leather—had been left behind, along with the possessions of all the other Jews, at the town hall in San Donato. They were left there a long time—I suppose waiting for the owners to come back. But after several years went by and nobody showed up for them, the bags were moved to the neighboring town of Alvito and that was where they remained. Some of the things were claimed by the survivors of the deceased, but not my mother's bag. It's still there. I have a witness who saw it. They refuse to give it to me, of course. I can't even look inside it. It's the same thing every time. I don't have proof I'm her son. They told me—and they're right, of course—that anyone could come along and claim he was her son. And that's that."

"But why would anyone do such a thing?"

Bloch/Appelbaum gave a shrug. "Maybe because Kafka is famous now?"

"Isn't that sad?" Lisette sighed.

"I ended up leaving Italy empty-handed. Still, apart from that, I learned a lot about my mother. I even met her last boyfriend. He was very gracious to me. He told me how unhappy and lonely my mother was, a bit on the adventurous side, according to him. He said she spoke of me often, and of Kafka, too. But she said I was dead. I suppose it was easier for her to bury me than to admit she had given me up. Her lover, Arturo, is an old man at this point. He's a clockmaker and an amateur photographer as well. He gave me a picture of Grete. It's the only one I have."

Bloch/Appelbaum pulled a small leather case from his breast pocket with a black-and-white picture inside, which he handed across the desk to Joachim.

Of course he recognized it as Grete immediately. She sat on a wicker rocking chair in a garden, wrapped in plaid, a large tabby cat nestled in her lap. She looked into the lens, head tilted sideways, eyeing the camera askance. Grete never looked at anyone directly; it was one of the reasons he hadn't liked her.

Joachim noticed his visitor studying him intently, his hand twitching, eager to have the picture back.

"I'm so sorry that all that happened," said Joachim, handing back the photo. "What more can I say?"

"Would you mind introducing me to your mother?"

"My mother? What for?"

"She and my mother were best friends. I'm sure she knows more than she lets on. She might know something about my adoption. Or have some proof, what do I know? Old letters from Grete, anything."

"My mother doesn't believe Grete had any children. What Brod wrote is gossip, as far as she's concerned."

"Gossip that my mother spread about herself? Pardon me, but why would she do such a thing?"

"Maybe to make herself interesting. Get attention, I don't know. It worked pretty well for her, didn't it? Listen, I'm sure what you're telling me is true from your point of view. I'm not accusing you of lying. There's no doubt in my mind that you really believe you're Grete's son, why not? And maybe Kafka's, too. I didn't mind listening to your story, but I would rather you not bother my mother with it. It would just be too upsetting. And I can guarantee she doesn't know any more about it than I do."

"Then write to Brod for me. He's the only one who can help."

"Why not do it yourself?"

"There's no point. He would take me for an impostor. I would if I were him. But if you wrote him we had met and you were convinced I was telling the truth, he might be more willing to help."

"In what way, exactly?"

"By acquiring my mother's belongings. The papers she left in Florence. And also the ones in Alvito. I need those documents!"

"So you think they would listen to Brod and hand them over to you?"

"Absolutely. If Brod told them to, they would do it. After all, there are letters from Kafka in there."

"Who told you that?"

"I know. I have witnesses who knew my mother when she was staying in Florence. She showed them a stack of letters from Kafka and even bragged about them. 'The one famous man in my life,' she said. It was those letters, the most valuable possession she had, that she placed in the care of the lawyer in Florence before she left for San Donato."

"And that's what you want."

"Of course. I believe there is something in them about me. Does your mother still have the letters that Kafka wrote to her?"

"I don't know. If she does, I've never seen them. And she's never mentioned them to me."

"I think it's very foolish of you not to take any interest in this. A whole Kafka craze has broken out. Do you know how much those things are worth?"

Joachim gave a shrug. "I don't. But now, if you'll excuse me, we're going to have to end this conversation. No offense, but I have a patient waiting outside."

Bloch, aka Appelbaum, sprang to his feet, almost overturning his chair. His cheeks were crimson red.

"Doctor, you will help me, won't you? Will you write to Brod?"

"I'll think about it."

Lisette rose from her seat as well. "I hope you aren't upset with me. I wouldn't have brought him if I hadn't thought it was important. And please, don't forget Reich. You really ought to help. Who else if not you?"

Joachim saw his guests to the door. When he opened it, little Virginia was sitting there waiting, just as he'd said.

After five, he left to catch the train.

Autumn twilight in Manhattan. Lights and traffic at every turn, a sense of excitement in the air. Lexington Avenue with its lit-up windows, cars and pedestrians rushing about, buzzing with mystery.

He turned to look at a pretty young woman in a fur coat. Did she just smile at him?

He was still attracted to Lisette; she was a very appealing woman. But crazy, too. He wanted nothing to do with her. Her or Reich and that orgone stuff, or Bloch, or whatever his name really was.

Daytime here reminded Joachim of Geneva and walking home from school past the lake at thirteen or fourteen. The wind, the splashing water, the solitude. Back then, he used to prolong the walk, not wanting to go home. Whereas now he was in a hurry, looking forward to it. To his wife and children, to the good supper she had ready for him, to a cozy fire in the fireplace and a glass of cognac to go with it.

By the time he walked home from the station, it was already dark.

It had showered here during the day, and the fallen leaves smelled of damp.

Their home stood on a slope. With its windows lit up, it looked like a ship. The instant he came within sight of the house, the front door flew open and his children came rushing out. They must have been counting the minutes since the time his train arrived. Then, emerging from the warm glow of the doorway behind them, the slim silhouette of Nina Perel appeared.

2019

Lyon

GRETE BLOCH'S LUGGAGE HAD been stored in the village of Alvito, not far from San Donato, probably until 1964. There were two witnesses to that fact.

First, Bruno Massa, son of Dr. Massa, who had treated Grete for free during her stay in San Donato and also helped her in other ways. Among her belongings were thank-you notes she had written him in Italian and the medical report he wrote that saved her from being deported to the women's concentration camp in Pollenza.

And second, Ettore Volante, a friend of Bruno Massa's and a surveyor by profession.

In 1964 the two men set out to find whatever traces they could of Grete Bloch and her alleged son. They did so at the request of television host and journalist Enzo Tortora, a common acquaintance of theirs who apparently smelled a blockbuster story in the discovery of never-before-published information about the child of a celebrated writer from Prague.

Tortora was a commentator on one of the most-watched shows on Italian TV, *La Domenica Sportiva*, or *Sports on Sunday.* The program was extremely popular with viewers, and Massa and Volante felt flattered that they were able to help.

The following letters come from the archive of Grete Bloch; the originals were written in Italian.

San Donato Val Comino Technical Studio
November 4, 1964

Dear Mr. Tortora,

Immediately after your departure from S. Donato, Mr. Massa's family and I extended a great effort to unearth every possible detail concerning Mrs. Bloch—and it seems our search has not been wholly unsuccessful.

We found a newspaper with an article about Grete Bloch, which was published years ago and which we have here available for you. We have also contacted the people Grete Bloch knew well during the hardest period of her isolation in San Donato.

Among these acquaintances, it seems that Mr. Cendrone Nazzareno, in whose house Grete Bloch lived at one point and with whom she apparently had certain relations, which the gentleman has never denied, is deserving of special attention.

This Nazzareno must have known a lot about Grete Bloch. He is also well informed about the history of her son, about her brother, who lives in Tel Aviv, and about the Czech author, whose one book he even owns, though he says it would take him a while to find it.

Thanks to the fact that Grete Bloch lived for a time in the Gaudiello inn, from the records we were able to track down some of the addresses of the families with whom she lived in San Donato after that.

We still want to take a closer look at the correspondence in the possession of the Massa family, which we hope may contain valuable documents.

I have had a chance to read your letter addressed to Bruno Massa and I hope that your meeting with Mr. Marco was useful.

I will be glad to be of further assistance to you. Warm regards from me, as well as from the rest of your friends in S. Donato.

Yours,
Ettore Volante

S. Donato
November 6, 1964

Dear Mr. Tortora,

I received your letter just this morning and I hasten to reply.

First, I must inform you that despite very thorough research I did not manage to find a single trace of Mrs. Blok's friend, the mysterious female art student, in the municipal office archives.

On the other hand, it is with great delight I share that, like good hunting dogs, we did succeed in discovering the location of the items which Mrs. Blok left at the scene at the time of deportation: clothes, letters, photographs of her deceased son, and also the mysterious album. I am not even going to tell you what it took me and my friend Hector to track them down, but believe me, we sweat through the proverbial seven shirts.

Also, I must inform you, we found a copy of the weekly *L'Europeo* with Zampa's article about Mrs. Blok. We also know Blok had a brother who in the years between 1941 and 1944 lived in Tel Aviv. His address was written on the reverse side of a photograph of Mrs. Blok, which is now in the possession of the magazine *L'Europeo.*

It was tough, but we did get some work done, I hope it will be of benefit to you. In any case, you can call or send me a telegraph at the municipal office.

Warm regards from me and all your fans in S. Donato,
Bruno Massa

"Zampa's article," which both Massa and Volante mention in their letters, was for a long time the only source of information on the fortunes of Grete Bloch in Italy. The author of the article was the Italian Germanist Giorgio Zampa, who in 1954, on the thirtieth anniversary of Kafka's death, paid a visit to San

Donato and attempted to hunt down everything that had to do with Grete.

No doubt he was inspired to do so by Brod's biography, which contained a reference to Kafka's having a child. Zampa neither confirmed nor denied the hypothesis of a son, but he returned from his trip with a number of intriguing details that he used not only in the article but later as well in his book *Rilke, Kafka, Mann: Letture e ritratti tedeschi.*

S. Donato
November 6, 1964

Mr. Tortora,

Just for clarification, I am taking the liberty of appending my letter to the one which Bruno sent you. It is true we were able to track something down for you.

I am happy to confirm the news of the famous article by Giorgio Zampa from 1954, which I have also had an opportunity to reread. It was written for the periodical *L'Europeo* and can be found in the archive in number 37 of 12.9.1954. We also have a copy here in San Donato, should you not want to look for it elsewhere.

The photograph of Margarete Bloch, which was printed in the magazine and subsequently also in the French newspapers, was given to Zampa by Mr. Arturo Carcone, a clockmaker, who lived and still lives in S. Donato.

The address of Mrs. Bloch's brother, who lived in Tel Aviv, was in fact noted on the back of this photograph, as Carcone had assured us.

My friend Bruno Massa and I have not missed any opportunity to obtain valuable information for you, and just a few hours ago we received assurance that the famous luggage belonging to Mrs. Bloch is, or at least was until a few months ago, securely stored not far from here. So we now know with absolute certainty where it has been the entire time since Mrs.

Bloch was taken away by the Germans in May 1944. But that is useless to us, since we are not legally authorized to access it.

If you wish, we can meet again and discuss it. However, I am rather of the opinion that you should come in person here, to S. Donato.

Sincere regards from your devoted friends in S. Donato, Ettore Volante

(The date Volante gives for Grete's deportation in his last letter is incorrect. The sixteen Jews from San Donato were arrested and taken away on April 6, 1944, not in May.)

Enzo Tortora in fact did go to San Donato after he received these exciting reports from his friends. But there was no blockbuster story.

In 1970, he published a recollection of his visit in *La Nazione.* In his article "Il misterioso figlio di Kafka," he writes that the moment he got the letter about the found luggage, he hastened in person to the place where it was stored. Upon his arrival, however, he was informed that, just "a few days" earlier, workers from the British Red Cross had come and taken away all of Grete Bloch's effects.

The disappointed reporter had no choice but to retrace the same steps described by Giorgio Zampa ten years earlier, in his article from 1954. The difference being that Zampa, despite saying nothing about it, most likely succeeded in getting into Grete's mysterious suitcase. The photographs that appeared with the article, and also in his later book, could only have come from there. In particular the photo of Grete with a child in her arms and the boy on the hospital bed.

Tortora never returned to the subject of Kafka again over the course of his career, but interestingly, the author of *The Trial* in roundabout fashion did return to him.

In 1983, the popular moderator was suddenly arrested and jailed on charges of colluding with the Mafia. During the trial, which went down in legal history as "Il Caso Tortora," it soon became obvious that the whole affair was a case of mistaken identity. Nevertheless, Tortora was sentenced to ten years in prison, of which he served two. He was fully rehabilitated and returned to work in television, but soon after, he fell sick with cancer and died.

What happened to Grete's luggage? Where did it go? I continued my search. In summer 1945, a year after Grete Bloch's deportation, the mayor of San Donato received a query from the British Red Cross concerning Grete's fate. The mayor replied that Grete had been transported to the east by the Germans, and that was all he knew. He also mentioned her belongings, which she had left behind in the village and for which, he wrote, she might return.

Since no one turned up to claim the luggage, however, it was moved from the town hall in San Donato into storage in the neighboring town of Alvito, and there it remained, until one day it vanished off the face of the earth.

Tortora's version struck me as unlikely. Why would the British Red Cross turn up out of nowhere, twenty years later, to reclaim Grete's belongings? The organization's archivist, when I reached out to him by email, confirmed that the British Red Cross had not retrieved any luggage during the sixties in Italy. But it could have been the International Tracing Service (ITS), whose mission was to search for missing persons displaced or killed during World War II. The ITS was originally founded in Germany, by the Allied forces, but later relocated to Geneva, under the International Committee of the Red Cross.

My letter to the ITS remained unanswered. In their archives, which are stored in Bad Arolsen, Germany, and accessible online, I found several Margarete Blochs, but none of them had a date of birth corresponding to Grete's and there was no reference to Italy.

My belief that Grete Bloch's luggage had gone missing was finally confirmed by an expert on the subject of Jews interned between 1940 and 1944 in the village of San Donato Val di Comino: Anna Pizzuti.

The first mention of Anna Pizzuti I came across was on the website of the Centro Primo Levi, in New York.

Pizzuti was a high school teacher of Italian and geography in San Donato until, one day, during a school project on historical memory, she discovered the town's involvement in the interning of Jews. Once she learned about it, she couldn't let it go; it became her personal mission.

Who were these people who had fled from every corner of Europe? How did they occupy their days in internment? Did they have any contact with the local population? Could their lives be held and weighed in your hand?

Several of them had survived; the rest had vanished without a trace. Pizzuti set about tracking them down. Letters, official memorandums and requests, as well as statements from witnesses at the time—one by one she collected them all, and assembled them into a picture, encapsulated in a book she titled *Vita di carta* (*A Life on Paper*). Eventually she expanded the scope of her research from just San Donato to the whole of Italy.

At this point, she has long since ceased to be a schoolteacher. She presents at conferences, organizes commemorative events, and manages websites where you can look up the names and fates of hundreds of Jewish refugees in Italy.

Pizzuti replied promptly to my brief letter, really just an attempt to establish contact. She even sent me a copy of her book as an attachment.

Dear Anna,

Thank you so much for sending me your book. I started translating it, and although the robotic translator is not perfect, it is still fascinating. It is just these kinds of details that are always missing from history and that you need so much when you are writing a book of fiction.

I will make my way through your book slowly, it will probably take me some time, but I am really excited to have this possibility.

To answer your question, I am working on a book partly based on the life of Felice Bauer—Franz Kafka's fiancée from Berlin, who immigrated to the USA in 1935. I was lucky to meet her family in New York, when I lived there, and ever since then I have had this desire to write about her.

Previously, I wrote two novels that are partly historical. One dealt with the life of Friedl Dicker Brandeis—a Viennese Jew who was a painter and art teacher of children in Terezín. The other deals with anarchism—and also with the life of Alexander Berkman and Emma Goldman.

I am not a historian, I studied philosophy, but I have always had this passion for the past, and for some reason I keep going back to the first half of the twentieth century.

Grete Bloch, who was interned in San Donato, was a close friend of Felice and her family. Of course she is mostly known for "having Franz Kafka's son." I think this is not true and she made up the story at some point when Kafka was getting famous. But this is not why I am writing about her.

I am really touched by the situation of a 50-year-old woman (I am 47 now) who is totally alone, caught up in this absurd, dangerous, and hopeless situation.

I have read everything that I can, but there is not much information about Grete. And it is all connected to this mysterious Kafka's son. Still, I was able to put together some picture from the pieces I was able to find. Then I came upon your book on the website of the Centro Primo Levi, and that led me to your website and mailing address.

I am really looking forward to spending time with your book. I am sure I will find in it many answers to my questions.

Sorry for the long letter. I hope Google will be able to help you with the translation.

Thank you so much again!

The mention of Google was relevant, given that Anna and I had no language in common. She spoke and wrote only Italian, and her book, *Vita di carta*, existed solely in Italian, which I don't know at all. I read her book using DeepL, while Anna translated my letters from English to Italian and hers from Italian to English with the help of Google Translate.

This lent them a peculiar, awkward charm.

Dear M.,

In the Italian edition of Letters to Felice there are also letters to Grete. When you look in the pdf file I sent you, under the name of Grete Bloch, you will find all the links to her there.

I described her story as a Jewish refugee in Florence and then during her internment in San Donato. I was working on her personal file, which contains documents relating to the Italian period. I am sending you the file, but if you would like, you can get the documents directly from Central State Archives in Rome. They are unfortunately in Italian.

All the best, Anna

P.S.: I visited Terezín.
P.S. 2: I also do not believe the rumor about Kafka's son. It was Max Brod who spread it.

Dear Anna,

If you permit, I have some questions concerning the precious documents you sent me.

1) What does "fu Luigi e fu Jenny Meyrowitz" mean?

2) Do you think Bloch really had a nephew in Italy? I know her brother Hans was in Palestine, but I am not aware of any other siblings or relatives.

3) In the letters of Bruno Massa and Ettore Volante to the journalist Enzo Tortora in 1964, I came across the name Nazzareno Cendrone and the information that Grete Bloch had an intimate relationship with him. Elsewhere there is mention of the clockmaker Arturo Carcone, who apparently also had a relationship with her. But in his 1970 article, Tortora mentions only Arturo Carcone, a clockmaker who had a relationship with Grete and with whom Tortora was able to talk. He doesn't mention Nazzareno at all.

My question is: Were there two different men (Carcone and Cendrone)? Or did Tortora or one of his informants mix things up? Did you come across any information about this?

4) It seems that Dr. Massa in San Donato was treating Grete for rheumatism, there was no talk of cancer. Do you think the certificate in her file was just made up to keep Grete from being deported?

5) My last question doesn't concern the documents but it is important. During your research in San Donato, did you come across any mention of Bloch's luggage, which (according to Massa and Volante) was stored in Alvito until 1964 when it was taken away by the Red Cross? This piece of the story seems very strange. Why would the Red Cross look for someone's bags twenty years after the war? And where would they take them?

Maybe some of the answers to my questions are in your book, which I still need to finish reading carefully. In that case, I apologize.

Dear Magdalena, I answer immediately:

1) In Italian "Fu" in front of the names of a person's parents means that these parents have died;

2) During internment, sometimes kinships were invented when the internment office was requested to change the location of the person interned. We were looking for someone to confirm this relationship. In the case of Grete, they made her write a wrong name. This Tokteni does not exist. I found who this person really was, I read it from the documents. It's a bit funny to read them, because it turns out that this person invented aunts or cousins in various places, but, I seem to remember, the transfer didn't come through;

3) Before answering, I must make a premise: I deal with the internment of foreign Jews and I have read thousands of documents and listened to many stories. I have always preferred, as a working method, to stick to the documents, but I have learned that even there we have to work hard to understand what the truth is. You can also see it in the documents I sent you: Did you notice that Grete is talking about a son in England? To understand this, you need to know the laws of fascism against foreign Jews said that foreign refugee Jews had to be expelled; subsequently it was established that if they had begun the process to emigrate, they could remain a few more months. Many had relatives who had already emigrated. Others, like Grete, I believe, invented them.

You will have noticed that Grete also changes the destination of her emigration. It was very difficult to emigrate, everyone said they are going to do it, but very few succeeded.

Why do I write this to you? To tell you that, if it is difficult to understand whether the documents, in these cases, say or not the truth, think how difficult it is to understand whether the testimonies of many years later can be completely true. I distrust a little (some more than a little).

So: There was Cedrone and there was also Carcone. Grete was a woman who grew up in big cities, mistress of herself;

you can imagine how she could feel lost in a small village like San Donato was then. So, surely she had to look for friendship, closeness (even if the laws forbade it), and this created gossip. The transfer to Pollenza was meant as punishment for her, and I am sure that Dr. Massa's medical certificate was supposed to help her stay in San Donato. It is sad to think that she would have been deported also from Pollenza, where there was a women's camp and the Nazi-fascists arrested almost everyone.

As for the baggage, a 1945 reply from the mayor of San Donato to the Red Cross states that the baggage was handed over to the authorities in Alvito (town where I was born, very close to San Donato). In reality, the luggage has disappeared. And this is the only truth.

I wrote in a hurry and apologize if you were expecting more in-depth answers.

Continue to send me your questions, I will try to answer you as I can.

1954

Los Angeles

OF THE THREE HANUKKAH BLESSINGS, she remembered two: *"Baruch ata Adonai, eloheinu melech ha'olam, asher kidshanu be'mitzvotav ve'tzivanu lehadlik ner shel Hanukkah."* And *"Baruch ata Adonai, eloheinu melech ha'olam, she'asa nisim le'avoteinu ba'yamim ha'hem ba'zman ha'zeh."* She could also recall the first two verses of "Mighty Rock of My Salvation," which they had sung in German at home. She kept forgetting where she had put her medical bills, what groceries she was supposed to buy, and whether or not she had been outside that day. Yet she could recollect prayers in Hebrew that she had heard as a child.

The short circuit that had run through her brain—a minor cerebral event, the doctor said—had apparently revived some long-unused connections while knocking out or disabling others.

A spread of goodies sat waiting on the table, under lids covered with dish towels so nothing would get cold: roast beef, potatoes sautéed with onions (one of Joachim's favorites), brussels sprouts sprinkled in bread crumbs, and a platter of jelly doughnuts with a heap of almond cookies Felice had baked herself. Whatever was left over, she would pack in a box for Joachim to take back with him to New York, so the children would have something sweet from her for Christmas. She had also baked them a genuine German stollen with marzipan.

On the sideboard—all that was left of her lovely dining room in Berlin—the silver menorah she had inherited from her grandmother in Neustadt sat perched atop a lace-trimmed tablecloth. Her mother had taken it with her when the family moved to Berlin, giving it a place of honor in the china cabinet. It was an antique, probably eighteenth century.

Neustadt in Oberschlesien, the town where Felice grew up. Among locals, it was known by the nickname "Fränkelstadt," after Samuel Fränkel, founder of the textile factory there. Now the town was called Prudnik.

It was all coming back to her. The little sewing-supplies shop she had loved so much, with its sweetish smell of cardboard boxes, buttons, and thread. The aroma of poppy-seed pastries, lemon rind, and fresh bread in the bakery on the square; of pickles and roast coffee from the merchant next door, whom everyone had called "lame Weisenstein" to differentiate him from the other Weisenstein, who owned the funeral parlor. Everyone in the little town had had their own nickname. And the fragrance of cobblestones after a rain and of fallen leaves in the park. And of warm wax and oil in the synagogue where her mother took her. And in the hallway of their building, the odor of stored potatoes and coal from the cellar, of roast meat, boiled cabbage, and apples. And of course the ever-present stench of smoke and the din from the Fränkel and Pinkus textile factory, with its giant steam-powered looms working day and night.

Supposedly, all the Jews had disappeared from Neustadt in Oberschlesien, now known as Prudnik. That was what Sophie told her, who had heard it from Max. Neustadt no longer existed. Even Fränkel's synagogue, the town's showpiece, which the Nazis had burned on Kristallnacht, was demolished after the war. It used to be featured on postcards titled "Gruss aus Neustadt, Ob. Schl.," along with the factory, the Marian column on the town square, and the fountain in the park. The synagogue had been built in Moorish style, while the factory was of neo-Gothic construction, predominantly red brick.

The factory was still in operation, from what she had heard, now in the ownership of the Polish state. Nothing was returned to the original owners, who had built not only the largest textile factory in Europe but also most of the town, including the schools, the hospital, the bathhouse, the library, and the park.

Did the young people in Prudnik still take trips to Castle Mountain on Saturday afternoons? Did people still go to the lakeside restaurant for trout? Did they still have a brass band playing in the gazebo at the park on Sundays after lunch?

"Baruch ata Adonai, eloheinu melech ha'olam, she'hecheyanu ve'kiyemanu ve'higianu la'zman ha'zeh."

Joachim supplied the third blessing, pronounced before lighting the candle on the first night of Hanukkah.

He lit the shammash and then used it to light the first candle, reciting the prayer with no mistakes. After all these years, he still remembered it. But he didn't join in on "Mighty Rock of My Salvation," leaving Felice to intone it on her own.

They sat down across from each other at the festively set table and Joachim tucked into the food with relish. It always tasted better to him at his mother's than anywhere else. Although Nina Perel tried her best, cooking from Felice's recipes, it wasn't the same. His mother must have added some special ingredient that she kept to herself.

"What do you think that Leo is up to? Weinberger, no? The one who went to Palestine. His father was a cantor. The two of you were best friends at one point. You were always running over to their place. Have you had any news from him? How is he doing?"

"I don't know. He became some government big shot. I haven't written him in ages. Anyway, he never forgave me for my 'failure,' as he put it. Though it wasn't a failure to me. I grew out of my faith like a baby grows out of diapers—that's how I saw it."

"I've started praying again before I go to bed," said Felice. "It helps me fall asleep. Do you remember how I taught you and

Lily the Shema Yisrael? I would have taught you more, but your father wouldn't hear of it. No child of his was being dragged back into the Middle Ages, he said. He was a German and a European, period."

"He was right about that. Why tie yourself down when you can be free?"

"Freedom isn't for everyone. You need something to hold on to."

"How is Lily doing? We haven't talked in a long time. She sent me a photo. That little girl of hers is growing into a real beauty. Whom do you think she takes after?"

"She came to see me recently. On her own. She said she wants to get a divorce, she can't take it anymore. But she's totally dependent on that man. She doesn't know how to do anything! She didn't even finish school. Now she's got it into her head to go work as a saleswoman or a cleaning lady somewhere. Said she'll scrape by somehow. Can you imagine?"

"Why not?"

"How long do you think she'll last?"

"You always managed to scrape by, too, Mom. Remember what that was like? How old were you when you learned to do massage? Or when you opened your store? Lily is still young. She could learn anything."

"But I've worked my entire life. Well, apart from those fifteen years when your father supported us. Lily has never worked. And she's never been interested in real life. It's all just a dream to her. She's always made it all up on her own and then been disappointed when things didn't work out. She's never listened to reason."

"I feel sorry for her."

"So do I. But I can't take her in."

"She asked if she could move in with you?"

"Her and the little one. She's too proud to ask him for anything. But tell me, where would I put them? I've got one room and a bedroom, and the kitchen is so tiny, I can barely turn around. We would be crawling all over each other. And I don't have money, either. All my savings have gone to doctors. I can barely get by on my own. I'm not complaining, mind you. I'm not asking anyone for anything. But I can't take care of her. Not anymore."

"Mom . . ."

"What is it now?"

Was he imagining it, or was there somebody else sitting with them at the table? The shadow of a bowed figure, rhythmically nodding its head as if it were reciting something.

Joachim closed his eyes, and when he opened them again, the shadow was gone.

Felice stared at her hands resting on the tablecloth.

"Let her chutzpadik husband take care of her. It's his responsibility. That's what I told her. She got offended."

Felice rose from her chair and reached for Joachim's plate. "Here, let me clear that away for you."

He stood up to help, but she pushed him back down into his seat. "Pour yourself some more wine. No more for me, thanks. And you can smoke if you want. I'll air the place out afterward."

She gathered up the empty plates and vanished behind the curtain that separated the kitchenette from the main room. He noticed she had a slight limp, probably a result of the stroke. He needed to ask about that. Ever since Else had died and his mother had been on her own, she had aged visibly.

From the kitchen came the sound of clinking dishes and running water. He could tell she was upset and didn't want to talk, so he left her alone. The next fifteen minutes or so passed in silence, with him smoking and Felice on the other side of the curtain. Her voice sounded calm when she called out again.

"Will you have some coffee?"

He couldn't bring himself to say the reason for his visit.

His mother thought he had come because Hanukkah was

starting and soon Christmas would be here. She had knit new sweaters and colorful caps for Nina Perel and the children, as well as making a whole box of cookies and three jars of orange marmalade. It made her glad to know Joachim would deliver the gifts to them personally.

He didn't want to ruin her joy.

But when he sat down for breakfast on the day of his departure and Felice brought him a soft-boiled egg and toast, he knew it could wait no longer.

"Before I forget, Mom. Schocken Books gave me a call."

"They called you up? Who gave them your number?"

"I'm in the phone book, Mom."

"Who was it who called?"

"Mr. Schocken."

"Hmm."

"He said he actually wanted to speak to you, but he didn't want to disturb you. Since you gave him the brush-off once before, he asked me instead."

"It's already been settled."

"Mom, listen to me."

"It has nothing to do with you. Or anyone but me. It's my personal business."

"Not entirely, Mom."

"What do you mean? They are my letters, aren't they? The person who wrote them trusted me. He certainly wouldn't have wanted them to be read by anyone else."

"But how can you be so sure? Mr. Schocken says—"

"I knew him. As far as I know, Mr. Schocken did not."

"How many letters do you have anyway?"

Felice silently rose from the table and went to the sideboard. She bent down, opened it up, and took a large Bata shoe box from one of the shelves. The table shook as she set it down, rather too abruptly, next to the butter and jar of preserves.

"Here they are. The famous letters. And here they will remain."

"Mr. Schocken is offering quite a bit of money, Mom. Eight thousand dollars. He said he can afford it now that Germany is paying him restitution. Eight thousand dollars would come in awful handy now that you can't work anymore. Think about it. It's an opportunity. What are you going to do otherwise? Of course you can always come stay with us, but . . ."

"I'd rather not."

"Then what are you going to do? I'm not in a position to be sending you money regularly, paying for your doctors. I've got a mortgage, a family."

"I'm not asking you to. I've never asked anyone for anything. And don't shout at me."

"Mom, please!" Now he really was almost shouting. Why was she so stubborn?

He hadn't told her the whole truth about his dealings with Schocken. The reality was, the publisher had phoned him up and, addressing Joachim in his typical overbearing manner, had instructed him to come for lunch the next day at the French restaurant Voisin on Park Avenue.

When Joachim showed up as agreed, at precisely half past twelve, the elderly gentleman was already there and waiting, seated at a table, sipping a glass of water. He dominated the conversation through most of the meal. Each time Joachim attempted to say a few words, Schocken listened politely but didn't respond to what he had said. Maybe the old man was going deaf and didn't want to let on.

Over Joachim's order of steak frites and Schocken's plate of trout with haricots verts (on his doctor's advice, he was eating light), the publisher related the full account of his campaign in beautiful, near-archaic German.

How at first he had assigned Max Brod, with whom he was in close contact, to write to Felice.

How then he, Schocken, had written Felice himself, and had now spent more than two years trying to convince her.

He couldn't see why Joachim's mother was so reluctant. The sale entailed no risk for her. She only stood to make money on it. All the terms were clearly spelled out in the contract he had offered. Felice would be paid in cash and the letters would be stored in a safe-deposit box, along with the other rare manuscripts, and wouldn't be published until five years after her death.

Once Schocken was through with the letters, he would donate them to the archive at the Hebrew University of Jerusalem, which he himself had helped to establish and in which he still had a guiding hand.

Isn't that what Kafka would have wanted?

In the two years Schocken had spent trying to win her over, Felice had answered him only once, briefly and dismissively. Kafka's letters were extremely personal, she said, and she didn't feel she had the right to make them public. After that, she had stopped responding.

Acquiring the correspondence was obviously very important to Schocken. His greatest fear, he told Joachim, was that Felice would destroy the letters before she died. What else could she have in mind for them? It would be a terrible, irreplaceable loss, not just for his publishing house but for literature as a whole. Who knew, she may have destroyed them already. He had to act, and quickly.

Furthermore, explained Schocken, there were all sorts of con men coming out of the woodwork now. One even trying to pass himself off as Kafka's son. An actor by the name of Appelbaum. He had been so bold as to turn up at the publishing house in person. Implausible as his story was, he was still capable of complicating the whole affair.

Salman Schocken rarely begged anyone for anything. But he would be truly grateful if Joachim could help. Would he fly out to Los Angeles and speak to his mother? Naturally, the publisher would cover the cost of the trip. This way, Joachim could verify with his own eyes whether the letters still existed and how many of them there were. No one else had seen them, after all, not even Max Brod.

It was not a request but an order, and Joachim had obediently nodded yes.

Now the Bata box rested on the table in between them. Joachim's stomach was tied in knots.

"May I have a look?"

"Why not?"

He carefully lifted the lid. There they were, along with the envelopes, all tied up in green ribbon. Two big bundles of letters.

He closed the box back up.

"What do you plan to do with them?"

"What do you think? I'm putting my things in order."

"Do you intend to burn them?"

She lowered her graying head.

"Is that what you intend to do?"

"Let's just drop it."

"Because if you don't, I am going to sell them once you're gone. I don't see any reason not to."

She carefully wiped her hands on the cloth napkin in her lap and rose from her seat. Then she picked up the box and put it back in the sideboard. "Well. That's that. Shall I make us some more tea?"

Joachim knew there was no point in pressing. She wasn't going to discuss the matter with him any further. He could only confirm to Schocken that the letters still existed.

Felice made him lunch and drove him to the airport, with the cookies, preserves, and sweaters packed in wrapping paper.

Before he got out of the car, she thanked him for coming and said his visit had brought her great joy.

Joachim felt ashamed.

His mother had always avoided emotional displays, keeping her good-byes quick and to the point. So it was this time, too. Instead of walking him into the terminal, she just stepped out of the car, gave him a hug, and kissed him on the cheek.

"God bless. Now off you go."

Joachim took a few steps, then turned and looked back.

His mother hadn't climbed back in the car and driven off as she usually did. Instead, she just stood there, next to the old Ford, one hand tucked in the pocket of her blue jacket, the other raised in farewell. The ocean breeze swept the green silk scarf off her head, tousling her graying hair.

He waved to her and turned to continue on his way. To the plane home and his family's house decorated in Christmas lights, and maybe with a dusting of snow, to Nina Perel and the children.

Then he stopped and turned around once more. She was still standing there. And all of a sudden he pictured her dead. Lying on her back, head turned to the right, eyes closed, a wisp of gray hair over her mouth.

1955

Los Angeles

HAD EVERYONE SUDDENLY LOST THEIR MINDS?

Brod wrote her again, this time directly, instead of through Sophie, and once more he enumerated all the reasons why she ought to sell her letters to Schocken.

Then, in early February, a few weeks after Joachim's visit, a stranger called on the phone. He spoke in German and said his name was Casimiro Appelbaum.

It struck her as unusual for someone in America to introduce himself over the phone using his full name.

He asked if he could visit her, saying he had something very important he needed to ask.

She said she was ill and not receiving visitors. If he wanted something from her, he could tell her over the phone.

"I am the son of Grete Bloch and Franz Kafka," he said. "The doctor might have told you about me when you saw him."

"What doctor?"

"Your son."

"You say you're the son of Franz Kafka?"

"And Grete Bloch, your friend. I didn't want to shock you like this, over the phone. Which is why I would rather come see you in person."

It took her a moment before she could bring herself to speak. Then it occurred to her to ask, "And where are you?"

"I'm in New York. But I can come anytime."

"Give me your number, I'll call you back." Practical, quick-witted Felice.

She took down his number, hung up, and dialed Joachim at his office. Luckily, he was on break and the secretary put her through right away.

Yes, that man, Appelbaum, had been to see him. Twice, as a matter of fact. The first time Joachim agreed to talk; the second time he refused. How the man knew Joachim had been to see his mother in L.A., Joachim had no idea; maybe his secretary had let it slip.

He did bear quite a resemblance to Kafka, he told her.

"Nonsense, sheer nonsense! The idea! Why didn't you tell me?"

"I didn't want you to be needlessly upset. I wasn't sure he was telling the truth, but he does know an awful lot of details about Grete, especially from the last few years. He says the story about the bayonet is a rumor and Grete died in Auschwitz. There are witnesses, or one anyway. Still, Mr. Schocken is convinced Appelbaum is an impostor."

She cried out, "Of course he's an impostor! And what does Schocken have to do with it?"

"Just calm down, Mom. Appelbaum went to see him, too. He wanted to know how much he would pay for Kafka's letters to Grete."

"He has Franz's letters?"

"Well, not yet. But he thinks he might be able to get them, if he can convince someone—like you—that he actually is Grete's son. He doesn't have any proof. His birth certificate and all his other documents were in some bag that went missing. Before she was deported, Grete placed her letters in the safekeeping of a lawyer in Florence, but obviously he isn't just going to hand them over to Appelbaum."

"Letters! Again with the letters. You really all have lost your minds. Brod, Schocken, and now to top it all off, this Appelbaum fake. Please, how could Franz have had a child with Grete? It's a lie."

"You're probably right, Mom. In any case, don't invite him over—don't even give him your address. If he calls again, just tell him to stop harassing you. But as for the letters, you really should get rid of them. With Schocken, at least they'll be in good hands and finally you can have peace of mind. Not to mention you need the money."

When they broke up, she didn't promise that she would destroy his letters, nor had he asked her to. On the contrary, he had always made it clear that he still wanted to be with her, even if only through his letters.

Now she had to get rid of them, though. She should have done it a long time ago.

After her conversation with Joachim, she hardly slept a wink all night. Every time she dozed off, Kafka's son, or whoever he was, came leaping out at her. In her last dream, she was trying to stab him with a knife, but it was an old jackknife and the tip just kept glancing off of him while he stood there laughing, until she stabbed him in the eye.

As morning came, she made up her mind to settle the matter then and there. No more putting it off.

She got out of bed. Day was just breaking, the birds chirping in the jacaranda boughs.

She took off her pajama top and, using a washcloth dipped in cold water, washed her face, breasts, and underarms, as she did every day. She rinsed out her mouth and got dressed, but instead of a house frock, she took from the closet a dark blue pleated dress. Finally, after pinning her hair up in a bun and smoothing the hair above her forehead into two neat waves, she hung a necklace of red coral beads around her neck.

She went into the kitchenette, brewed her morning coffee

with milk, toasted some bread, and ate breakfast, more festively than usual, at the table in the living room.

Once she had eaten, washed the dishes, and swept up the crumbs, she was ready.

The Bata shoe box traveled from the sideboard to the dining room table.

She opened the lid.

Here we go.

It almost felt like the letters were cowering from her.

All night long she had been thinking about how to destroy them, mulling over the various options in her mind. She couldn't burn them. She didn't even have a stove. She remembered how swiftly her own letters, which she had brought with her from Prague, had disappeared in flames. There had been a pretty nice stack of them, too. While Felice fed the stove, her mother had stood looking on from behind, making cutting remarks. She had known all along her relationship with Kafka would come to nothing.

Throw them in the trash as is? Impossible.

She had to tear them up.

Rip them into tiny shreds that no one could ever piece together. Then pour them back into the box, take them to the ocean, and bury them in the sand. Find a spot that even he would have liked and lay them to rest. The thought of it appealed to her.

She untied the ribbon and picked up the first letter, the one he had typed. She took it out of the envelope and set it aside.

Slowly she made her way through the first bunch, then the second, until she was holding one of the last letters. Written in the summer of 1917, a year after their accord in Marienbad. The end of the war was not yet in sight. Again he made excuses for why he couldn't marry her, again enumerating all of his bad attributes, his unsuitability for marriage, his writing. He was living at the time in a damp, freezing apartment with no kitchen or bathroom, though it did have a view of the garden; he commended it for that. Nor was he eating properly; no wonder he had fallen ill. Europe was burning, yet he wrote only of himself. For her, Felice, he felt sorry, too, although not because it was hard for her surviving in that third year of war while supporting her mother and sister besides, no. He felt sorry for her only because she loved him. It was an ugly, selfish letter. That one definitely deserved to disappear.

It was two densely handwritten pages on thin wartime paper. She slowly tore it into two halves. The paper was old and put up no resistance, surrendering with a soft crinkling. She laid one half on top of the other, then tore them in two again, as easily as the first time. It wasn't until she tried to rip up several scraps together, laid one on top of the other, that she had to exert her strength. Her hands were shaking by the time she was through.

But she didn't give up. She picked up another envelope and removed from it the next letter, even worse than the one before.

The little bits covered with spidery writing floated down to the floor around her, featherlight flakes a mere puff of air could have blown away. They were nothing.

Dust you are, and to dust you shall return ran through her head, which was throbbing from lack of sleep. She was cold.

She got up, leaving the letters on the table, and dragged herself to bed. She climbed in, fully dressed, and pulled the blanket up to her neck. Tears ran down her temples, tickling her in her hair and behind her ears. She was useless. She had destroyed only two letters and was already too drained to go on. Meanwhile, there was still a whole stack of them left. This was going to kill her. And anyway, it was all going to end up with Schocken, who was just waiting for her to die. Joachim wouldn't think twice about selling him the letters; he had already threatened he would.

Schocken, Joachim, Brod, and now this Appelbaum fellow to boot. Circling her like a pack of hyenas smelling blood.

She couldn't trust anyone.

Exhausted, she finally fell asleep. When she opened her eyes again, she was feeling somewhat better and had an appetite. She knew now what to do. She would call up Masha and ask her to come over after she closed the shop. Then she would tell her friend everything. Masha had no personal connection to any of it, and this would be her first time hearing about the letters. She was a sensible, honest person, the kind you could count on for good advice.

Masha hurried right over. Felice barely had time to gather together the letters, put them back in the box, sweep up the scraps of paper, make tea, and spread a piece of bread with butter and jam.

She settled her girlfriend down at the table, poured her a cup of tea, and explained the whole thing to her. Well, not the whole thing, but enough for her to be able to help Felice reach a decision.

Masha wasn't too interested in literature. She had heard Kafka's name; that was about it. Yet she immediately grasped how difficult, if not impossible, it would be for Felice to hand over the letters. With her kind heart, she could sense it; she didn't need a lot of words.

"Here's what I think," Masha said, stroking the back of Felice's hand. "If this Kafka person really was as great a writer as you say, destroying the letters would be a shame. I think they're right about that. And when it comes down to it, it's not about the money, although eight thousand dollars, in your situation, is certainly nothing to sneeze at. The thing is, if you don't give them the letters now but you also don't destroy them, which I don't think would be good and you don't really want to do, either, you won't have any control over what happens to them later. Who knows whose hands they might fall into? This way, you don't have to worry. From everything you've told me, it sounds like this Schocken's a reputable man, someone you can trust. It's funny, I had no idea he had anything to do with books." She smiled. "I remember the department stores—we used to go shopping at Schocken. The one in Frankfurt had a lovely café."

Masha went on: "You don't have to sell him all of them, either. No one but you knows how many there are. I can go through them with you if you want. You can pick which ones you don't want anyone to see and we'll burn them together. I'll help you. Then the rest you can sell to Schocken, and that'll be the end of that."

1955

Musso and Frank, Los Angeles

Felice had heard tell that Salman Schocken, former owner of one of the largest department store chains in Germany, publisher and patron of Jewish literature, was a forceful, stubborn man who refused to give up on an idea once he got it into his head. Even if, to get what he wanted, he had to chop down the forest and dry up the sea like a hero in a fairy tale.

But she hardly could have imagined the whirlwind she would unleash with a single telephone call to New York.

Less than an hour after she had called Joachim to tell him she was accepting Schocken's offer, her telephone rang. Even the ring sounded urgent. And the deep voice on the other end was bubbling over with enthusiasm.

"You've made me a happy man," Schocken declared. You would have thought she had accepted his marriage proposal. "This is one of the happiest days of my life."

He informed her that he was flying to Los Angeles first thing in the morning. He was bringing the contract and money with him, and taking Felice to lunch. Assuming she agreed, he suggested they meet at Musso and Frank. The last time he was there, he said, Charlie Chaplin was sitting at the next table. Did she like Chaplin? Did she like going to the movies?

Yes, she liked going to the movies.

"So tomorrow at one, then, agreed?"

"All right, see you tomorrow."

She took a taxi to the restaurant. It was still chilly, so she put on the best piece of clothing she had, the coat with the silver fox collar. She had had it resewn a couple of times, but the fox still looked like new. The one thing Felice knew was how to take care of clothes. To go with it, she wore a blue silk dress and a hat. Then she put on a light touch of lipstick and powdered her face so she wouldn't be too pale.

She had to laugh at herself a little, getting all dressed up like that. Why bother? For Schocken's sake? Or in case she ran into Gregory Peck along the way? Checking herself in the mirror before she left home, making sure every hair was neatly in place beneath her small round hat, it suddenly dawned on her why.

She wanted to look her best so that Franz would be proud of her.

Schocken was waiting for her outside when she arrived. Pacing back and forth nervously like a young man on his first date, holding an enormous bouquet of red, yellow, and orange tulips wrapped in silk paper. He was dressed in a suit and vest, with a dark caped overcoat and a gray felt hat, which he doffed in greeting as she approached. He sported a white mustache to go with the wreath of white hair on his head, and his eyes were dark and lively.

"For you. Do you like tulips? For us this is the time of year when spring is in the air."

"For you in New York?"

"For us in Berlin, dear Madam Felice. May I call you by your first name? You aren't offended? For some reason I feel like we have known each other forever. And yet we've only just met. Are you hungry?"

He offered her his arm and led her through the entrance. Once inside, the waiters immediately took charge of them, steering them to a table along the side, with a good view of the dining room, yet also affording them privacy.

"Just take a look around," he said as the waiter helped them out of their coats and slid back a chair for Felice. "No need to be embarrassed. If you're lucky, you might see one of your favorite actors or actresses. I confess I don't go to the cinema much. I mostly read in my free time. Though Marilyn Monroe I would recognize, I suppose."

He asked the waiter for a bottle of champagne and instructed Felice to order the lobster, explaining that the restaurant was renowned for it.

"Steak, my dear, we can have anytime! Go ahead and bleed me for all I'm worth. The old geezer Schocken deserves it." His body shook with a wholehearted laugh. He was in a marvelous, exultant mood.

His gaiety was infectious; she couldn't help but laugh with him.

He reminded her of the way her father used to get at family parties, after a few glasses of wine, when he would unwind and forget his daily troubles.

"So where you are from, Madam Felice? Where were you born?"

"I come from a small town near the Czech border. In our day, it was known as Neustadt in Oberschlesien, if that means anything to you. When I was twelve, we moved to Berlin."

"Fränkel and Pinkus, textiles, how could I not know them? Compared to Margonin, where I grew up, Neustadt was an opulent town. It had a park and a fountain. We only had a pond with ducks. We were poor, but then again, not so poor it crushed us, if you know what I mean. We never lost the ability to dream. On the contrary, dreams were our main sustenance. Margonin had a direct line to God, long before the phone was invented. Well, I got out of there as fast as I could. I wanted to be a writer. Which one of us Jewish boys didn't? Fortunately, it didn't take too long for me to realize that I didn't have the knack for it and I was much more talented in business.

"Neustadt in Oberschlesien. I remember it well. I visited Max Pinkus there in the twenties. Truly a rare man, though even back then he was already getting on in years. A humanist, a philanthropist, people like that existed in those days. I was one myself. I believed that people could be transformed by beauty and art. You yourself know how that turned out, what a comical error in judgment that was. That dream of mine took the longest to die and it also hurt the most. Before, that was my backbone, my mainstay, so to speak. Without it, there wasn't much left for me. Money? Is that enough for a man to go on living? Books? And yet we live. And sometimes we even find a good reason for it, so let's drink to that now, shall we?"

Despite all the energy bristling from him, Felice noticed a great sadness harbored in his dark-colored eyes. Especially when he paused for a moment.

"So anyway, this Pinkus," Schocken went on, "had a large collection of books and artwork, mostly things related to Silesia. The Nazis blew it completely to bits. Fortunately, he didn't live to see it. He died in '34. I was at his funeral. His heart gave out, sitting there writing in his library. I can only wish such a death for myself. His son Hans, who inherited his estate, lives in England. Sadly, I have heard his affairs are not coming along so well. He has the misfortune that most of his family's properties are in Poland, in the Russian zone, and they won't give him back a thing. I at least got something out of Germany, although most of my department stores are merely ruins at this point."

The waiters brought their lobsters. Felice generally avoided fish. When she was little, her mother had instilled in her a fear of bones getting caught in her throat, especially if she ate fish together with potatoes. But the tender white flesh of the lobster was delicious. She hadn't tasted it in ages, probably not since her last trip to the south of France, when she and Robert were still in Geneva. There was a restaurant on the promenade des Anglais where he had taken her on every one of their visits to Nice. He ordered lobster for her and roasted fish for himself and a bottle of white wine to go with it.

"Pork I can easily do without, Madam Felice, but why should Jews voluntarily deprive themselves of such a sumptuous delicacy, don't you agree? Kosher or not. You know, I find it so odd that we never crossed paths in Berlin. We must have had plenty of friends in common, as I'm sure we would discover if we were to start naming names. I didn't become close with Brod until Palestine, though of course we knew each other before, since he did publish with me. Have you noticed how friendships in exile take on a different dimension? Our friends become our homeland. They are the only witnesses of what was. And then, once they're gone, well . . ."

Felice knew from Sophie, who had it from Brod, that Schocken had divorced his wife shortly after relocating from Jerusalem to New York. He had always had mistresses, Sophie said. That was common knowledge. Schocken was a notorious connoisseur when it came to beautiful books, houses, furniture—and women. But he wouldn't have left his wife for a mistress. When he filed for divorce, he said the reason was they didn't love each other anymore, can you believe it? After fifty years of marriage! Now he lived alone and reportedly claimed to be delighted to be a free man at last. Talk about selfish.

Again it reminded Felice of her father, who a few years before his death left her mother for a younger woman and only returned home to die.

"You've never considered emigrating to Palestine?"

"Robert went there to look into it, for a month, in '32. But he came back convinced that it wasn't for us. He insisted America was the only place our children could build a life in freedom. In Palestine it was impossible, he said."

"Your husband was a very farsighted man to get you all out of Germany as early as he did. I had many influential friends in Palestine, I traveled there often before the war. In 1925, I was one of the cofounding patrons of the Hebrew University. I thought I would be happy there. I had plans. I built a library. I bought a local paper and turned it into a modern daily for news and culture, along the lines of the *Frankfurter Allgemeine Zeitung*. I kept on publishing books. But your husband was right, Madam Felice, it isn't the place for us. It's too foreign, too poor, too dirty. Forgive me, but too ugly. I'm a European and always will be. I enjoy comfort and nice things. I'm no ascetic, nor a pioneer. They practically pride themselves on their rudeness there, to them it's a sign of equality. And everything is a constant debate. Everyone's got their opinions, everyone's a prophet. Jerusalem is exactly like Margonin, I tell you. And Tel Aviv wasn't much better, although my eldest son, who's living there now, insists I wouldn't even recognize it today, everything is so modernized. It's German money behind it all, obviously, reparations. Far be it from me to blame the Zionists for taking it. My son says there are new buildings all over the place—theaters, hotels, roads, cars, restaurants—and there hasn't been food rationing for two years now. They even managed to clean up the beaches, which a few years ago were so dirty, the city council shut them down. Swimming there meant taking your life in your hands. They didn't have sewers, they just dumped it all in the sea. My son writes they don't have to stand in line like they used to anymore, either. Bus stops, grocery shopping, the movies—the lines they had you wouldn't believe! Anyway, my son is happy. He runs my publishing house and the newspaper, and he's building the state of Israel. Israel needs support, and I've always been happy to give it. But live there? No one can make me do that."

The entire lunch, Schocken didn't mention Kafka or the letters even once. As if the only reason he had come to California was to reminisce about old times over lobster and champagne with Felice.

He even talked her into ordering the *île flottante*: whipped, foamy egg whites afloat on a thick vanilla cream. He himself had a cognac to go with his coffee. Then, having waited until they were finished, he pulled two leather folders from his spacious briefcase and pushed aside the cut-glass vase, in which the waiter had arranged a bouquet of tulips.

"Here is the contract. One copy for you and the other for me. Shall we do it?"

He handed her a pen.

"You don't even need to read it. It's all there, the way I explained it to you in our correspondence and over the phone. The contract is with Schocken Books, and it's binding on my heirs as well, which is crucial, since you're sure to outlive me by many years, Madam Felice. To your health!" He took a sip from his glass. "Very nice. I gave up smoking, at my doctor's insistence. But there are pleasures in this world I have no intention of giving up. I may as well just climb into the coffin otherwise."

She signed the two copies of the contract using her full name; Schocken added his sprawling squiggle underneath. Then he snapped the folders shut and slipped them into his briefcase.

"They wouldn't fit in your purse, would they? I also brought the money, of course, and I'll give it to you just as soon as we have a bit of privacy. I could escort you home and pick the letters up now, if it's convenient for you. If not, we can make an arrangement for tomorrow. I'm happy to wait."

"That won't be necessary," said Felice. "I assumed we would settle it straightaway."

As they got out of the taxi in front of her building, Schocken asked the driver to wait, so he could take him back to his hotel afterward.

Felice lived in a new apartment house with an elevator. Each unit had its own little balcony and plenty of light, and Felice was content to be there. Still, riding up to her place with the former owner of the Schocken department stores, she couldn't help but reminisce about her old apartment in Berlin. Comparing the luxury of her situation then with the two small rooms and kitchenette that she had now. Though things could have been a lot worse. She could have been dead a long time ago.

Holding his hat in his hand, Schocken stepped inside the apartment and looked around. His eyes came to rest on the sideboard. "Well, what have we here? An honest-to-goodness Berlin buffet, the cornerstone of marital bliss. Greetings, old friend. I'm sure there was a whole dining room that went with this piece."

He was teasing her a bit. After all, this was a man whose furniture had been designed by Bauhaus artists and whose department stores had been referred to in the press as "temples of functionalism."

He ran his eyes over the walls. An oil painting of a bridge in Berlin, a landscape, and a portrait of Felice in a blue dress. "That's a very good likeness."

He had her tell him the name of the painter, who had once been quite well known in Berlin, but it didn't ring a bell.

"I've always been more interested in writers than painters. There are other people for that."

She took his hat and laid it on the sideboard. He declined to take off his coat.

Felice removed her coat and hat and attended to the tulips. They almost didn't fit in the vase. The petals on the more fully open flowers were upturned like the outer wings on a flying beetle, yellow pistils encircled by black stamens at their center.

She stood the bouquet on the sideboard. "Please, have a seat. I'll make us some coffee."

Sitting on the table, which was covered with a crocheted tablecloth, was the brown shoe box with the Bata logo on it.

"Is that them?" He sat down at the table and lightly stroked the lid of the box with his palm. "May I?"

The thought suddenly flashed through her mind that when Schocken opened it up, Franz would be lying there inside. She sometimes saw him like that in her dreams.

"Mr. Schocken, I have to let you know, there are several letters in there that weren't written to me, but to Grete Bloch, a friend of mine and Franz's. Sadly, she died during the war. At one point she entrusted me with the letters, and I don't know whether I have the right to give them to you. There may be somebody else with a greater claim to them."

"You mean Miss Bloch's brother in Tel Aviv? Don't worry. I'm only buying your part, not Miss Grete's letters. Provided you agree, I would take hers solely for safekeeping, till the matter is sorted out."

"I'm not talking about her brother. . . ."

"Then who? She has no other heirs. Ahhh . . ." He slapped his palm on the table. "You mean that impostor? He came to see you, too? That's outrageous! The audacity!"

"He called me up on the phone, claiming to be Grete and Kafka's secret son. It's such nonsense. Why, Franz couldn't even cheat a tram conductor! I will never understand how Brod could spread such rumors, given how well he knew him. As it happens, Grete did have a child. But not with Kafka. The boy was adopted by a childless family in Munich. I had always assumed that he died. But what if he didn't? Even my son wasn't positive that the man was an impostor. Supposedly he knew all sorts of things about Grete, things a person could hardly invent."

"He didn't invent them. He read them in an Italian newspaper. There was an article published last summer, on the anniversary of Kafka's death, and—poof—Kafka's son appeared in the fall. Talk about a coincidence. A German professor in Italy decided to get to the bottom of the mystery of Kafka's alleged son, and took a trip to the village in the mountains where Miss Bloch was interned. He interviewed the survivors, and apparently he was even allowed a peek inside some bag of hers that got left behind when the Germans took them away. He unearthed a few photographs, which didn't prove a thing. No documents. He also spoke with Miss Bloch's last lover, a clockmaker, and in Turin he looked up a lady by the name of Rosa Myler, who was Grete's best friend in San Donato and witnessed her death in Auschwitz. She debunked Brod's tall tale about the bayonet. And neither she nor the lover believed in the existence of any child with Kafka. Apparently, Grete was delirious in her final months, insisting she was Kafka's wife and reading his books out loud to the clockmaker in German. The poor man didn't understand a word of it.

"Appelbaum is an actor by profession. I think that says it all. My guess is he read the article and succumbed to the idea that he was Kafka's lost son. He saw it as a chance to get rich and make a name for himself. I don't mean to be unfair. Maybe he really is adopted and doesn't know who his real parents are. But he isn't Kafka's son, most likely he's not Grete's, either, and you, dear Madam Felice, have every right to entrust me with the letters of your friend."

She walked off into the kitchen.

When Felice returned, bearing a tray with two hot cups of coffee, a sugar bowl, and a plate of cookies clinking on it, Schocken had taken the letters out of the box and divided them into three equal stacks. Next to them stood a fourth stack of one-hundred-dollar bills.

"Eight thousand. Please, go ahead and count it. And here is your copy of the contract."

Felice obediently counted the money while Schocken took out three large envelopes, carefully slipped the letters inside, and deposited them in his briefcase, then clicked the lock shut.

"There. That should do it. And now let's the two of us have a cup of good German coffee. Thank you so much. I tremendously enjoyed reminiscing with you today. My entire spirit was lifted. If only we had known at the time what fate had in store for us and how precious an experience it was that we were going through, eh? We might have appreciated it more. Now all we can do is fish for the splinters of a sunken ship. Well, thank you for these." He tapped the briefcase.

"Now I had better run, or my driver will fall asleep," he said, rising to his feet.

She walked him to the door and handed him his hat.

"Thank you. I can find my way out on my own. Have a lovely day, my dear Felice, and give my regards to your son. He's a clever young man. You can be proud of him."

This time, instead of a kiss, he gave her hand a hard squeeze, then slowly started down the stairs. At the bend in the staircase, he turned one last time. "I'm dying to know if these are really all the letters there are. But I realize there's no point in asking now that our business is settled." He lifted his hat in good-bye. "Adieu."

She stepped back into the apartment, closing the door behind her.

Slowly, Felice made her way to the table, where, alongside the empty box, the two coffee cups, the sugar bowl, and the untouched cookies, lay the bundle of bills and the folder with the contract inside.

She sat down.

Silence, emptiness. She would have to live with that emptiness from now on.

Taking a cube from the sugar bowl, she stuck it in her mouth and crunched it between her teeth.

The empty cardboard box.

The letters in Schocken's leather briefcase.

The letters that are waiting. And being awaited.

Hurry up, woman, die! Kafka's readers want to know it all.

A gag in the mouth to keep her from screaming.

It'll be fine, don't worry.

1955

Tel Aviv

WAVE AFTER WAVE LICKS THE BEACH, sand washing over sand, as the water retreats and leaves behind a swath of tiny seashells and the stiff, glistening fronds of cast-up seaweed. Some small creature burrows into the wet dark of the sand to wait out the day. A tiny crab scurries to safety as the sky pales in the east.

Otto gets up earlier in the morning than his wife. He sits on the balcony, smoking and watching as, drip by drip, the night dissolves into dawn. The sun is approaching from somewhere beyond the horizon and the birds chirp with increasing excitement, hopping about the oleander bush and the leaves of the low-growing palm, climbing the vines of bougainvillea and shaggy branches of tamarisk. Their beating wings set the hibiscus blossoms aquiver. Back home in Prague, they had had a potted hibiscus plant, and he never could have imagined what a wealth of flowers it would produce in a climate where it was native. Of course there were lots of things in Prague that he couldn't have imagined.

Like the knot of scrawny cats sleeping off their nightly rambles at the foot of the rickety shed in the yard, surrounded by tin cans their ground-floor neighbor keeps filled with water for them. She also secretly brings them food. Not all the neighbors approve of the feline colony, complaining of the stench and their yowling at night.

Once the sun finally climbs above the horizon and the uproar in the branches subsides, Otto abandons his observation post. He goes to the kitchen and squeezes some orange juice for Ilse, who has just gotten up, and, to judge by the rhythmic huffing and puffing coming from her room, is performing her daily gymnastics workout.

Ever since their daughters moved out of the house, both he and Ilse have had bedrooms of their own. A person no longer sleeps so soundly after reaching a certain age, and a partner's sighs and tossing and turning interferes with sleep, not to mention other things.

Otto washes and shaves quickly, freeing the bathroom up for his wife, and goes to get dressed. Gray pants, shirt and tie, light sports jacket. After breakfast he'll go shopping. He had parted with his vest after their first few months in Tel Aviv as one of his first concessions to the local climate. He wears one now only to go to concerts or the theater.

As soon as he's ready, Otto moves into the kitchen. He glances out the window again at the yard. It really does look like a jungle. He never was one much for botany, and he still doesn't know the names of all the bushes and flowers and trees, but he marvels at the shapes and colors of their blossoms. In the Czech lands, everything was in moderation, always just the right amount, whereas here there is either too much or not enough. Too many scents, too many colors, too much noise, too much sun, and a moon so huge it feels like you could just reach out and touch it. Not enough water.

Now that he has more time to think, since he no longer needs to go to work, Otto often catches himself staring at his surroundings in amazement. As if he were only here in this exotic country as a tourist, and once the trip was over, he would be going home. As if there were a home to go to.

But who says there isn't? Maybe life in Prague is still going on as before, and he just doesn't realize it. Maybe the person making breakfast and staring out the window, amazed at the pink blossoms of bougainvillea, isn't the real Otto Heinrich Hoffe, but his double. Meanwhile, the real Otto is getting out of bed in his big Vinohrady apartment, shaving, getting dressed, eating breakfast, and tramping the same daily route to the stop for the streetcar that takes him to his job as the manager of a branch factory in Vršovice.

The idea that he might be his own double is oddly comforting to him.

He makes his coffee in a *cezve,* the way he learned from their Arab neighbors. With a soft-boiled egg and a slice of white bread spread with jam.

The locals breakfast on a salad of chopped vegetables and other things like that. Healthier, no question, but for someone who had been eating bread, butter, and jam in the morning ever since he was little, a salad didn't appeal. If only the bread here was more like the Czech bread.

On the days she goes to work, Ilse doesn't eat breakfast. She just downs a glass of juice and is ready to go. A half hour's fast walk on an empty stomach is another one of the regular exercises she uses to keep her figure slim and firm.

She looks fresh and young in a blue summer blouse that goes with her eyes and fair hair, and a beige knee-length skirt.

"It's going to be a hot one," he says.

"Probably."

"At least it isn't humid."

"Do we have anything for this evening?"

"Not today. Tomorrow we've got a concert. What are you doing today?"

"I'm going to do the shopping, then some reading. Answer a few letters."

"So we'll have ourselves a quiet night tonight, yes?"

"Is Max coming over?"

"No, but Eva will drop by."

Ilse latches the door shut behind her, swings her bag the way she did with her school bag when she was little, and skips down the few steps to ground level. Once on the street, she resumes the respectable stride of a middle-aged lady.

Straight, left, right, straight, third street to the left. Her step is fast and light. It's a glorious morning, sparkling with colors. She feels good in her linen jacket as a cool wind wafts from the mainland, probably down from the mountains. She hops across a stream of dirty water splashed across the sidewalk by a vegetable vendor.

The stores are just opening up, along with the cafés. Mixing with the aroma of fresh-baked bread and ground coffee is the odor of unemptied trash cans, rotting fruit peels, scraps of fish. A cat bolts out in front of her near Trumpeldor Cemetery, a tabby, thin as a bone.

She buys a bag of crispy bread rolls at the Polish bakery and a couple of early peaches from the Arab's next door, hoping by now they'll be sweet and juicy.

She unlocks the house with her own key. On the third floor, where Max lives, she stops a moment and listens. A faint sound of music is coming from the apartment. She knocks on the door, as always, before slipping the key in the lock. Max knows she's coming, but she still considers it polite to warn him in advance.

She steps into the entryway, quietly closing the door behind her, and calls out, "Good morning, Max."

No reply.

She sets the rolls and peaches down in the kitchen and walks into the next room. The door to the bedroom is open, but Max isn't there. Nor does she see him in his study, where she notices at a glance that the materials they were working on the day before are still there, carefully spread out on the table.

She finds him in the living room, in an armchair of leather and stainless-steel pipe, his favorite Bauhaus chair. He had it shipped in from Prague, not realizing how sick and tired of functionalism he would become after moving to Tel Aviv. How living amid its simple, bright, hurriedly purpose-built homes, with no embellishments, but also *no substance*, as he so often said, he would long with all his soul for the thick-walled labyrinths, the superfluous alcoves, projections, ornaments, corridors, and staircases of buildings in Prague.

The air is cloudy with cigarette smoke and Max, who normally takes such care of his appearance, even in front of her, or especially in front of her, is sitting without his glasses on, disheveled and in his pajamas, just as he got out of bed, with tears rolling down his cheeks. He doesn't bother to wipe them away, letting them drip freely onto the breast of his pajama top, which is already soaking wet.

Ilse reaches out and strokes his white neatly trimmed hair.

"Max."

"Good morning, Esther," says Max. "Don't you find this clarinet concerto unbelievably tender? Where does that tenderness come from?"

"It's beautiful," Ilse says.

"There must be a loving God, Esther. Mozart couldn't possibly have composed this music otherwise. But assuming there is such a God, how can there be evil? Does it exist inside of God? Or is it something distinct from God? I believe I answered this one question at one point. But now I don't know anymore."

"Is anything wrong?"

He shakes his head. "I had a dream about Prague. But that's almost every night. There was a café—the Louvre, I think—then I was roaming the streets. Felix was with me. My mom was waiting at home."

"And then?"

"Then nothing. I woke up and got out of bed as usual. Put on Mozart. I was about to wash up and get dressed and make coffee for us for breakfast, read through my notes from yesterday. And then it all hit me at once." He leans forward and buries his face in his hands.

She kneels on the ground beside him, stroking his back, his hair, until he settles down.

"My darling."

The concerto is over, the record spinning silently in circles.

Ilse stands and walks to the turntable, lifting the needle. "Should I put on something else?"

"Not now. Could you open the windows, please?"

"Of course. It's so refreshing out."

"And could you make the coffee? I'll tidy myself up a bit in the meantime."

"Of course."

"And then we'll get to work."

"Has the mail arrived?"

"Not yet."

Returning to the kitchen, Ilse arranges the rolls on a plate and slices the peaches. "You know, Max," she says, calling to him in the other room, "I had an idea about Kraus. Which quote you should use. It came to me yesterday on my way out, so I didn't have time to tell you."

At nine o'clock sharp, the mailman rings the doorbell.

"Good morning, professor. How are you doing today?"

To the ginger-haired little man from somewhere in Galicia, Mr. Brod—who even at home wears a vest and a tie, and receives more letters than anyone else on the block by far, and all the way from Europe and America, if you please—could only be a professor.

There is a mailbox on the ground floor, of course, as there is in every building, but the mailman refuses to use it, preferring instead to tramp up to the fourth floor every day, so he can hand the professor his mail personally and wish him a nice day. In return, he gets an envelope of stamps every now and then to give to his little boy Itzik, who collects them.

Max returns with the bundle of letters to his study, where

he and Ilse, over a second cup of coffee, review the notes and materials for the revised edition of his autobiography, specifically the chapter on Karl Kraus. On his dispute with Kraus. On this point it is essential to be extremely precise and ensure that everything is documented in detail. Because, incredible as it seems to him in this day and age, there are still people, and more than a few, who admire Kraus, regarding him as something of a genius. He was brilliant in his way. But no one could persuade him, Brod, that the Austrian's flashes of literary prophecy and wit—for that matter, frequently in poor taste—were able to compensate for the abundance of lies and poison he sowed. Kraus was a perfect example of the self-hating Jew, lashing out at anything and everything around him. Being in his favor or falling foul of him, the result was the same in the end: nothing but fickleness, caprice, rage, and recklessness, particularly dangerous in those difficult times when the world was on the verge of collapse and humanity was girding itself about with fire and sword. Back then, anyone with the ability to distinguish good from evil and beauty from ugliness had an obligation to contribute to positive work, rather than sowing hatred. Back then, yes, back then it had still been possible to fight for humanism.

"Here it is, Max. This is everything."

The materials that need to be read through once more for possible quotation lie separated into a pile at the edge of the table. A few old letters, some handwritten notes by Max, three issues of *Die Fackel*, Max's short story, Werfel's first collection of poems, and the *Arkadia* yearbook of poetry. The corpus delicti.

Max tosses the letters from the mailman onto the table and settles into a chair. "Here's the mail. Let me just have a look."

He riffles through the envelopes, glancing at the return addresses. Two American universities, neither of which he has heard of. Italy, Spain. All of it clearly regarding Kafka. They could answer those later. Oh, not that guy again! He tosses aside one of the letters with a snort. If only he could dispose of the letter writer that easily.

The worst specimen of a species whose most courteous members are still at best a nuisance. They don't give him a moment's peace. Obsequious in their letters, then slandering him behind his back. Flattering him in a blatant attempt to pry what they can out of him: Could you tell me if Kafka prayed? Did he read Kierkegaard? Was it true that he visited brothels? What did he eat for breakfast? All writing dissertations.

And then there's this German fellow, another one who merely makes a show of being polite while keeping a dagger hidden beneath his cloak of courtesies. He is out to skewer Brod the way he skewers Brod's every word, and Brod is well aware of that. For a bard like him, the ultimate satisfaction, the greatest feat he is capable of, is to demonstrate—in a slew of boring, condescending essays—that he, Max Brod, has distorted Kafka's texts, changing the meaning or jumping to erroneous conclusions. Nowadays everyone and their brother claims to understand Kafka better than he does, yet all they are doing is stringing together a whole load of nonsense in an effort to be original, and whining that Brod is trying to keep Kafka to himself and that his interpretation—which, begging your pardon, isn't founded on fantasies and conjecture, but on hours and hours of intimate conversation, dozens of personal letters, and more than twenty years of loyal friendship—that this interpretation is being canonized by him, Max Brod. So much for human gratitude.

Meanwhile, if not for Brod, for his courage and indefatigable work, there wouldn't even *be* anything to research, the chutzpaniks.

Without him there would be no Kafka, and that's a fact.

They wouldn't have those cozy positions of theirs at all the universities adding "Kafka studies" to the curriculum, because where there's demand, there will be supply, so if you want to make money, you'd better move fast! They fight over Kafka while spitting on him, Brod, and yet they keep coming back, because without him they have nothing and they constantly want to know more, like that cheeky German fellow.

"The gall!" shouts Max. "Inventing theories about Kafka. He should write about his sisters instead, the ones the Germans murdered."

And Ilse—his guardian angel, his helper, his savior, his mistress, on whom he bestowed the name of Esther the queen; the woman who took him in thirteen years ago, at the darkest time of his life—doesn't ask who Max is talking about. She knows. She knows almost more about Max's affairs than Max does himself. Being much younger and very attentive, she remembers everything, down to the smallest detail.

She points to one of the letters he set aside. "That one is from Schocken."

"Really? I didn't notice. Open it up."

New York
April 20, 1955

Dear kind friend,

I hope that my letter finds you in full health and creative vigor. As for me, I certainly can't complain.

I am pleased to inform you that the correspondence of F. K., which had been in the possession of Madam Felice, has been secured. The purchase went smoothly. I saw to it myself. It consists of more than five hundred letters addressed to F. B., plus several incomplete letters to Grete Bloch. Some of the correspondence was likely destroyed by the owner, but the bulk of it has been preserved. I have written you already regarding the terms of the sale. Work on the transcriptions and notes may begin immediately upon the death of the recipient, and the letters may be published as a book five years thereafter. Until then they will remain securely locked in my safe. This acquisition brings me greater joy than all of my previous achievements put together, I suspect because the owner was so difficult to convince.

I suggest that, insofar as it can be managed, the letters to Felice should be published together with the letters to Miss Bloch. Bearing that in mind, therefore, I beg you to renew your search and undertake all possible steps that might lead to the acquiring of the items in Florence.

I must also draw your attention to the fact that various impostors have surfaced recently, laying false claim to be related to Kafka. I say this so that you will be prudent and not trust just anyone. Even if in your case, dear Max, warnings like these are like carrying water to the sea. I know no one more circumspect than you, at least in all things concerning Kafka.

Cordially yours,
Salman Schocken

Brod leaps out of his chair and paces the room with the jerky stride that makes him easy to recognize from a distance. "So it actually worked, Esther. Splendid! This will be absolutely critical."

He stops short mid-stride and raises his index finger. "I'm inviting you to lunch. This is cause for celebration. I'll ring Otto right now to join us."

At noon, linked arm in arm, the two of them relocate to the restaurant Stará Praha, where Otto is already waiting. The minute he sees them, Otto announces a small miracle: Today they're offering roast duck with cabbage and dumplings. Unbelievable after years of rationed food.

They order a round of beers to go with the duck and reminisce about old times, the restaurants and cafés of Prague. They make plans for a trip together to Europe. Max tells stories from the theater, where a new play is in rehearsal, and Otto laughs out loud. Who wouldn't laugh to be drinking beer and eating roast duck in such good company?

In the end, it's a beautiful day.

After lunch, Otto goes home to lie down and Max and Esther return to work. But first they stretch out for a while, too, as they do every day. Their bellies are too full for lovemaking, but Max at least gently caresses Esther's breasts.

1959

Pontresina, Switzerland

SALMAN SCHOCKEN, BEFORE THE WAR, owner of one of the largest department store chains in Germany, later a publisher and a collector of rare prints and manuscripts, nicknamed "Bismarck" by his coworkers, stepped out of a plane on the morning of August 5 at the international airport in Zurich feeling relatively fresh. After the supper served on board, he had taken a pill and fallen asleep for a good six hours. He wouldn't have slept any longer even at home in bed; his daughter had worried for nothing.

He preferred to travel alone, and that hadn't changed with age; if anything, quite the opposite. In recent years, he had had even less patience for the various delays and requirements of others. He had no desire for anyone to accompany him to the mountains, let alone one of his children or grandchildren. In his suitcase he had a few favorite books, a notebook, and a pen, and he was looking forward, looking forward a great deal.

The taxi driver carried Schocken's luggage to the car and whisked him to the main station, where, while the gentleman had a hearty breakfast in the café, the driver secured a ticket for the train. He then accompanied the elderly man to his coach, found him a seat by the window, and deposited his bags in the netting above his seat, all without a word and for just a few dollars extra. In Chur, Schocken was helped with his bags by a handy young man. The little red train, an electric line that climbed into the mountains, was already sitting there waiting. To transfer he had only to walk across the platform.

By three o'clock he was standing at the station in Pontresina, breathing deep into his lungs the warm fragrance of drying hay, freshly cut pine trees awaiting pickup, and the frosty breeze from the glaciers. The summer clouds frayed against the saw-toothed mountain peaks and regrouped themselves in the limitless blue overhead.

How well he had done not to be dissuaded from the trip! What could some puny little doctor, who had never set foot outside New York, know about a place like Pontresina and its salutary effect on his old and weary heart?

He recognized immediately the driver from the hotel who came for him at the station; he even remembered his name: Mario. He recalled that Mario's family lived down under the mountains, close to Bergamo.

During tourist season, Mario hired himself out to the management of the Grand Hotel Kronenhof. He slept with the other short-term workers in a dormitory in the attic and was quite content with his lot. He once boasted to Schocken that he earned as much in tips over the three summer months at the hotel as he did for a year of hard labor in the field and vineyard at home. And on top of that, he had some fun and got out from under the watchful eye of his stern parents, who would rather have seen him living at home and married in a cottage, but could hardly object, given how much money he brought in.

How glad he was, it struck Schocken, to see again this cheery lad, with whom, true enough, he could communicate only in his shaky Italian, picked up from operas and holiday travels, but still, he probably knew more about him than he did about his own grandchildren. He had only to hear Mario speak, in that singsong voice of his, and his whole world lit up. He instantly got a craving for a glass of red wine and a proper steak au poivre.

Unexpectedly moved by his reunion with the hotel driver, Schocken grew misty-eyed. He patted Mario, who fortunately didn't notice, on the shoulder, and the boy grabbed the suitcases and walked ahead to the car, the old man trailing more slowly behind.

They crossed the little bridge over the shallow Ova da Roseg, then curved sharply left onto the main road, to a turnoff over the green rapid-filled waters of the Bernina. The confluence of the two mountain torrents, which continued on under the name Flaz, was visible out the window of Schocken's room, number 333, which he reserved every year. He hadn't skipped a year even once since the war. Before, he and his family used to come here in the winters. But those were different times.

As they drove, he showered Mario with questions: What had the weather been like this year? Had they had a lot of guests? How about storms? Fires? Had anyone in the village died? Were there any children born? And what about Mario, was he finally getting married?

Really he was just trying to get the boy talking.

The whole welcoming committee was awaiting him at the reception desk, including the hotel manager. Loyalty was valued at the Kronenhof, especially loyalty proven in the difficult postwar times. Guests who hadn't abandoned them even after the war were bowed to here.

The manager himself saw the old man up to his room, in order to make certain that everything was in order. Waiting on the side table were a bouquet of roses, a bowl of fruit, and a box of chocolates. "Compliments of the house," the manager said under his breath, his cheeks turning red.

On his way out, the manager asked if the gentleman needed any help unpacking and whether he wished to eat right away, or would wait until dinner, which was served beginning at half past six.

"I won't be needing help and I'll wait," replied the old man. He shook the manager's hand once more and closed the door behind him.

He stepped out onto the balcony.

The Flaz bubbled past directly below, freshly born from the waters of the Bernina and Roseg rivers, the latter of which gave its name to the entire valley, extending toward the south and at this time of day still suffused with sun. The train station building, where he had arrived just a short while ago, was visible from where he stood, tracks gleaming in the afternoon light. Forests of spruce, pine, and larch climbed the slopes of the mountains, whose jagged peaks lined the valley to either side. He had come to know almost all of them by name over the years, just as he had the hotel staff: Piz Rosatsch, Piz Surlej, Piz Arlas; to the left, Piz Chalchagn, Piz Boval, and Piz Tschierva. All the way in the back shone the brilliant white ridge of the highest peak in this part of the Alps, Piz Bernina, whose crest, four thousand meters in elevation, ran along the border with Italy. And in the distance, beyond its white-capped dome, beyond its precipitous flanks and shadowy gorges, spread the heavenly Valtellina valley, with its excellent red wine, which the Romans began to cultivate more than two thousand years ago.

That's what he'd have for dinner. A *demi-bouteille* of sforzato and beef bourguignon with buckwheat polenta. And, as an appetizer, olives and a slice or two of bresaola, air-cured in the fragrant wind that blew nowhere else but in the valley blessed by the gods.

And he wasn't going to get emotional about it all and keep tearing up like an old lady. What was wrong with him?

At six thirty on the dot, he was sitting at his usual table in the plate glass–windowed dining room—with a panoramic view of the surrounding mountain peaks, as the tourist brochures said. He was engaged in a friendly chat with the old waiter Niccola, one of the last who still remembered the visits of Monsieur and Madame Schocken, along with their four children, who after months of lazing about in school needed to strengthen their lungs, as Madame Schocken put it.

Together, they were trying to figure out, though only because it seemed to matter so much to Niccola, how long Schocken had been coming to the hotel. Including the interval of the war, it came to thirty-five years.

"That alone is cause for celebration," Niccola declared, pouring a glass of dark red wine into a glass. "We are glad to have you here with us again, monsieur."

By eight o'clock Schocken was back in his room. Just in time to catch the sunset's final act. Gazing out from his balcony, as the sky faded to gray and the mountain peaks went dim, it almost appeared that the actors had taken their leave for the day. However, anyone who wasn't here for the first time knew it was just a mock exit, to be followed by the *bouquet final*, like the grand finale in the fireworks show that the hotel management put on for guests from time to time.

It began inconspicuously, with a trace of blush on the right side of the cliff at the end of the valley. Then the glow increased in intensity, engulfing the mountain up to its peak, where the snow lay in angled layers. The sky, catching fire from the mountain, was now no longer gray but a saturated orange. Then it all faded again to a soft shade of pink and the woods were blanketed in a cloak of purple darkness. But this was still not the end. Somewhere on the other side of the mountains, a stream of sunlight broke through a pass and the sky once more abruptly turned to gold. It was nearly unbelievable how long it was possible to prolong the performance.

In conclusion, a patch of bright green sky appeared between the two mountaintops, and planted in it was the night's first star.

Before dinner he had taken a bath and had a nap, and now he didn't feel sleepy at all. On the contrary, his senses were unusually keen and his mind was alert, even agitated. Probably due to the strong wine, of which he had drunk a bit more than he should have.

He changed into his pajamas and robe, cleaned his dentures over the sink, then closed the door to the balcony, to prevent the nighttime insects from flying in, and switched on the lamp by the desk. He would try to write for a while.

He hadn't confided his plan to anyone, but he had left for the mountains this summer with the intention of starting his memoirs. Over the course of his life he had come into contact with so many interesting people, it would be a shame not to bear witness to it. Not only had he provided financial support to several Jewish writers who had gone on to be famous, but he had also personally helped to lay the cornerstones of Israel: the university in Jerusalem, and the national library.

In prewar Germany, he had made his name as a pioneer of modern architecture and the modern lifestyle. The items in his department stores were designed by Bauhaus artists. Young Germans fought to get positions at his firm, which was constantly modernizing and improving. He built a vacation colony in the German mountains where employees of his and their families could stay. He arranged summer camps for their children. And paid for talented young people to go to school. Yes, he sincerely believed that, with all the twentieth century's achievements and technology, there was no reason why anyone should still be living in poverty and ignorance. He saw enormous potential, intellectual and spiritual, in ordinary working people. All they needed was a nudge in the right direction. To be educated and surrounded with beautiful, not just practical, things.

Especially in Germany, which had given the world Kant and Schiller, Schelling, Heine, and Novalis, but first and foremost Goethe—Goethe, who had once upon a time made him, a young shop assistant from Margonin, dizzy with possibilities, and opened up both his mind and heart alike.

Schocken had with him his well-thumbed copy of *Faust*, from which he was never parted for long. He had yet to read to the end of this masterwork, which Goethe had spent almost his entire life writing, allegedly fifty-six years in all, naturally with breaks. All the wisdom he had acquired over the course of his life was there within its pages. The pinnacle of Western culture illuminated by the beaming smirk of a fallen god; the cynicism of experience and the sweetness of faith; the wretchedness and the nobility of the human condition in the fullness of its complexity. Yes, in those days nobility, good, and beauty were still associated with reason, the Greek *nous*, not to be confused with the calculation, conniving, and practical skill of present-day ape-men.

There had been clumsy attempts to prove that Goethe had something to do with Auschwitz. That Auschwitz and the other horrors of World War II were the outcome of a specifically German type of idealism. Nonsense.

While ape-men perhaps differed in their external attributes, in the degree of their dexterity or ability to organize, otherwise they were the same the world over, in America as in Germany. They were all just waiting for their chance—their historical moment, as that other German, Hegel, would have put it. Though for that matter, Schocken had never been fond of Hegel, who struck him as trying too hard.

He had a similar impression when it came to Wagner as well.

Leaving aside the rare moments of inspiration, the composer's pompous music, intended to uplift the souls of the German bourgeoisie, made him feel nothing but depressed and bored and genuinely sorry for the singers, who worked themselves ragged for the sake of a spectacle that dazzled only, if at all, thanks to its deafening volume. Well. He could put it all in his memoirs. But he had to start somewhere.

"I was born in Margonin, Prussia, in 1877. My father, a poor street vendor, selling nuts, dried fruit, and beans . . ." No, strike that. That's no good.

"I was born in 1877 in the small town of Margonin, which at that time was Prussia, though it is now part of Poland. My parents were poor, so I was unable to study, and at age twelve I embarked on an apprenticeship with a merchant." No, strike that, not good at all.

"I was born in a world that no longer exists. When did it cease to be? Some say it was the moment when Adolf Hitler became chancellor. Others claim it was still earlier, in the trenches of World War I. That, they say, was when man ceased to be human.

"But I am afraid that it may never have existed at all, this world in which we lived, we, lovers of beauty and progress, readers of Goethe. Perhaps from beginning to end it was nothing but an illusion, hiding behind it the true face of man, the sneering grin of mass graves and gas chambers. Some of the artists whom I have had the good fortune to meet in my life, whether in person or through their work, have been gifted with a special clairvoyance, which enabled them to see which way humanity was heading, or rather in which direction modern civilization was dragging it. . . ."

The old man suddenly ran out of breath, as if he were walking up a steep slope. Modern civilization—what did he actually mean by that?

He could hear the voice inside his head, thin and squeaky: Who are you trying to fool, you Jew? Goethe and Schiller? Don't make me laugh! A Yid is what you are, a filthy Yid.

He heavily rose to his feet and, crossing the room to the balcony door, threw it open wide. In an instant the room was filled with the sounds of night: the burbling of the stream, the whirring of the cicadas, the hooting of a night owl.

He walked back to the desk.

It kept returning; it would always keep returning. That hateful face at the bend in the dirt road: "Don't make me laugh, Jew!"

He was too upset. He would read for a while instead.

Oh, look, it's my dad. What are you doing here? Why do you look so young, Daddy?

Here, Son, take my hand.

He could still hear the burbling stream and the whirring of the cicadas, but the room was somehow brighter. His bald pate shone in the lamp's yellow glow. His sweaty forehead on an open book.

He could see himself from above. His shoulders in the green silk robe, a long-ago gift from his wife. How shriveled he'd become over the past few years. He looked like a broken puppet slumped over the desk.

Which page of *Faust* had he opened to?

Es war ein König in Thule,
Gar treu bis an das Grab,
Dem sterbend seine Buhle
einen goldnen Becher gab.

Es ging ihm nichts darüber,
Er leert' ihn jeden Schmaus;
Die Augen gingen ihm über,
So oft er trank daraus.

It was foolish of him to have left the key in the lock from inside. In the morning they would have to break open the door.

1960

Rye, New York

"WHAT DATE IS IT TODAY, NURSE?"

"October fifteenth."

"The fifteenth already? Put down 'Probable cause of death, cardiac arrest.' What time did you find her?"

"Seven thirty."

"Put down 'Cardiac arrest, apparently in her sleep.'"

"Dr. McCabe?"

"Nurse Lee?"

"Given the patient's condition, there was no way to know if she was awake or asleep."

"That's why we put 'apparently,' Nurse Lee. Understood?"

"Yes."

"Have you notified the family?"

"Not yet."

"Then please do. And take care of the body. But you don't need me to tell you that."

Felice lay in the hospital bed, head turned to the side, a wisp of gray hair lying across her cheek and mouth. As Nurse Amanda Lee bent over her to brush the hair out of the way, she felt a puff of air on the nape of her neck. As if someone was blowing on her neck from behind.

"Doctor!" She quickly straightened herself. She really was not in the mood for fooling around right now.

She turned to look, but no one was there. Dr. McCabe had already left.

Huh, thought the nurse. A draft must have found its way in from the corridor. The window was closed.

She straightened the old lady's head, rearranging her unruly hair. Smoothed the blanket and pulled it over the dead woman's face. She would take her down to the cooler and then go call her son.

Shame, he was just here yesterday, along with his kids. Like they had a feeling the end was near and they wanted to say good-bye. The whole family had come. They talked to their grandma, but she didn't even open her eyes.

But really, why say *shame*? She was better off, poor thing, now that it was over with. A life like that was no life anyway. It wasn't the way Amanda would've wanted to go.

The lady's son was nice. A doctor, too, supposedly. Lived with his family not far from here. One of them came at least once a week, even though she couldn't talk. When they first brought her to the hospital, yes. She could even tell people apart, she'd heard. But that was before Amanda's time. For as long as she could remember, the lady had only been able to answer questions with her eyes, and then not even that. Her son spoke German to her—the lady was a German. He used to take her out to the garden in her wheelchair.

Nice family.

She would send Eileen in to clean up. Needless to say, they'd be getting a new admission.

Amanda Lee pushed the bed down the hall toward the elevator. The morgue was downstairs, in the basement.

Felice, she thought, what a pretty name. Felicity was even nicer. If she ever had a little girl, maybe she would call her that.

Felicity meant happiness, right?

2020

Lyon

"In sleep, souls communicate; awake, bodies separate," wrote the Taoist Master Zhuang.

The images emerge unbidden, floating up to the surface from sleep, at 5:00 a.m., 5:30; outside it's still dark. I am in the novel, entirely inside of it. Not residing within it like a home, but more like in a stream, mid-flow.

I see a young woman on the seashore. Behind her the city hums: lights, intersections, flat roofs and peeling plaster; oleanders and flocks of sleeping birds. Around her prevails the dark of night. Flat waves lick the beach, shifting back and forth sand, pebbles, clams. Come morning the beach will be covered in the patterns like writing they leave behind.

The woman is barefoot, in a light summer dress, arms exposed. She registers the rhythmic pounding of the waves, the surface of her skin in the warm, balmy air, and the cool pressure of the red beads strung around her neck.

I have always belonged here. On the shore of this sea. To the scent of sedimented salt, washed-up kelp, dead fish.
Soles in warm sand
and the stars.

Liquid stars
in my tears, as I raise my head and softly howl. Beneath my body's surface I am sinking. Layer by layer.
Who will be rescued? Who will be saved?
The throngs buried in the hills of Jerusalem?
Stones soaked in blood. O world of pain. And ecstasy.
Dip a finger in the shiny ravages, touch all of those sweaty foreheads and kiss—to the point of annihilation. Laws of beginnings and ends.
But before all else, the dark miracle of creation, when everything could still be arranged otherwise.
My warm feet in the sand.
The lengths to which I extend myself like a string
and the word again becomes vibration and everything points back to its beginning.
Grace. And peace.

When Felice died, it left behind a void.

Thinking of nothing better to do, I baked a sponge cake using Felice's recipe, which her granddaughter Leah had sent to me.

Mix baking powder with pastry flour. Beat butter to a foam. While beating, slowly add sugar one tablespoon at a time, lemon zest, juice from half a lemon, and, still beating, sprinkle in flour. Then stir in an egg yolk and, finally, whipped egg whites.

I beat the dough using a wooden spoon, and by the time I was done, my palm had bloody blisters on it. It hurt, but the connection with Felice was tangible.

The calluses on my hand were my admission ticket to Hades, the sacrifice I needed to make in order to enter.

My writing is coming to an end. It is fall again, as it was ten years ago in New York when I first began my search for Felice

Bauer. Perhaps there really is some symmetry to the world, a symmetry whose meaning escapes us.

There are many things I can't explain and don't even want to. Maybe it comes with aging. No longer trying to bend reality to my will and offer justifications where there are none. No longer trying to tell myself that things are under my control. It may bring some uncertainty to take the opposite approach, but it enables me to keep going further into the open.

2000

New York

ISN'T IT STRANGE HOW THE WAY that others look at us depends on our appearance? And how easily looks can deceive?

Those two white, apparently Jewish children, who just walked past the bench with their Black nanny, undoubtedly saw just another old man possessed of the usual attributes (cane, white hair, spectacles), who stood out from the anonymous ranks of similar old men perhaps only in the degree of his elegance. Little children are hardly equipped to judge that sort of thing. His love of fine clothes and shoes was a trait he had inherited from his mother.

If only they could have seen inside. Behind the wrinkle-creased forehead. Into his batiste shirt–covered chest, through his coat of fine English wool.

Old man? Hardly. He was a boy. Ten years old at most.

When he looked back on his life, or whatever cliché he chose to use, when he flipped through the individual events of his life in the order they had played out, he realized there was only one phase when he had felt truly grown-up. He was a little over thirty and had just opened his own private practice in Manhattan. He had a beautiful wife, whom he loved very much, and two healthy children. He had just bought a house. He spoke at conferences on the psychoanalysis of children and had published a few articles in professional journals. He had shaken hands with Anna Freud at the New York Psychoanalytic Society.

At the time, he had thought it was just the beginning, yet later it turned out to have been the height of his career, the only strong, self-confident phase in a life that, outwardly, progressed with relative success, but underneath it all, he had never ceased to wrestle with doubt.

How long had that phase lasted? Approximately ten years. From 1950, when his father passed away, until his mother's death.

He glanced at his watch: 10:35. The man should have been here by now. Had he described it well enough when they talked over the phone? The bench by the pavilion that rents model sailboats. It was the only building around like it; he couldn't possibly miss it. But maybe the man wasn't that familiar with Central Park—who knew where he was coming from? It was the first place that had come to mind when Joachim was trying to think of where they could meet. He brought his grandsons here whenever he came to New York with them, so he knew for a fact that the public restrooms here were decent. Of course he had no idea what sort of shape the other man was in, but he must have been at least a few years older than Joachim, so he, too, was likely to appreciate having the toilets nearby.

After all these years, it was unbelievable hearing from him.

Here came someone now, shuffling along. A little man with a long white beard and a cane, wearing a black coat, with a hat on his head. For the love of God, he couldn't understand how people dressed like that. He must have dug those crummy old shoes out of a trash can.

The man stopped at the sailboat-rental concession and took a look around. Then, walking a bit faster, he headed toward the bench.

Could it be . . .

"Good day," he called in German, without breaking his stride. "Do you recognize me?"

"Good day," said Joachim, politely rising to his feet. "But of course. Now that I see you up close. You haven't even changed that much. How are you?"

"You've sure gotten old." The little man laughed. "Well, it has been fifty years almost. Pardon me, but is there a men's room nearby?"

"Right over there," said Joachim, gesturing to a door on the side of the building. "Just go ahead. I'll wait."

He sat back down on the bench.

Two remote-control model boats raced across the artificial pond, ringed with stone. Colorful leaves bobbed on the surface of the water. Despite its being October, the sun was still pleasantly warm.

"I'm back," Joachim heard the voice beside him say. "May I join you?"

"Please."

"I was here once with my boys. I've got three boys and a daughter, just so you know. This was '69 or '70. I'm certain of that because the boys were still little and my girl hadn't been born yet. They kept saying they wanted to rent a boat. 'You promise me you won't fight over it?' I said. They fought over *everything.* 'No, Papa, we promise.' 'All right, if you can behave yourselves all week, we'll come back on Sunday and you can rent one then.' Well, they didn't behave. I said maybe the following week. Again they didn't behave. So we kept putting it off, for about a month or so, until finally I felt sorry for them. Sunday came around and I said, 'Let's go, boys.' We traveled halfway across the city and I rented a boat for an hour. Cost an arm and a leg. 'You'd better appreciate this,' I said. 'I won't be paying for that again.' The boys reverently took the boat from the man at the concession and carried it to the pond. They launched it onto the water, and guess what? No wind. It was about to rain and the lousy thing didn't move an inch. I didn't realize there had to be wind. I figured since it was remote control, it didn't need any wind. But that's why they call it sailing, right? Boy, were they disappointed! Here they were, all excited to get their boat out there on the pond and race against the others, and now it was barely crawling. They put their hands in the water and stirred it up, making a storm, till one of the guards came over. Little rascals. I could cry when I look back. You have two children, don't you?"

Joachim nodded.

"How many grandchildren?"

"Three. Two boys and a little girl. She's a big young lady now."

"What do your children do?"

"You really want to know?"

"Of course."

"My daughter got a degree in medicine. She's a child psychiatrist, like me. My son is an attorney. One of my grandsons wants to be a musician, the other one says he's going to study astrophysics. My granddaughter is studying art. She just left for a year in Europe. Supposedly, she's got talent, but I wouldn't know how to judge."

"Astrophysics? So he wants to study the universe?"

"That's right. Have you seen the photos from the Hubble telescope? They're fascinating."

"Yes, yes." Appelbaum tugged at his beard and nodded his head. "Children are the greatest wealth. I have four, as I said, but I got a later start than you, so my grandchildren are still little. Just four of them, too, so far. All boys. The Hubble telescope, yes, yes. Penetrating the mysteries of God's creation. And how is your wife?"

"Nina Perel is fine, since she went into retirement."

"Did she work outside the home?"

"Not until the children grew up. She got her degree in social work. Worked with paroled prisoners."

"Prisoners? Really?"

"Yes. But toward the end, mentally, it took a toll on her. Reintegration rarely works out the way one hopes. Most of the people end up back behind bars. It's depressing. What about your wife?"

"Long story." Appelbaum laughed. "I'd rather talk about you. What was the name of that young lady who took me to see you that time?"

"Lisette."

"Beautiful woman. I remember wondering why you let her go. You were married, right?"

"Only briefly."

"Very attractive woman. How is she doing?"

"Lisette passed away. I just found out last week from a common acquaintance of ours. I thought maybe that was the reason why you called."

"May the earth be light upon her. No, I had no idea. I didn't really know her. The last time I saw her was at your office. So she died, then. Any idea where and how?"

"In Boston, cancer. Lisette lived in Boston. She married someone from Reich's circle. She had a practice in psychotherapy, quite successful, from what I hear. She called and wrote me after Reich had his trial, then again, once he was in prison. I'm sorry, Wilhelm Reich. I assume you know who he was? She begged me to do something, put in a word with Eissler. Kurt Eissler, he was a leader of the New York Psychoanalytic Society. She wanted Reich's former colleagues to stand up for him, afraid he wouldn't survive if he was sent to prison. Which is what ended up happening. His heart gave out just before he was released. Reportedly they found him on his bed, in a suit with no shoes.

"I followed the trial, that whole witch hunt. It was unbelievably cruel. Incomprehensible. Even before his imprisonment, federal agents forced him to destroy all his devices and burn all the books he had published in the United States."

"But why did they see Reich as such a threat?"

"They considered him a crook. He claimed his experiments enabled him to extract this sort of cosmic energy, which he called orgone, and which he insisted he could harness and even use to treat cancer. He saw this energy, this orgone, as God, and was completely open about it. The witch hunt was started off by a couple of prudish reporters who were outraged by Reich's theories on sex and his accumulators, which he sold as medical devices. Remember them, the boxes? The papers called them 'sex boxes.' Of course, they always go with whatever looks good in the headlines. The government didn't get involved until later. By that time, the libel campaign against Reich was in full swing. Of course it didn't help that he used to be a Communist, when he was still in Europe. He was actually lucky, though. In the fifties they could easily have charged him with espionage and executed him."

"So, did you help?"

"There was no point in talking to Eissler. For him, Reich didn't exist. You see, in his eyes, Reich had deserted Freud. To be honest, part of the reason why I didn't rush to get involved was that I was afraid to be associated with Reich. I didn't want to lose my license or my patients. I'm not proud of myself."

"I see. And Lisette?"

"After Reich's death, I didn't hear from her again. At one point, in the late sixties, I got hold of her address and wrote to her, but she never replied. Why am I telling you this anyway?"

"Because I asked."

"True."

"Do you still have your practice?"

"I do, but I only take appointments two days a week."

"And in your free time?"

"I read a lot. Spend time with my grandsons. Travel. I used to go quite a bit to Asia and the Middle East. I've got a nice collection of carpets and works of art. But now I just fly to Europe. I took my grandsons there last year, to keep them from getting stupid."

"To Germany? To look for your roots, as they say?"

Joachim shook his head. "I've only been to Germany once and that was by myself. In Berlin, in '84."

"And?"

"I lasted exactly four days."

They watched the leaves floating on the surface of the pond.

"Is your family home still standing?"

"It is. They did a nice job of restoring it after the war. You can't even tell that it went a while without a roof. I took a walk around our neighborhood, went to the zoo, the aquarium, peeked in on the sea horses.

"Apart from that, I played tourist. The typical American. I couldn't bring myself to speak German. The whole four days I didn't talk to anyone, other than my wife, whom I called from the hotel every night. You know, ever since I was ten and our father took us away to Geneva, I had been pining for Berlin like a lost paradise. I knew of course nothing was the same there anymore, but somehow I didn't believe it. I couldn't talk myself out of the feeling. It's not the sort of thing you can control with your mind, you know. You can think and imagine whatever you want, but somewhere deep down inside you is that little boy who just wants to go home. I went to Berlin, but at the same time I was afraid to."

"So, did it help?"

"A little, yes. I realized there was nowhere to return to. No matter how badly I longed for it. How about you? Have you gotten used to it here?"

"Yes and no. I didn't have any paradise to leave behind. This is my home. My family is here."

"Your wife and children."

"Not only them. You may find it strange, sir, but you're like family to me, too. Or, more precisely, the closest thing to family that I've ever had. My adoptive parents probably knew more than they managed to tell me, but now it's too late. I'll never find out."

"Where did you wait out the war?"

"England. Partly in an internment camp. As you know, they were arresting Germans, even German Jews. But never mind the war. Do you realize you're the only person I know, not counting those villagers in Italy, who ever met my mother? Do you have any memories of her?"

"From Berlin, just vaguely. When it comes to my parents' friends, I always get them mixed up. But she visited us in Geneva, before we left for the U.S. She was fleeing Germany at the time and didn't have a job. She stayed with us a month or so, maybe even more. She and my mother were always whispering to each other, going into the big room together and closing the door. My sister, Lily, and I found it strange, since my mother was the type of person who always made a point of being open and direct. She always taught us if you couldn't say something out loud and in front of everyone, then you shouldn't say it at all. I remember Grete smoked a lot and hardly ate. She said she couldn't sleep at night. After that she met a man named Ernst. I don't recall his last name. He was quite a bit younger than she was. From our place she left for Palestine, where her brother was, but she didn't stay there long before returning to Europe again. By that time we were gone."

"Did she look like she does in the photos?"

"She was prettier. Tiny and full of life. She liked to dress nicely—she and my mother had that in common. She was a smart lady and loved having an audience. When she sat down at the table, everything had to revolve around her."

Appelbaum smiled and shook his head. "I definitely don't take after her in that. I'm more shy when it comes to people."

"How can an actor be shy?"

"Actor?"

"You are an actor, aren't you?"

"I'm sorry, but how did you come up with that? I've always made my living in business. Before I retired, I sold pet food and supplies. I've been watching you all these years, you know, even if just from a distance. When your mother died, in 1960, I wanted to write you, but I didn't dare. I was afraid you would take me for an impostor, like old Mr. Schocken. Where does your mom have her grave?"

"We buried her in Los Angeles."

"Why didn't you bury her closer? That way, you could visit."

"She wanted to be next to my father."

"I also found out when your sister died. In 1965. What a tremendous blow. I cried along with you. She wasn't even fifty, right? Cancer?"

Joachim nodded.

"I thought so. We had our second boy in 1964. A year and two months after the first. And the third one was not long in coming. They just came bursting out like chestnuts, one after the other. Then last came Rachel, the most beautiful one of them all."

"When did you get married?"

"In February '62. In 1961, I went to Israel and everything changed for me. I came back a different man. Do you mind if I tell you about it?"

"I've got plenty of time."

"I went in early June. That spring, the trial of Eichmann had begun, if you recall. It was all over the papers. I wasn't too interested, though, I confess. I'd gone to Israel to look for my mother's brother, my uncle, assuming he was still alive. Or anyone else from his family. I was hoping to meet my relatives and speak to Brod in person. It was sort of a last-gasp attempt."

"So how did it turn out?"

"My uncle was no longer living, and I wasn't able to track down anyone in the family. When I went to see Brod at the theater, he practically had a heart attack. He was working as the dramaturge for the Habima Theatre, as I'm sure you know. The theater was in a new building, pretty ugly, if you ask me. He had this tiny office, overflowing with papers and books, kind of a dump. At first he invited me in, offered me a seat, said he was always glad to have visitors from Germany. But the moment I told him who I was, he tried to get rid of me. He told me Schocken's heirs already had the letters from Florence, along with the correspondence from your mother, and it was all going to be published together in Germany. That was all he knew of. If I wanted to, he said, I should contact Schocken's heirs. He wouldn't even speak to me about my mother, saying he only knew her in passing, through Kafka. He didn't want to hear about her life in Italy, or her death. 'I have a weak heart,' he shouted, waving me off like an insect. 'Please, just go away!' And here I'd thought he'd be happy to see me. You can see how naïve I was. Remember what he wrote in his biography of Kafka? 'It is impossible to imagine what a beneficial effect it might have have had on Kafka had he known he had a son.' Anyway, looking back, I don't really know what I expected."

"But are you truly convinced? You don't have any proof."

"I don't. The only thing I know for a fact is who my mother was. The rest I learned from Brod's book, like everybody else. How else could I have found out? After all, it was he who published my mother's private letter saying that Kafka was the father of her child.

"But after that disastrous visit to his office, I realized that Brod had never actually believed in my existence. I was just a theory to him, an attractive and safely remote proposition that served to bolster his status as the one true expert on Kafka. He kept repeating to me that Kafka's son was long dead. As if he had proof. As if he had any evidence whatsoever. Yet there was no birth certificate, no record of death, nothing at all but a single letter from my mother, in which she doesn't even name anyone. And the testimonies of a few survivors in Italy. And then, of course, there was me."

Applebaum slapped his hand against his thigh as if attempting to convince himself of his tangible existence.

"Chances are you're not even Kafka's son."

"Chances are I'm not. Does it matter? I don't even care anymore. I am what I am, period. Dust in the face of the Almighty. But my wife . . . my wife is a truly exceptional woman. And my children are truly exceptional children. And I won't even mention my grandchildren."

Appelbaum smiled happily, then after a moment went on. "I've since forgiven him, but at the time I was quite upset by how he treated me. From Tel Aviv I went to Jerusalem. I was hoping to find Felix Weltsch. I'm sure you've heard of him. He was friends with Kafka, too, back in Prague. If not Brod, I thought maybe he might be able to shed some light on the matter.

"I took one of those overcrowded buses that you literally have to squeeze into, and tumbled out of it, half dead, at the stop outside the Old City walls. By then it was dark and the moon was coming up—it was almost full. It was warm, but not hot like in Tel Aviv. The air was pleasant, refreshing. The bushes and trees were filled with buzzing cicadas. I had no idea where I was going to sleep, and I was absolutely famished. Outside the Jaffa Gate, in this little street to the left, there was an Arab bakery open, so I bought a burek and a bottle of soda, and sat down on a stone step with it.

"I've told my children this story many times. When I was done, I got up and slowly made my way down the main street, past the Tower of David. I didn't have any destination in mind, I was just wandering. I thought I might stumble across someplace where I could spend the night. There were Jews passing me on either side. In pairs, small groups, or on their own, girls and women, too. All walking with their heads down, like they were in a hurry, and turning off into a little side street. So I followed them and picked up my pace. There was something drawing me.

"At first I kept pausing at every intersection to see which way I was going, but then I stopped paying attention and turned without even looking, as if by memory. Finally I walked down a dark passageway, and came out at the top of a staircase. Below, to my left, was a large open space strewn with people. Everyone had their backs turned to me and their hands over their eyes. Some were bowing and saying or chanting something—I couldn't hear what. A lot of them had books in their hands. I can still picture it to this day, down to the smallest detail. Then

I saw the wall and it dawned on me where I was. Up until that moment, I didn't have a clue.

"I mean, yes, I knew there was a wall in Jerusalem that was part of a temple that had been destroyed and that it was known as the Wailing Wall, but I didn't realize it was something I could see with my own eyes. I was deaf and blind and all I cared about was me and my unhappy history. I was searching for my parents, but I never thought to search for my true origins.

"There was a step there, so I sat down on it and cried. No one even noticed. I forgot all about Brod and Kafka, even about my mother. All of a sudden I couldn't have cared less who my father was or wasn't and who had done me wrong. I saw the multitude of my ancestors, my brothers and sisters. I had never experienced anything so powerful in my life. I spent the whole night sitting there, letting everything pour out of me with my tears. All the weight and the pain. The next morning, I tell you, I was carefree as a child."

Appelbaum pulled out a large cloth handkerchief and blew his nose.

"So. I let Weltsch go. I came back to New York and started going to synagogue. Got married, and the rest you already know. Do you go to temple?"

"No."

"Why not?"

"If you ask me, Mr. Appelbaum, the temples ought to be knocked down. Churches, synagogues, mosques, every last one. The evil that organized religion has done in the world, and continues to do to this day, can never be balanced out by any speck of good it might bring. That's the conclusion I've come to. In the end, evil will always prevail. That's just how it is when people have power. And religion and power go hand in hand. Every man for himself, I say. Though believe me, I get it. Our longing to fit in, to belong to something, is incredibly strong. I wish I had someone to protect me, too, when I can't sleep at night. And clearly, the illusion that there is a God who cares about us will always be more attractive than accepting that we're just a lonely island of consciousness awash in a sea of darkness."

"So you don't even pray?"

"Praying is for the weak and unfortunate. It just makes you feel a little bit better, that's all."

"And your children?"

Joachim shook his head. "I raised them to be freethinkers. My wife tried it once when they were still little. Her family wasn't religious, but she respected tradition. They always at least kept the holidays. She felt like the children needed community, some sort of cultural framework, let's say. She wanted them to grow up in Jewish culture, so she told me she wanted to take them to temple, but I wouldn't allow it. Then one time she took them while I was away. She couldn't even last till the end. Everything the rabbi said just got on her nerves, and the children wouldn't keep quiet. She kept having to hush them. Once was enough, she decided. The children would just have to make do with what we had. And that was a reformed temple. Can you imagine what she would have said if they'd banished her off to the women's section?"

Appelbaum threw up his hands. "I'm constantly in conversation with God. I argue with him and debate—that, too, is prayer. And I truly would be weak and unfortunate, just as you say, if he didn't make himself known to me. Well, one never knows. Your children might surprise you yet, or maybe your grandchildren. You can never wander so far that there is no way back. I remember Kafka put it quite nicely in one of his letters to your mother. He said—"

"I'm sorry, but I have to go to the bathroom." Joachim rose to his feet. "And then I need to go."

"I'll walk with you. Where are you headed?"

"East Seventy-second. I managed to park right by the entrance. Where are you going?"

"I live in Brooklyn."

"I'll drop you at the subway."

Appelbaum shuffled along beside him, leaning heavily on his cane. Joachim had to hold himself back to keep from getting too far ahead. When they finally reached the car, he unlocked the door and held it open for the older man. Appelbaum shook his head. "Thank you, but I'd rather walk. It's just a few blocks. With my legs, it's easier than climbing in and out of a car."

Joachim slammed the door shut and stood there, lost for words. How should they say good-bye? Would they ever see each other again? It wasn't likely.

The other man was probably having similar thoughts. He tapped the tip of his cane on the sidewalk, staring at it as if he hoped it might offer advice.

"There's something else I'd like to ask," Joachim said finally, working up the nerve. "For nearly fifty years you watched me from afar, but you never wrote or called. So why do it now? Why did you want to meet with me?"

Appelbaum stopped tapping his cane. Then, very slowly, measuring out his words, he said, "Why now, why not later . . . what do I know? That's just the way it worked out. All these years I've been thinking, You have to meet with him. You have to ask him one more time about your mother. He's the only one who might remember how she smelled."

"Unfortunately, I don't."

"I kept putting it off," continued the old man, "because I was afraid you would chase me away again. Until one morning I woke up and found this bump on my neck. . . ." He reached his hand up and felt behind his left ear. "So I called. I haven't been to the doctor yet. Even my wife has no idea."

He raised his head and they looked each other in the eye.

Yes, Joachim thought, there really is something strange about those eyes of his.

He extended his hand. "Better get that checked, Mr. Appelbaum. I hope it's nothing serious. Good luck. And good-bye."

"It'll be fine," said the older man. He shook Joachim's hand and gave a slight bow. It seemed he was about to go, but then he changed his mind.

"To finish what I was saying about Kafka. In one of his letters to your mother from 1913, he wrote that the most important thing was to have a constant inner connection. To something infinitely high or deep. A relationship to the infinite. And that relationship is all that matters, nothing else. Very precisely put, don't you think? So long. And be well."

Joachim looked at his watch and opened the car door again, but he didn't get in. Instead, he remained standing, following with his eyes the dark, bowed figure of the man in the hat as he turned the corner with the help of his cane.

It was true, he had chased him away, the second time that Appelbaum had turned up at his office. He hadn't even tried to be polite, though he didn't yell or wave his hands around like Max Brod.

Joachim lifted his head and scanned the surroundings. Somewhere in the area, on the rooftops along the edge of the park, he had been told there was a hawk's nest. He was hoping he might see it.

Why had he lied to that man anyway? It wasn't true he didn't pray.

Sometimes he would recite the Shema Yisrael before going to bed, the way his mother had taught him. In doing so, he invoked her presence, her soft hand and gentle caress.

Author's Note

This book is a work of fiction. Some of the characters bear the names of people who actually lived, while others are based on real people whose names have been changed. There are also characters and events that are completely invented.

As for the documents and letters cited in my book, they are all of my invention except for those listed below:

pp. 138–146: Letters quoted from Franz Kafka, *Letters to Felice*, trans. James Stern and Elisabeth Duckworth (New York: Schocken Books, 1973).

pp. 165–172: Letters from the Grete Bloch Collection, housed in the archives of the Leo Baeck Institute, New York.

pp. 175–179: Correspondence between the author and Anna Pizzuti.

p. 227:

There was a king in Thule,
Was faithful till the grave,
To whom his mistress, dying,
A golden goblet gave.

Nought was to him more precious;
He drained it at every bout;
His eyes with tears ran over,
As oft as he drank thereout.

Translation by Bayard Taylor, in
The Works of J. W. von Goethe, vol. 9, p. 130

Acknowledgments

Thanks to Jiří Zavadil for his valuable insights into the text, and for his love and support, without which this book would not have been possible.

Thanks to Alice Marxová, Veronika Tuckerová, and Daniela Hodrová, who read the manuscript at various stages and whose comments helped me to complete it.

Special thanks belong to Anna Pizzuti in Italy, who shared with me the results of her many years of research.

Bellevue Literary Press is devoted to publishing literary fiction and nonfiction at the intersection of the arts and sciences because we believe that science and the humanities are natural companions for understanding the human experience. We feature exceptional literature that explores the nature of consciousness, embodiment, and the underpinnings of the social contract. With each book we publish, our goal is to foster a rich, interdisciplinary dialogue that will forge new tools for thinking and engaging with the world.

To support our press and its mission, and for our full catalogue of published titles, please visit us at blpress.org.

Bellevue Literary Press
New York